HOLLYWOOD

Charles Bukowski was the legendary Californian writer who became famous for his semi-autobiographical books about low-life America. Novels such as *Post Office* and *Factotum* made this one-time bum, and lifelong alcoholic, rich and famous, and culminated in the making of *Barfly*, a major Hollywood movie based on his life starring Mickey Rourke and Faye Dunaway. He died in March 1994.

BY CHARLES BUKOWSKI

The Days Run Away Like Wild Horses Over the Hills (1969)

Post Office (1971)

Mockingbird Wish Me Luck (1972)

South of No North (1973)

*Burning in Water, Drowning in Flame: Selected Poems
1955–1973* (1974)

Factotum (1975)

Love is a Dog from Hell: Poems 1974–1977 (1977)

Women (1978)

*Play the Piano Drunk Like a Percussion Instrument Until the
Fingers Begin to Bleed a Bit* (1979)

Shakespeare Never Did This (1979)

Dangling in the Tournefortia (1981)

Ham on Rye (1982)

Bring Me Your Love (1983)

Hot Water Music (1983)

There's No Business (1984)

War All the Time: Poems 1981–1984 (1984)

You Get So Alone at Times that It Just Makes Sense (1986)

The Movie: 'Barfly' (1987)

The Roominghouse Madrigals: Early Selected Poems 1946–1966
(1988)

Hollywood (1989)

Septuagenarian Stew: Stories & Poems (1990)

The Last Night of the Earth Poems (1992)

Screams from the Balcony: Selected Letters 1960–1970 (1993)

Pulp (1994)

Living on Luck: Selected Letters 1960s–1970s, Volume 2 (1995)

Betting on the Muse: Poems & Stories (1996)

Bone Palace Ballet: New Poems (1997)

*The Captain is Out to Lunch and the Sailors Have Taken Over
the Ship* (1998)

Reach for the Sun: Selected Letters 1978–1994 (1999)

HOLLYWOOD

CHARLES BUKOWSKI

CANONGATE

This Canons edition published in Great Britain in 2019 by Canongate Books

First published in Great Britain in 2007 by Canongate Books Ltd,
14 High Street, Edinburgh EH1 1TE

Published in the United States of America in 2002 by Ecco, an imprint of
HarperCollins Publishers Inc., 10 East 53rd Street, New York, NY 10022

First published in the United States of America in 1989
by Black Sparrow Press, California, USA

canongate.co.uk

4

British Library Cataloguing-in-Publication Data
A catalogue record for this book is available on request from the British Library

ISBN 978 1 78689 167 9

Typeset in Fournier by Palimpsest Book Production Ltd, Falkirk, Stirlingshire

Printed and bound in Great Britain by Clays Ltd, Elcograf S.p.A.

for Barbet Schroeder

Introduction

When Charles Bukowski writes about Hollywood he is not usually referring to the movie industry, but to the place where he lived for many years: a scruffy residential district, at the unfashionable end of Sunset Boulevard, known as East Hollywood. Here in rundown apartment buildings in the smoggy basin of Los Angeles, below the HOLLYWOOD sign, live the working poor of LA, newly arrived immigrants and those who have all but given up on life. Night sounds include sirens, arguments, bottles smashed into trash cans and gunshots. This is Bukowskiland – the setting of many of his poems, stories and novels, of which there are six. This book is his fifth novel, first published in 1989, when the writer was in his late sixties. In contrast to the rest of his work, when Bukowski writes here about 'Hollywood', he *is* concerned with the movie business.

Before the story gets underway we read a prominent disclaimer: 'This is a work of fiction and any resemblance between the characters and persons living or dead is purely coincidental, etc.' While it is usually a mistake to assume that people in novels are facsimiles of people in life, this disclaimer is disingenuous, as the sarcastic 'etc.' indicates. Bukowski's working method had always been to create characters based closely on himself and those around him, and seldom was this more true than with *Hollywood*, which is best described, perhaps, as a *fictionalised journal*. The subject matter is the author's recent experiences writing a screenplay, *Barfly*, about his early life, and the process of seeing *Barfly* made into a Hollywood movie. In working on the picture, the author met a parade of celebrities and *Hollywood* is also a *roman à clef* in that it is a book in which many of the characters are famous people in disguise, the point partly being to satirise their extravagant personalities and reveal their sometimes bizarre behaviour. The making of the film, and the story told in *Hollywood*, is studded with outrageous episodes, many of which are quite hilarious. At one point in the book Bukowski's autobiographical hero, Henry Chinaski, compares his odyssey through low-life America to show-business and has to conclude that: 'my past life hardly seemed as strange or wild or as mad as what was occurring now'.

Before delving deeper into the book let's remind ourselves of that 'past life', recapping how Bukowski went from sleeping on park benches to having a movie made about himself: not the usual experience of the average bum, though he was never merely that.

Born in Andernach, Germany, to an American serviceman father and a German mother just after World War One, Henry Charles Bukowski Jnr. (Hank to friends) was taken to the United States as a child and grew up in Los Angeles, which became his home town. In material terms, the Bukowskis lived a comfortable, lower-middle-class life. Nevertheless, Hank's childhood was miserable. He revisited his boyhood time and again for his books, never tiring of writing about Chinaski's bullying father, his ineffectual mother and the acne that further blighted Chinaski's youth, as it did the author's. The saga is recounted most fully in Bukowski's fourth novel, *Ham on Rye*, also published by Canongate.

As he grew older, Bukowski shunned society, turning his face against the conventional life his parents had prepared him for, having sent their only child to a good school followed by college (which he dropped out of). When he left home, he chose to work manual jobs in order to earn just enough to rent cheap rooms where he would spend his free time alone, drinking and listening to classical music on the radio, while typing stories and poems. For brief periods during his youth, mostly when he was travelling around the country, he sank lower than this and knew what it was to go hungry and sleep rough as a bum.

Whether he had a roof over his head or not, Bukowski lived a hermit-like existence and was always, to a large degree, shy of people. As a result he remained almost entirely inexperienced sexually until the age of twenty-seven, when he met Jane Cooney Baker in a Los Angeles drinking den. A thirty-eight-year-old woman with an unhappy past, Jane was a 'barfly', that is, she lived her life largely in bars, doing whatever she had to do in order to buy her next drink. She and Hank discovered they had much in common: they both believed alcohol could blot out their misery, and they felt most people weren't worth a damn. The couple moved in together and, though they fought, Jane was the love of Bukowski's life, as well as being the inspiration of some of his best work, not least the poems of love and grief in his wonderfully titled and highly recommended book *The Days Run Away Like Wild Horses Over the Hills*.

Poems of grief as well as love poems because Jane drank herself to death when she was fifty-one, while life for Bukowski went on. For years he worked unhappily for the US Postal Service, as a delivery man, then mail sorter, choosing to make his home in East Hollywood, in the shadow of the movie business, which he had nothing to do with at this time. He was still there – in a shabby apartment on De Longpre Avenue – when he started to become successful in the early 1970s, having been discovered by several admirers including a publisher named John Martin. With John's encouragement and financial support, Hank left the US Postal Service when he was forty-nine, making the momentous decision to become a full-time writer. (He didn't tell John he was about to be fired from the post office anyway.)

Gradually, Hank started to make a living from his pen, his books selling especially well in translation. By the late 1970s he had a large readership in France and Germany, his fan-base growing in Great Britain and the USA, and was earning enough money as a result to buy his first home, a detached property in San Pedro, south of LA. Soon he also acquired a BMW car. Hank shared this new, lucky life with a young woman named Linda Lee Beighle, whom he married in 1985, and who encouraged him to adopt a healthier lifestyle. Under Linda Lee's influence, Hank cut down on his intake of beer and whisky, for example, drinking wine instead.

So we can picture our hero – that is to say, both the author Bukowski and his alter ego Chinaski – at the time of this novel: a man in his sixties who, though battered and buffeted by life, has reached a point in his career where his books are selling and his home situation is comfortable. Hank was probably as happy now as he had ever been.

Several filmmakers were interested in adapting Bukowski's work for the screen. In 1981, director Marco Ferreri made *Tales of Ordinary Madness*, based on a Bukowski short story. The picture set the standard for most of the Bukowski movies that followed in that it focused on the shock value of his stories while failing to convey the subtlety, wisdom and wit of the writing. Around the same time Taylor Hackford attempted to make a film of Bukowski's novel, *Post Office*, but couldn't get the project off the ground. Shortly thereafter Hackford became a well-known director of major Hollywood pictures, including *An Officer and a Gentleman*. When it came to making *Barfly*, Bukowski discovered that Hackford – husband of the actress Helen Mirren, and the inspiration for the character Hector Blackford in this novel – still owned the rights to his principal characters and could therefore block the project if he wished. Fortunately, Hackford gave way to Bukowski and his new director, Barbet Schroeder, to whom *Hollywood* is dedicated, allowing the film to go ahead.

Barbet Schroeder is an exotic fellow: born in Iran in 1941 to a German father, and educated in France. He is also a somewhat eccentric filmmaker, whose previous projects included a picture about an ape and a documentary profile of Ugandan dictator Idi Amin. Like many people who come across Bukowski's work – as happened with me when I started reading Bukowski, and felt compelled to write his biography – Schroeder became infatuated with Hank, who, as well as being a highly engaging writer, possessed a magnetic personality and great integrity. Here in LA, a town where most creative people aim to sell out as soon as possible, was a writer who had never compromised his art. He had been tapping out his unique poems and stories for decades, when hardly anybody cared to read them, or indeed had laughed at him. Now, finally, the world was coming around to his way of thinking.

The screenplay contract offered to Bukowski by Schroeder was worth $10,000, but with his books selling briskly Hank wasn't motivated primarily by cash. Rather he pecked out the screenplay as an intellectual exercise when he could be bothered, and though he was unfamiliar with the conventions of screenwriting he eventually had a draft to show Barbet. *Barfly* was the story of Hank's relationship with Jane when they were living together in the 1950s, drinking so heavily that Bukowski hadn't been able to do much writing. 'While the time had not been an unhappy time,' Chinaski reflects in *Hollywood*, 'it had been mostly a time of void and waiting.'

So we begin to tuck into what is a layer cake of autobiography: the novel *Hollywood* being about the making of a movie, which had in fact been made, and was about Bukowski's real early life and the woman he had loved. The action in *Hollywood* begins decades after Hank and Jane lived together, and long after she had died. In the first chapter, in his old age, Henry Chinaski is being wooed to write the screenplay of a picture called *The Dance of Jim Beam* by Jon Pinchot (a foreign film director who once made a documentary about a dictator named Lido Mamim – one example of how close to life the characters are drawn). The first sentence is classic Bukowski: 'A couple of days later Pinchot phoned.' Immediately we are into the story, which is told in Bukowski's elegantly simple prose, with plentiful dialogue, whereby characters talk as people do in life; they don't give speeches. Bukowski's humorous tone makes the reader snort with laughter and the pages fly by.

In the story, Pinchot strikes a deal with an independent Hollywood production company called Firepower, run by a couple of wheeler-dealers apparently based on Menahem Golan and Yoram Globus, whose Cannon Group made *Barfly*. Pinchot is then driven to distraction by the vacillations of the executives who promise him money, then run out of cash, leading the director such a dance that he is reduced to living in a shack in Venice Beach. This was very close to the truth, as John Martin recalls: 'Barbet first asked Hank to write the screenplay for

Barfly, and then set out to get the picture produced, and *Hollywood* is a novel about that process, from hopeful beginning to bitter end. I especially love the part where Barbet is stranded in Venice, and Hank is working on the screenplay, and nothing is going right . . . every character and event in *Hollywood* is terribly true to life.' For my part, I relish the scene in Chapter 25 when the movie is cancelled and the director responds by taking an electric saw into a meeting with executives, threatening to amputate one of his fingers unless they put the movie back into production. It is in the light of extraordinary episodes such as this that Chinaski reflects that nothing in his past life, mad though that had sometimes been, compared to the world of movies.

Chinaski encounters numerous famous people while making his movie, and many of the characters in *Hollywood* are strongly reminiscent of real celebrities, their identities so thinly disguised that the reader feels invited to guess who they are. This is especially tempting if you know a little of the background story to *Barfly*. For example, early in the book we read about a meeting between Chinaski and Mack Austin, a reformed Hollywood wild man, and his actor friend Tom Pell, who has recently married 'the famed pop singer' Ramona. Mack Austin is surely based on Dennis Hopper, who did want to direct *Barfly*, while Tom Pell sounds very much like Madonna's husband at the time, Sean Penn, who wanted to play the lead. In life, as in the novel, Barbet objected strongly to Hopper taking over what Barbet saw as his picture and so Hopper was out, Penn too.

As an indirect result, Mickey Rourke took the lead in *Barfly*, playing Chinaski in a pugnacious style that, while not uninteresting, has little to do with the Chinaski we know from Bukowski's books. In *Hollywood*, the star is named Jack Bledsoe. The female lead, Wanda, based on Jane, went to Faye

Dunaway, who was really too good-looking for the role. In this book, the lead actress is named Francine Bowers, portrayed by Bukowski as a faded but still egocentric diva who insists that Chinaski write a new scene in which she can show off her legs.

Meanwhile, Chinaski is invited to a succession of Hollywood parties, where he avails himself of the ubiquitous free bar. One evening he is at the Chateau Marmont to meet Victor Norman, 'the best known novelist in America'. This was Norman Mailer, who confirmed to me that the story told in *Hollywood* was essentially true: when Bukowski had had a few drinks at the hotel he challenged Mailer to a fight. Mailer, who trained as an amateur boxer at the time, says he fixed Bukowski with a steely look and warned him in his customary macho style: 'Hank, don't even think about it.'

None of the celebrities I spoke to in connection with *Barfly* contradicted what Hank wrote in *Hollywood* to a significant degree. And while they didn't all bother to read the whole book, I suspect most did at least look themselves up in the novel. One filmmaker mentioned in the story told me, typically perhaps, that he read *the bit about himself*, that is where he apparently appears as a character. The point is that many of these celebrities recognised themselves in a book that is presented as a work of fiction. While bearing in mind that changes have been made, not least for legal reasons, and we must therefore accept that the characters are *not* facsimiles of real people, as you read *Hollywood* you are probably justified in assuming that, say, Frances Ford Lopalla, who pops up on page 27, may be based on Francis Ford Coppola; Jon-Luc Modard is probably meant to put one in mind of Jean-Luc Godard; celebrity couple Manz Loeb and Rosalind Bonelli are dead ringers for David Lynch and Isabella Rossellini; while the photographer Corbell Veeker is strongly reminiscent of Helmut Newton. You will find numerous other examples.

At the same time there is a close biographical correlation between the story told in *Hollywood* and Bukowski's private life in the mid-1980s. Like Chinaski, he was spending his days at the race track at this time; dining out at Musso & Frank's restaurant; and writing in the evenings in an upstairs room in his new house, which he shared with a young woman. The companion, named Sarah in the book, is the spitting image of Linda Lee Bukowski. Meanwhile, the making of the movie leads the author to think back on that time of 'void and waiting' he shared with another woman who haunts *Hollywood*, as she did his whole life. Interestingly, in the novel Bukowski calls her by her real name.

Jane Cooney Baker died in 1962, a maid in a fleapit Hollywood hotel. Her funeral was sparsely attended and when I visited her grave, years later, it had no marker. The only picture of Jane ever published, to my knowledge, is the grainy high school photo in my biography of Bukowski, *Charles Bukowski: Locked in the Arms of a Crazy Life*. Despite my best efforts, I found hardly anybody who had known Jane in life, and could not locate her relations. It may well be that they did not want to be found. In any event, Jane would have been forgotten almost entirely, I am sure, had Hank not made her posthumously famous. Now Jane is a legend. She is a central character in his novels *Post Office* and *Factotum*, as well as appearing in stories and poems beyond count. And Bukowski resurrected her again as Wanda in *Barfly*, shot partly on location in an old apartment building on Alvarado Street, where they once lived. It is clear from reading *Hollywood* that it was a disconcerting experience for Bukowski to be on set, in that same LA tenement, watching Faye Dunaway playing his ex: 'Strange and chilling indeed.'

As we near the end of *Hollywood* – wishing it was longer – *The Dance of Jim Beam* is edited and ultimately released, with Chinaski's endorsement that it is a faithful adaptation of his screenplay. This was the case in life. Schroeder didn't change a word of *Barfly* without Bukowski's consent, a rare honour to a screenwriter, though Chinaski notes that the true indication of the writer's status in Hollywood is that the star of *Jim Beam* earns 750 times the screenwriter's fee. In the closing pages of the book Chinaski attends the premiere, and informs us that the critics greeted the picture with mixed reviews. *Barfly* received considerable media attention, the film being seen as a comeback for Faye Dunaway; also because it was a natural story for journalists to write about 'the bum whose life became a movie'. Bukowski's profile was raised considerably as a result, which helped his book sales, but the film was a disappointment.

Bukowski himself was never entirely happy with the lead actors: he considered Mickey Rourke's costume too scruffy and thought the bar fights unrealistic. Bukowski wrote the screenplay, of course. 'But I had very little input once the film got going,' he commented. 'Some of the scenes I didn't think fit the reality enough . . . ' In truth, he had never been much interested in films, and the experience of making a movie confirmed his prejudices about the medium and the people who work in the industry. In *Hollywood* he lambastes movie folk as 'dumb cunts and bastards' and from what we read there was some truly asinine behaviour on set. Take the whim of the leading man, Jack Bledsoe, to have a certain colour Rolls Royce at his disposal, then his decision to walk on the bonnet of the Rolls for publicity photos, causing $6,000-worth of damage to the bodywork. One cannot say whether this actually happened, but there is the ring of truth to it, and to Pinchot's weary comment to Chinaski as they watch the vandalism: 'We have to keep the children happy.'

Apart from Bukowski's reservations, what else is wrong with *Barfly*? Well, the chief pleasure of reading the author is the enjoyment of his use of language: the spare style of his poetry and prose, the clever turns of phrase. While language defines a book, films are concerned principally with images. *Barfly* looks authentic, thanks to the care Barbet Schroeder took with the production – that it is to say it looks like Bukowskiland – but watching the film we don't get the same rich experience that comes from reading a book like this. Stripped down to movie dialogue, there isn't enough Bukowski writing to engage us in *Barfly*. And the writing was not on a level with Bukowski's best work. He wasn't a seasoned screenwriter, after all. Disappointingly, *Barfly* doesn't make us smile, let alone laugh. Contrastingly, there are many laughs – by which I mean laughter at the recognition of truth, which is what Bukowski is all about – in *Hollywood*.

The authorial tone of voice in *Hollywood* is slightly different from Bukowski's previous novels. When he composed his first novel, *Post Office* (1971), and his second, *Factotum* (1975), Bukowski was not yet successful, and there is a concurrent edginess, a real sense of desperation, to the writing. These are truly notes from underground, to borrow a phrase from Dostoyevsky, whose *Notes from Underground* was one of Bukowski's favourite books. His third novel, *Women* (1978), is different again: a delightfully rambunctious account of his adventures as a middle-aged rake. Published in 1982, *Ham on Rye* is grimly serious for the most part. Turning next to *Hollywood*, one is struck by the genial tone of a book that was written by Bukowski towards the end of his life, when he was financially comfortable and settled with his new wife. Speaking of whom, the novel concludes in classic Bukowski style when Sarah asks Chinaski what he'll do now the movie is finished:

'Oh, hell, I'll write a novel about writing the screenplay and making the movie.'
  'Sure, I guess you can do that.'
  'I can, I think.'
  'What are you going to call it?'
  '*Hollywood*.'
  '*Hollywood*?'
  'Yes . . .'
  And this is it.

And this is how it happened. After *Barfly* was released in the autumn of 1987, Bukowski started writing this book. He wasn't feeling at all well as he did so. During the making of *Barfly*, he imbibed heavily, as is evident in *Hollywood*. 'I winced when I read the manuscript,' remarks John Martin. 'It was, in the end, a bad environment for Hank, as at every turn alcohol was omnipresent, and Hank's drinking was prodigious. [I] thanked Hank's lucky stars that he finally escaped alive.' The alcoholic bender took a toll on his constitution, however. The day after he completed the novel, in the autumn of 1988, Bukowski collapsed with what was later diagnosed as tuberculosis. He conquered TB after a long battle, but was left a much frailer, more elderly-looking man. Other health problems followed and in 1993 Bukowski was diagnosed with leukaemia, dying the following year aged seventy-three.

Due to failing health, *Hollywood* is one of the last Bukowski books published during his lifetime. In it we find our hero, Henry Chinaski, who we have followed through so many adventures and tribulations, finally experiencing worldly success. It is heart-warming that in reality Bukowski also lived to enjoy popularity as a writer. Reading *Hollywood* we feel glad for Chinaski, and for the author whose singular journey through life had, despite all the odds, turned out happily in the end. I know you will enjoy this book.

Howard Sounes

Chapter One

A COUPLE OF days later Pinchot phoned. He said he wanted to go ahead with the screenplay. We should come down and see him?

So we got the directions and were in the Volks and heading for Marina del Rey. Strange territory.

Then we were down at the harbor, driving past the boats. Most of them were sailboats and people were fiddling about on deck. They were dressed in their special sailing clothes, caps, dark shades. Somehow, most of them had apparently escaped the daily grind of living. They had never been caught up in that grind and never would be. Such were the rewards of the Chosen in the land of the free. After a fashion, those people looked silly to me. And, of course, I wasn't even in their thoughts.

We turned right, down from the docks and went past streets laid out in alphabetical order, with fancy names. We found the street, turned left, found the number, pulled into the driveway. The sand came right up to us and the ocean was close enough to be seen and far enough away to be safe. The sand seemed cleaner than other sand and the water seemed bluer and the breeze seemed kinder.

'Look,' I said to Sarah, 'we have just landed upon the outpost of death. My soul is puking.'

'Will you stop worrying about your soul?' Sarah responded.

No need to lock the Volks. I was the only one who could start it.

We were at the door. I knocked.

It opened to this tall slim delicate type, you smelled *artistry* all over him. You could see he had been *born* to Create, to Create grand things, totally unhindered, never bothered by such petty things as toothache, self-doubt, lousy luck. He was one of those who *looked* like a genius. I looked like a dishwasher so these types always pissed me just a bit.

'We're here to pick up the dirty laundry,' I said.

'Ignore him,' Sarah interspersed. 'Pinchot suggested we come by.'

'Ewe,' said the gentleman, '*do* come in . . .'

We followed him and his little rabbit cheeks. He stopped then, at some special edge, he was charming, and he spoke over his left shoulder as if the entire world were listening to his delicate proclamation:

'I go get my VOD-KA now!'

He flashed off into the kitchen.

'Jon mentioned him the other night,' said Sarah. 'He is Paul Renoir. He writes operas and is also working in a form known as the Opera-Movie. Very avant-garde.'

'He may be a great man but I don't want him sucking at my ear lobes.'

'Oh, stop being so defensive! Everybody can't be like you!'

'I know. That's their problem.'

'Your greatest strength,' said Sarah, 'is that you fear everything.'

'I wish I had said that.'

Paul walked back with his drink. It looked good. There was even a bit of lime in there and he stirred it with a little glass stick. A swizzle. Real class.

'Paul,' I asked, 'is there anything else to drink in there?'

'Ewe, sorry,' he said, 'please *do* help yourself!'

I charged into the kitchen right upon the heels of Sarah.

There were bottles everywhere. While we were deciding, I cracked a beer.

'We better lay off the hard stuff,' suggested my good lady. 'You know how you get when you're drinking that.'

'Right. Let's go with the wine.'

I found a corkscrew and got a bottle of fine-looking red.

We each had a good hit. Then we refilled our glasses and walked out. At one time I used to refer to Sarah and me as Zelda and Scott, but that bothered her because she didn't like the way Zelda had ended up. And I didn't like what Scott had typed. So, we had abandoned our sense of humor there.

Paul Renoir was at the large picture window checking out the Pacific.

'Jon is late,' he said to the picture window and the ocean, 'but he told me to tell you that he will be right along and to please stay.'

'O.K., baby . . .'

Sarah and I sat down with our drinks. We faced the rabbit cheeks. He faced the sea. He appeared to be musing.

'Chinaski,' he said, 'I have read much of your work. It is wild shit. You are very good . . .'

'Thank you. But we know who is really the best. You're the best.'

'Ewe,' he said as he continued to face the sea, 'it is very very nice of you to . . . realize that . . .'

The door opened and a young girl with long black hair walked in without knocking. Next thing we knew she was stretched out up on the back of the sofa, lengthwise, like a cat.

'I'm Popppy,' she said, 'with 4 "p"s.'

I had a relapse: 'We're Scott and Zelda.'

'Cut the shit!' said Sarah.

I gave our proper names.

Paul turned from the sea.

'Popppy is one of the backers of your screenplay.'

'I haven't written a word,' I said.

'*You will . . .*'

'Would you, please?' I looked at Sarah and held up my empty glass.

Sarah was a good girl. She left with the glass. She knew that if I went in there I would start in on sundry bottles and then start in on my way to being nasty.

I would learn later that another name for Popppy was 'The Princess from Brazil'. And for starters she had kicked in ten grand. Not much. But it paid for some of the rent and some of the drinks.

The Princess looked at me from her cat-like position on the back of the couch.

'I've read your stuff. You're very funny.'

'Thank you.'

Then I looked over at Paul. 'Hey, baby, did you hear that? I'm funny!'

'You deserve,' he said, 'a *certain* place . . .'

He flashed toward the kitchen again as Sarah passed him with our refills. She sat down next to me and I had a hit.

The thought then occurred to me that I could just bluff the screenplay and sit around Marina del Rey for months sucking up drinks. Before I could really savor that thought, the door burst open and there was Jon Pinchot.

'Ah, you came by!'

'Ewe,' I said.

'I think I have a backer! All you have to do is write it.'

'It might take a few months.'

'But, of course . . .'

Then Paul was back. He had a strange pink-looking drink for the Princess.

Pinchot flashed toward the kitchen for one of his own.

It was the first of many meetings which would simply dissolve into bouts of heavy drinking, especially on my part. I found it to be a needed build-up for my confidence as I was really only interested in the poem and the short story. Writing a screenplay seemed to me an ultimately stupid thing to do. But better men than I had been trapped into such a ridiculous act.

Jon Pinchot came out with his drink, sat down.

It became a long night. We talked and talked, about what I was not sure. Finally both Sarah and I had drunk too much to be able to drive back. We were kindly offered a bedroom.

It was in that bedroom, in the dark, as we poured a last good red wine, Sarah asked me, 'You going to write a screenplay?'

'Hell no,' I answered.

Chapter Two

THE NEXT CALL from Jon Pinchot came 3 or 4 days later. He knew Danny Server, the young producer-director who had an entire movie studio down in Venice. Danny was going to lend us his screening room so we could see Pinchot's documentary, *The Laughing Beast*, about a black ruler who did it his way with bloody gusto. We were to meet first at Pinchot's for a few drinks. And so, it was back to Sailboat Lane again . . .

Jon answered the door and Sarah and I entered. Jon was not alone. A fellow stood there. He had a strange head of hair: it looked white and blond at the same time. The face was pink, going toward red. The eyes were a crazy round blue, very round, very blue. He had the look of a schoolboy about to play a horrible prank. That look, I would learn, never left him. He was likeable right off.

'This is François Racine,' said Jon. 'He acts in many of my films, and in others.'

'And in the others, I get *paid* . . .' He bowed. 'How do you do?'

Jon went for the drinks.

'Please pardon me,' said François, 'I will be finished in a moment.'

On the table he had a little roulette wheel, electrically controlled, it was set off whirling with the push of a button.

He had stacks of chips and a long sheet of paper full of calculations. There was also a betting board. He placed his chips, pushed the button, said, 'It is my Lady with the Spinning Head. I am in love.'

Jon came out with the drinks.

'When François is not actually gambling, he is usually practicing or at least thinking about it.'

The wheel stopped and François raked in his reward.

'I have studied the permutations of the wheel and I have it,' said François, 'so no matter where it stops, I have guessed and I win.'

'And his system works,' said Jon, 'but when he gets to the casinos he does not always stay with his system.'

'I am often defeated by the Death Wish,' François explained.

'Hank gambles,' said Sarah. 'He plays the horses. He's there every day they run.'

François looked at me. 'Ah, the horses! You win?'

'I like to think I do . . .'

'Ah, we go some day!'

'Sure.'

François went back to his little wheel and we sat with our drinks.

'He has won and lost hundreds of thousands,' Jon told us. 'The only time he wants to be an actor is when he is dead broke.'

'Makes sense,' I said.

'By the way,' said Jon, 'I have talked to the producer Harold Pheasant and he is very interested in the screenplay. He is ready to back it as a movie.'

'Harold Pheasant!' said Sarah. 'I've heard of him. He's one of the biggest producers in the business.'

'That's right,' said Jon.

'But I haven't *written* a screenplay,' I countered.

'No matter. He knows your writing. He's ready.'

'It doesn't seem plausible.'

'He often works that way and he makes nothing but money.'

Jon went for the bottle.

'Maybe you *ought* to write a screenplay,' Sarah suggested.

'Look what it did to F. Scott Fitzgerald.'

'You're not Fitzgerald.'

'No, he gave up drinking. That killed him.'

François was still at his little roulette wheel. Jon came out with the bottle.

'We'll have one more and then we should go.'

'O.K.,' I said.

'Listen, François, are you coming along?' Jon asked.

'Oh no, please pardon me, I must do more research here . . .'

Chapter Three

IT WAS A nice screening room. Off to one side was a fairly large bar, with bartender. The screening room even came with a projectionist. Danny Server wasn't about.

There were 7 or 8 people at the bar. I didn't know who any of them were. I switched to vodka 7's and Sarah was drinking something purple or green or green-purple. Jon was off setting up the film with the projectionist.

There was a fellow down at the end of the bar, staring at me. He kept it up.

I finally looked at him.

'Just what do you do?' I asked.

He paused a moment, had a drink, looked back:

'I blush to the very toes of my shoes to tell you this, but . . . I make films.'

I was to find out he was Wenner Zergog, the noted German filmmaker. He was kind of crazy, off the end of the stick as they say, always taking insane chances with his own life and everybody else's.

'You ought to get into something worthwhile,' I told him.

'I know,' he answered, 'but I don't know how to do anything else.'

Then Jon was there.

'Come on, it's about to start . . .'

Sarah and I followed him into the screening room. Some of the others at the bar came along, including Wenner and his lady companion. We seated ourselves and Jon told us, 'That was Wenner Zergog at the bar. Last week he and his wife had a pistol fight, they emptied their guns at each other, hitting nothing . . .'

'I hope his aim in his films is better . . .'

'Oh, it is.'

The room darkened and *The Laughing Beast* spread across the screen.

Lido Mamin was a large man, in size and ambition, but his country was poor and small. With the big countries he played his cards both Left and Right, bargaining and counter-bargaining with both factions for money, food, weapons. But, actually, *he* wanted to rule the world. He was a bloody bastard with a marvelous sense of humor. He realized that, basically, all life was worthless, except his. Anybody the least suspect in his country was quickly murdered and dumped into the river. There were so many bodies floating in the river that the croco-diles became bloated and could eat no more.

Lido Mamin loved the camera. Pinchot had had Mamin stage a council meeting for the camera. His underlings sat before him trembling as Mamin asked questions, made statements of policy. He grinned continually, showing huge yellow teeth. When he wasn't killing somebody or ordering somebody killed, he was fucking. He had a dozen or more wives and more children than he could remember.

At times, during the council meeting, he stopped smiling, his face became the Will of God, he could do anything, and might. He could sense the fear of his cohorts and he delighted in and used that fear.

The council meeting ended without anybody getting murdered.

Then he called a meeting of all the doctors in the country.

He assembled them at the main hospital, in the huge operating room, and they sat in the seats that circled above and Mamin stood down there in the center and spoke to them.

'You are doctors but you are nothing unless I tell you that you are something. You think you know certain things but this is an illusion. You are only trained in one small area. Let that training be useful to our country and not to yourselves. We live in a world where only the final survivors will be proven right. I will tell you how to use your surgical tools and your lives. Please do not be foolish and go against my wishes. I do not wish to waste your education and your skill. You must always remember that you know only what you have been taught. I know *more* than what is taught. You will always do as I suggest, I want to make this VERY CLEAR. Do you understand me?'

There was silence.

'Please,' continued Mamin, 'is there anybody who wishes to counter what I have just said?'

Further silence.

Mamin was a doll, a monstrous doll, and in a way you could like his gross and terrible style – as long as you didn't have to view the actual killings and torturings.

Next, for the camera, Lido Mamin showed off his Air Force. Only he didn't have an Air Force. Not yet. But he had the aviators and the uniforms.

'This,' Lido Mamin said, 'is our Air Force.'

The first aviator came running down a long row of boards. He ran very swiftly. Then when he reached the end of the runway of boards he leaped into the air and flapped his arms. Then landed.

Then the next aviator came running along. Repeat.

Next aviator.

Next.

There must have been 14 or 15 aviators. As each one leaped he gave a little yell and upon each face there was laughter and elation. It was very strange after you got the feeling of it: for each was laughing at how ridiculous it was, yet each *believed*.

After the last take-off and landing, Mamin faced the camera.

'As foolish as this must look, it is very important. What we do not have in actuality, we are ready for in spirit. Someday we will have our Air Force. Meanwhile, we do not sulk in shadows of unbelief. Thank you very much.'

Then there were some interior shots of the torture chambers. Nobody in them. But there was dung. Chains. Blood on the walls.

'This,' said Lido Mamin, 'is where the traitors and the liars finally tell the truth.'

The final scene was of Mamin in a huge garden with many bodyguards, with all his wives and all his children. The children didn't smile or jump about. They faced the camera silently as did the bodyguards. All the wives smiled, some of them holding babies. Lido Mamin smiled, showing his big yellow teeth. He looked very likeable, maybe even loveable.

The final shot was of the river of fat crocodiles. They just floated, vastly overweight and listless, eyes just rolling a bit as the bodies drifted by. Finis.

It was a fascinating documentary and I was happy to tell Pinchot as much.

'Yes,' he answered, 'I like strange men. That is why I have come to find you.'

'I am very honored,' I said, 'to be one with Lido Mamin.'

'It's true,' he said, and then we left to go back to his place.

Chapter Four

WHEN WE RETURNED, François Racine was intent over his little spinning roulette wheel. He had evidently drunk a great deal of wine. His face was quite flushed and he had a large stack of chips in front of him. A huge ash was about to drop off the end of his cigar. It fell to the table.

'I have won one million, four hundred and fifty thousand dollars . . .'

The little ball stopped at a number. François raked in the chips:

'That's enough . . . I mustn't be greedy.'

We walked to the front room, sat down. Jon went for the wine and the glasses.

'What are you going to do with all the money you've won?' Sarah asked.

'I'm going to give it away. It's nothing. Life is for nothing. Money is nothing.'

'Money is like sex,' I said. 'It seems much more important when you don't have any . . .'

'You talk like a writer,' said François.

Jon was back. He opened the first bottle, poured drinks all around.

'You ought to come to Paris,' he said to me, 'you are well-regarded there. Your own country treats you like an outcast.'

'Do they have a racetrack there?'

'Oh, yes!' said François.

'He hates to travel,' said Sarah, 'and they have racetracks here.'

'Nothing like in Paris,' said François. 'You come to Paris. We'll go to the track together.'

'Hell, I gotta write a screenplay.'

'We'll play the horses and then we'll write.'

'Let me think it over.'

Jon lit a cigar. Then François found a new cigar and lit it. The cigars were long and round and made sizzling sounds at the lighted end.

'May the Lord save me,' said Sarah.

'François and I went to Vegas the other night.'

'How'd you make out?' asked Sarah.

François took a big swallow of his wine, inhaled on his cigar, blew out a vast, magic plume of smoke.

'Listen. Listen to this. I am five thousand dollars ahead, I am in control of the world, I hold Destiny in my hand like a cigarette lighter. I know Everything. I am Everything. There is no stopping me. The continents tremble. Then, Jon taps me on the shoulder. He says, "Let's go see Tab Jones." "Who is this Tab Jones?" I ask. "Never mind," he says, "let's go see him . . ."'

François emptied his wine glass. Jon refilled it.

'So we go into this other room. Here is this Tab Jones. He sings. His shirt is open and the black hairs on his chest show. The hairs are sweating. He wears a big silver cross in these sweating hairs. His mouth is a horrible hole cut into a pancake. He's got on tight pants and he's wearing a dildo. He grabs his balls and sings about all the good things he can do for women. He really sings badly, I mean, he is *terrible*. All about what he can do to women, but he's a fake, he really wants his tongue up some man's anus. I am to puke, listening to him. And we paid this good money too. And when you pay for a nightmare, you are *really* a fool! Who is this Tab Jones? They pay this fellow thousands for wearing a dildo and grabbing his balls and letting the lights shine on the cross. Good men starve in the streets and here is this ID-IOTE . . . being ADORED! The women are *screaming*! *They* think he is real! This *cardboard* man who sucks on shit in his dreams. "Jon," I say, "please, let's leave, my mind is sliding away, I am offended and about to get sick in my lap!" "Wait," he says, "maybe he'll get better." He doesn't get better, he gets worse, he is louder, his shirt opens more, we see his bellybutton. A woman sitting next to me moans and reaches down into her panties. "Madame," I ask her, "did you lose something?" The bellybutton, it's like a dead eye, it's dirty. Even a bird would be offended to leave his droppings there. Then this Tab Jones turns and shows us his behind. I can see behinds anytime, anywhere, and I don't even want to, and here we have to pay MONEY to see this fat, soft, ugly ass! You know, I've had bad times, I've been beaten by the police, for instance, for nothing. Well, almost for nothing. But looking at those dumb buttocks I felt worse than when the police were beating me for nothing. "Jon," I said, "we must leave or my life is over!"'

Jon smiled, 'So we left. I just wanted to see Tab Jones.'

François was now actually in a fury. Little white flecks were forming at the corners of his mouth. Bits of spittle flew as he spoke. The end of his cigar was soaked darkly.

'Tab Jones! WHO IS THIS TAB JONES? What do *I* care for Tab Jones? Tab Jones is a fool! I am five thousand ahead and what do we do? We go see Tab Jones! Who is this Tab Jones? I know of no Tab Jones. My brother's name is not Tab Jones! Not even my mother's name! This Tab Jones is a fool!'

'So,' said Jon, 'we went back to the wheel.'

'Yes,' said François, 'I am five thousand ahead and we have seen the dead dildo sing. My concentration is broken. Who is this Tab Jones? I've seen better men picking up seagull dung! Where am I? The wheel spins and it is a stranger! I am like a baby dumped into a barrel of tarantulas! What are these numbers? What are these colors? The little white ball leaps and buries itself in my heart, eating from the inside out. I have no chance. My concentration is broken! Dildoes parade as the idiots scream for more! I am dizzied. I leap in with a rush of chips. I see my skull already in the stupid casket. Who is this Tab Jones? I lose. I don't know where I am. Once the concentration is broken, once you begin to fall, there is no return. Knowing I had no chance, I played all the chips away. I made all the wrong moves as if an enemy had taken over my body and my mind. I was finished. And why? BECAUSE WE HAD TO GO SEE TAB JONES? I ask you, WHO IS THIS FUCKING TAB JONES?'

François was finished, exhausted. His cigar fell out of his mouth. Sarah picked it up and put it in an ashtray. François immediately found a new cigar in his shirt pocket, slid it out of its silver tube, did the licking and the priming, rolled it, stuck it into his mouth, gathered himself and lit it with a fine flourish. He reached for the bottle, poured drinks all about, straightened up, smiled:

'Shit, I probably would have lost anyhow. A gambler without an excuse is a gambler who can't continue.'

'You talk like a writer,' I said.

'If I could write like one, I'd write that screenplay for you.'

'Thank you.'

'What's he paying you?'

I made a motion through the air with my hand: nebulous answer.

'I will write it for you and we will split it in half, all right?'

'All right.'

'No,' said Jon, 'I will be able to tell the difference.'

'All right, then,' said François, 'Tab Jones will write it with his dildo.'

We all agreed on that, lifted our glasses in a toast. It was the beginning of a good night.

Chapter Five

I WAS LEANING against the bar in Musso's. Sarah had gone to the ladies room. I liked the bar at Musso's, bar just as bar, but I didn't like the room it was in. It was known as the 'New Room'. The 'Old Room' was on the other side and I preferred to eat there. It was darker and quieter. In the old days I used to go to the Old Room to eat but I never actually ate. I just looked at the menu and told them, 'Not yet,' and kept ordering drinks. Some of the ladies I brought there were of ill-repute and as we drank on and on, often loud arguments began, replete with cursing and spilling of drinks, calls for more to drink. I usually gave the ladies cab fare and told them to get the hell out and I went on drinking alone. I doubt they ever used the cab fare for cab fare. But one of the nicest things about Musso's was that when I returned again, after fucking up, I was always greeted with warm smiles. So strange.

Anyhow, I was leaning against the bar and the New Room was full, mostly with tourists, they were chatting and they were twisting their necks and they were giving off rays of death. I ordered a new drink and then there was a tap on my shoulder.

'Chinaski, how are you?'

I turned and looked. I never knew who anybody was. I could meet you the night before and not remember you the next day. If they dug my mother out of her grave I wouldn't know who she was.

'I'm all right,' I said. 'Can I buy you a drink?'

'No, thanks. We haven't met. I'm Harold Pheasant.'

'Oh yeah. Jon told me you were thinking of . . .'

'Yes, I want to finance your screenplay. I've read your work. You've got a marvelous sense of dialogue. I've read your work: *very* filmatic!'

'Sure you won't have a drink?'

'No, I have to get back to my table.'

'Yeah. What ya been doing lately, Pheasant?'

'Just finished producing a film about the life of Mack Derouac.'

'Yeah? What's it called?'

'*The Heart's Song.*'

I took a drink.

'Hey, wait a minute! You're *joking*! You're not going to call it *The Heart's Song*?'

'Oh yes, that's what it's going to be called.'

He was smiling.

'You can't fool me, Pheasant. You're a real joker! *The Heart's Song*! Jesus Christ!'

'No,' he said, 'I'm serious.'

He suddenly turned and walked off . . .

Just then Sarah came back. She looked at me.

'What are you grinning about?'

'Let me order you a drink and I'll tell you.'

I got the barkeep over and also ordered another for myself.

'Guess who I saw in the Old Room,' she said.

'Who?'

'Jonathan Winters.'

'Yeah. Guess who I talked to while you were gone.'

'One of your x-sluts.'

'No, no. Worse.'

'There's nothing worse than those.'

'I talked to Harold Pheasant.'

'The producer?'

'Yes, he's over at that corner table.'

'Oh, I *see*!'

'No, don't *look*. Don't wave. Drink your drink. I'll drink mine.'

'What the hell's wrong with you?'

'You see, he was the producer who was going to produce the screenplay that I haven't written.'

'I know.'

'While you were gone he came over to talk to me.'

'You already said.'

'He didn't even want a drink.'

'So you screwed it up and you're not even drunk.'

'Wait. He wanted to talk about a movie he had just produced.'

'How'd you screw it up?'

'I didn't screw it up. *He* screwed it up.'

'Sure. Tell me.'

I looked in the mirror. I liked myself but I didn't like myself in the mirror. I didn't look like that. I finished my drink.

'Finish your drink,' I said.

She did.

'Tell me.'

'That's twice you've said, "Tell me."'

'Remarkable memory and you're not even drunk yet.'

I motioned the barkeep in, ordered again.

'Well, Pheasant came over and he told me about this movie he produced. It's about a writer who couldn't write but who got famous because he looked like a rodeo rider.'

'Who?'

'Mack Derouac.'

'And that upset you?'

'No, that didn't matter. It was fine until he told me the title of the movie.'

'Which was?'

'Please. I am trying to drive it out of my mind. It's utterly stupid.'

'Tell me.'

'All right . . .'

The mirror was still there.

'Tell me, tell me, tell me . . .'

'All right: *The Furry Flotsam Flies.*'

'I like that.'

'I didn't. I told him so. He walked off. We lost our only backer.'

'You ought to go over there and apologize.'

'No way. Horrendous title.'

'You just wanted his movie to be about *you.*'

'*That's it!* I'll write a screenplay about myself!'

'Got the title?'

'Yeah: *Flies In the Furry Flotsam.*'

'Let's get out of here.'

With that, we did.

Chapter Six

WE WERE TO meet Jon Pinchot in the lobby of the Beverly Hills Cheshire at 2 p.m. It meant missing a day at the track, which did bother me, but Jon had insisted. There was a fellow there who had the ability to raise money, to back films. This fellow, Jean-Paul Sanrah, had no money himself but it didn't matter: they said he could jack off a statue in the park and money would emanate from the genitals. Great. Suite #530. Sounded more like quitting time.

Also, lounging around Suite #530 was Jon-Luc Modard, the French film director. Pinchot said he more than liked what I wrote. Great.

Dear Sarah was along in case I needed help getting back home. Besides, she believed there might be starlets in #530 flashing their navels.

We got there and Jon was in the lobby sitting in a big leather chair, looking for freaks and madmen. He saw us, then rose, puffing out his chest. Jon was a big fellow but he always liked to appear larger than he was.

We exchanged words of greeting and followed Jon Pinchot to the elevator.

'How's the screenplay coming?'

'It's jelling.'

'What's it about?'

'A drunk. Lots of drunks.'

The elevator door opened. It was nice in there. Padded green, dark fluffed green material and if you looked into the green you could see peacocks there, many many peacocks. They were in the ceiling too.

'Class,' I said.

'Too much,' said Sarah.

It stopped at 5 and we moved out. The rug was made of more fluffed green with more peacocks. We were walking on peacocks. Then we were at #530. It was a large heavy black door, much larger than ordinary doors, maybe twice as large. It looked more like the gate beyond the moat.

Jon rapped with an iron knocker shaped into the head of Balzac.

Nothing.

He knocked again. Louder.

We waited.

Then the door slowly opened. A little man almost as white as a sheet of paper opened the door.

'Henri-Leon!' said Jon Pinchot.

'Jon!' said Henry-Leon. Then, 'Do, all of you, please come in!'

We walked in. It was spacious. And everything was over-size. Large chairs, large tables. Long walls. High ceilings. But there was a strange musty smell. For all the vastness there was the feeling of a tomb.

We were introduced about.

The fellow as white as a sheet of paper was Henri-Leon Sanrah, the brother of Jean-Paul Sanrah, the money-getter. And there was Jon-Luc Modard. He stood very still, said nothing. You got the idea that he was posing, being a genius. He was small, dark, looked like he had shaved badly with a cheap electric razor.

'Ah,' Henri-Leon Sanrah said to me, 'you brought your daughter! I've heard about your daughter, Reena!'

'No, no,' I said, 'this is Sarah. She's my wife.'

'There are drinks on the table. Many wines. And food. Please help yourself. I'll go get Jean-Paul,' said Henri.

With that Henri-Leon offed to the other room to find Jean-Paul. And with that, Jon-Luc Modard turned and walked to a dark corner, placed himself there and watched us. We went to the table.

'Open the red,' I said to Pinchot. 'Open several reds.'

Pinchot began working the wine opener. There was food everywhere on silver platters.

'Don't eat the meat,' said Sarah. 'Or the cakes: too much sugar.'

The gods had sent Sarah to add ten years to my life. The gods kept driving me toward the blade, then, at the last moment, lifting my head off the block. Very strange, those gods. Now they were driving me to write a screenplay. I had no appetite for that. Of course, I knew if I wrote it it would be a good one. Not a great one. But a good one. I was hot with words.

Pinchot poured the wine. We all lifted our glasses.

'Umm Hummm,' said Sarah.

'French,' said Pinchot.

'I forgive you,' I said.

As we drank, I was able to see into the other room. The door, as they say, was ajar. And Henri-Leon was trying to rouse a large body resting on this large bed. The body would not rouse.

I saw Henri-Leon reach into a bowl and grab a handful of ice cubes. Two hands full. He pressed the ice cubes against both sides of the face and on the forehead. He opened the shirt and rubbed the ice on the chest.

The body still didn't rouse.

Then all at once it sat up, screamed: 'YOU SON OF A BITCH, WHAT HAVE YOU DONE? I'M GOING TO HAVE TO DEFROST MYSELF!'

'Jean-Paul, Jean-Paul . . . you have . . . visitors . . .'

'VISITORS? VISITORS? I NEED VISITORS LIKE A DOG NEEDS FLEAS! GO OUT THERE AND STUFF FROGS IN THEIR MOUTHS! PISS ON THEM! BURN THEM!'

'Jean-Paul, Jean-Paul . . . you had an appointment . . . with Jon Pinchot and his screenwriter . . .'

'All right . . . shit . . . I'll be right out . . . I'm going to jack-off first . . . No, no, I'll wait . . . something to look forward to . . .'

Henri-Leon came out and spoke to us.

'He'll be right out. He's been under terrific pressure. He thought his wife was leaving him. Early today, a cablegram from Paris: now she has changed her mind. It was a mortal blow, like great oxen being ripped apart by a pack of mad dogs . . .'

We didn't know what to say.

Then Jean-Paul came trundling out. He was dressed in white pants with wide yellow stripes. Pink stockings. No shoes. His hair was all in brown curls, didn't need combing. But the brown hair looked bad. Like it was dying and couldn't make up its mind what color to be. He was undershirted and scratching. He kept scratching. Unlike his brother, he was big, and pink . . . no, red, a red that flamed and faded, faded away one moment to his brother's white, then flamed, redder than ever.

The introductions went around.

'Ah, ah, ah,' he said.

Then, 'Where's Modard?'

Then, he looked around, saw Modard in the corner.

'Hiding again, huh? God damn, I wish he'd do something *new*.'

Suddenly Jean-Paul turned and ran back into the bedroom, slamming the door.

Modard let out a little cough from his corner and we poured some more wine. It was all really excellent. Life was good. All you had to do in their little world was be a writer or an artist or a ballet dancer and you could just sit or stand around, inhaling and exhaling, drinking wine, pretending you knew what the hell.

Then Jean-Paul came crashing back through the door. I thought he'd hurt his shoulder. He stopped, felt his shoulder, dismissed it, scratched himself and charged forward again. He began circling the table at a quick and even pace, shouting:

'WE'VE ALL GOT ASSHOLES, RIGHT? IS THERE ANYBODY IN THIS ROOM WITHOUT AN ASSHOLE? IF SO, SPEAK UP AT ONCE, AT ONCE, YOU HEAR ME?'

Jon Pinchot dug his elbow into my side: 'See, he's a genius, see?'

Jean-Paul circled at the same quick pace, screaming: 'WE'VE ALL GOT THIS SLICE IN THE BACK, RIGHT? DOWN THERE, ABOUT IN THE MIDDLE, RIGHT? THE SHIT POURS OUT OF THERE, RIGHT? OR AT LEAST WE HOPE IT DOES! TAKE AWAY OUR SHIT AND WE ARE DEAD! THINK HOW MUCH SHIT WE SHIT IN A LIFE-TIME! THE EARTH, AT THE MOMENT, ABSORBS IT! BUT THE SEAS AND THE RIVERS ARE GAGGING UP THEIR VERY LIVES WHILE SWALLOWING OUR SHIT! WE ARE FILTHY, FILTHY, FILTHY! I HATE US ALL! EVERY TIME I WIPE MY ASS, I HATE US ALL!'

Then, he stopped, seemed to see Pinchot.

'You want money, right?'

Pinchot smiled.

'Fucker, I will get you your god damned money,' said Jean-Paul.

'Thank you. I just told Chinaski, here, that you were a genius.'

'Shut up!'

Then Jean-Paul looked at me.

'The best thing about your writing is that it excites the Institutionalized. Also those that should be excited. And that figure goes into the many millions. If you can only remain pure in your stupidity, someday you may get a phone call from hell.'

'Jean-Paul, I've already gotten those.'

'Yeah? Huh? Who?'

'X-girl friends.'

'YOU DULL ME!' he screamed and began circling the table again, scratching himself as he did so.

Then, after one last big circle, he ran to the bedroom, slammed the door and was gone.

'My brother,' said Henri-Leon, 'is not feeling well today. He is upset.'

I reached around and refilled the glasses.

Pinchot leaned toward me and whispered, 'This suite, they've been here for days, eating and drinking, they don't have to pay the bill . . .'

'Really?'

'It's paid for by Frances Ford Lopalla. He thinks Jean-Paul is a genius . . .'

'Love and Genius are two of the most over-used words in the language,' I said.

'You're starting to talk silly now,' Sarah told me, 'you're starting to get stinko.'

With that, Jon-Luc Modard emerged from his corner. He walked up to us.

'Give me a fucking wine,' he said.

I poured it tall. Jon-Luc drank it right down. I poured another.

'I've read your shit,' he said. 'Best thing about it, it's so simple. You have a case of brain-damage, no?'

'I might. I lost almost all the blood in my body in 1957. I was in the basement of a charity ward for 2 days before some crazy intern with a conscience found me. I think maybe I lost a lot of things then, more mental than physical.'

'It is one of his favorite stories,' said Sarah. 'I love him, but you have no idea how many times I've had to listen to that story.'

'I love you too, Sarah,' I said, 'but somehow, the telling of old stories, again and again, seems to bring them closer to what they were supposed to be.'

'O.K., Popsy, I'm sorry,' Sarah said.

'Listen,' said Jon-Luc, 'what I want to ask you to do is to write the English dialogue for the sub-titles of my new movie. Also, I have a scene I want to use from one of your stories, where the man gets a blow job under the desk and just goes about his business, answering the telephone and all that crap. Is it a deal?'

'It's a deal,' I said.

Then we just pulled up the chairs and started drinking. And Jon-Luc started talking. He talked and he talked, looking only at me. At first, I felt flattered, then after a while, I felt less than that.

Jon-Luc kept right on talking. He was being dark and playing Genius. Maybe he was a Genius. I didn't want to get bitter about it. But I had had Genius pushed at me all through school: Shakespeare, Tolstoy, Ibsen, G.B. Shaw, Chekov, all those dullards. And worse, Mark Twain, Hawthorne, the Brontë sisters, Dreiser, Sinclair Lewis, it all just laid on you like a slab of cement, and you wanted to get out and away, they were like heavy stupid parents insisting upon regulations and ways that would make even the dead cringe.

Jon-Luc just kept right on talking. That's all I remember. Except now and then, my good Sarah saying, 'Hank, you shouldn't drink so much. Slow down a little. I don't want you dead in the morning.'

But Jon-Luc was on a roll.

I no longer understood what he was saying. I saw lips moving. He was not unpleasant, he was just there. He needed a shave. And we were in this strange Beverly Hills hotel where you walked on peacocks. A magic world. I liked it because I hadn't seen anything like it before. It was senseless and perfect and safe.

The wine poured and Jon-Luc kept going.

I lapsed into my pathetic cut-off period. Often with humans, both good and bad, my senses simply shut off, they get tired, I give up. I am polite. I nod. I pretend to understand because I don't want anybody to be hurt. That is the one weakness that has lead me into the most trouble. Trying to be kind to others I often get my soul shredded into a kind of spiritual pasta.

No matter. My brain shuts off. I listen. I respond. And they are too dumb to know that I am not there.

The drinks poured and Jon-Luc kept on talking. I'm sure that he said many astonishing things. I simply focused on his eyebrows . . .

The next morning in my own place, in Sarah's and my bed, the phone rang about 11 a.m.

'Hello?'

It was Pinchot.

'Listen, I have to tell you something!'

'Yes?'

'Modard NEVER TALKS. There has been NOBODY, NOBODY WHO HAS EVER CAUSED HIM TO TALK LIKE YOU DID! HE TALKED FOR HOURS! EVERY-BODY WAS ASTONISHED!'

'Oh, O.K.'

'YOU DON'T UNDERSTAND! HE NEVER TALKS! HE TALKED TO YOU FOR HOURS!'

'Listen, Jon, I'm sorry but I'm sick, I have to sleep.'

'All right. But I must tell you one more thing.'

'Shoot.'

'It's about Jean-Paul Sanrah.'

'Yes?'

'He says that I must suffer, that I haven't suffered enough and that when I have suffered more he will get me the money.'

'All right.'

'He's strange, isn't he? A real genius.'

'Yes,' I answered, 'I think that he is.'

I hung it up.

Sarah was still asleep. I turned on my right side, toward the window, because sometimes I snored and I wanted to direct the sound away from her.

I had just fallen into that gentle dark, that last rest given to us before death, when Sarah's favorite cat, Beauty, stepped off her own special pillow by Sarah's head and walked across my face. One clawed foot tore into my left ear, then she jumped to the floor, walked across, and leaped up onto the sill of the open window facing east. As the bloody sun moved up I was not gripped by entrancing thoughts.

Chapter Seven

THAT NIGHT, SITTING at the typer, I poured two drinks, I drank two drinks, I smoked 3 cigarettes and listened to Brahms' Third on the radio, and then I realized that I needed something to help me get into the screenplay. I punched Pinchot's number. He was in.

'Allo?'

'Jon, it's Hank.'

'Hank, how are you?'

'Fine. Listen, I'll take the ten.'

'But you said it might hinder your creative process to take it in advance.'

'I've changed my mind. There hasn't been a creative process.'

'You mean . . . ?'

'I mean, I've worked it out in my mind but there is nothing yet on paper.'

'What do you have in mind?'

'It's about a drunk. He just sits on this barstool night and day.'

'Do you think the people would care about such a man?'

'Listen, Jon, if I worried about what the people cared about I'd never write anything.'

'All right. Should I bring the check over to you?'

'No. Just put it in the mail. Tonight. Thank you.'

'Thank you,' said Jon.

I walked over to the typewriter and sat down. It worked right away. I typed:

THE DRUNK WITH THE BLUE AND YELLOW SOUL

EXTERIOR/INTERIOR – DANDY'S BAR – DAY

The CAMERA PANS DOWN FROM ABOVE; IT MOVES SLOWLY through the bar entrance and INTO THE INTERIOR BAR.

A YOUNG MAN sits on a barstool as if he had been there for eternity. He lifts his glass . . .

I was into it. All you needed was the first line, then everything followed. It was always there, it only needed something to set it running.

That bar came back to me. I remembered how you could smell the urinal from wherever you sat. You needed a drink right off to counteract that. And before you went back to that urinal you needed 4 or 5. And the people of that bar, their bodies and faces and voices came back to me. I was there again. I saw the draft beer again in that thin glass flared at the top, the white foam looking at you, bubbling just a bit. The beer was green and after the first gulp, about a fourth of the glass, you inhaled, held your breath, and you were started. The morning bartender was a good man. The dialogue came and took care of itself. I typed on and on . . .

Then, the phone rang. It was long distance. It was my agent and translator from Germany, Karl Vossner. Karl loved to talk the way he thought hip Americans talked.

'Hey, motherfucker, how ya doin'?'

'All right, Karl, you still riding your joystick?'

'Yeah, my ceiling is riddled with flakes of dry sperm.'

'Good man.'

'Thanks, baby. I learn all the good things from you. But, baby, I got good news. You wanna hear, motherfucker?'

'Oh, yeah, yeah, baby!'

'Well, besides whistling "Dixie" out of my asshole, I've translated 3 of your books: poems, *The Lice of Doom*; short stories, *Cesspool Dreams*; and your novel, *Central Station Arson*.'

'I owe you my left ball, Karl.'

'O.K., send it airmail. But, baby, there's more . . .'

'Tell me, tell me . . .'

'Well, we had a book fair here last month and I met with the 6 biggest publishers in Germany and let me tell you, they are hot for your body!'

'My body?'

'Your body of work, you know. Dig?'

'I dig, baby.'

'I got these 6 big publishers in a hotel room, I laid out the beer and the wine and the cheese and the nuts. Then I told them it would be open bidding for the advance on the 3 books. They just laughed and got into the booze. I had those assholes playing right into our hand. You are a hot number and they know it. I told a few jokes to get them loose, then the bidding started. Well, to get to the short-hairs, Krumph made the largest bid. I had the motherfucker sign a contract. Then we all hung one on together. All us assholes got stinko, Krumph especially. So, we scored. We're in like Flynn!'

'You're one cool dude, Karl. What's my cut?'

'Baby, it should amount to around 35 grand. I'll wire it to you within a week.'

'Man oh man, that's really *rowdy*!'

'It beats blowing glass, motherfucker.'

'And how, baby. Hey, Karl, ever heard this one? What's the difference between a chicken's asshole and a rabbit's asshole?'

'No, what's the difference?'

'Ask little Dick.'

'I got it! Far out!'

With that, our conversation was over.

Within an hour I was 45 thousand dollars richer. 30 years of starvation and rejection were starting to kick in.

I walked back to the typer, poured a good tall drink, belted that, poured another. I found 3/4's of a stale cigar, lit it. Shostakovich's Fifth was on the radio. I hit the typer:

The Bartender, Luke, leans forward over bar, eyeing the young man.

LUKE

Listen, you're in this place night and day. All you do is sit and suck up the booze.

YOUNG MAN

Yep.

LUKE

O.K., look, I don't mean to hurt your feelings or nothing but like maybe this shit don't lead nowhere.

YOUNG MAN

That's all right, Luke, don't worry about me. Just keep them coming.

LUKE

Sure, kid. But ain't there another part of you somewhere?

YOUNG MAN

Hey, Luke, you ever heard this one? What's the difference between a chicken's asshole and a rabbit's asshole?

LUKE

I don't want to hear no jokes, man. I want to know: Isn't there another part of you somewhere?

YOUNG MAN

Well, shit. I was in the 6th grade, I think. The teacher asked us to write something about our most moving experience. And I don't mean like moving to Denver.

LUKE

Yeah.

YOUNG MAN

Anyhow, I wrote about this frog I found in the garden. He had one of his legs caught in a wire fence. He couldn't get away. I got his leg out of the wire fence but he still wouldn't move.

LUKE
(*yawning*)

Yeah?

YOUNG MAN

So I held him in my lap and talked to him. I told him that I was trapped, that my life was caught in something too. I talked to him for a long time. At last he hopped out of my lap and hopped across the lawn and vanished into some brush. And I said to myself that he was the first thing that I had ever missed in my life.

LUKE

Yeah?

YOUNG MAN

The teacher read it to the class. Everybody cried.

LUKE

Yeah. So?

YOUNG MAN

Well, I thought that some day I might be a writer.

LUKE
(*leaning forward*)

Kid, you're nuts!

I decided that was enough screenplay writing for one night.
I just sat by the typer and listened to the music on the radio. I
didn't remember going to bed. But in the morning, I was there.

Chapter Eight

VIN MARBAD CAME highly recommended by Michael Huntington, my official photographer. Michael snapped me constantly, but so far there had been no large call for these efforts.

Marbad was a tax consultant. He arrived one night with his briefcase, a dark little man. I had been drinking quietly for some hours, sitting with Sarah while watching a movie on my old black-and-white tv.

He knocked with a rapid dignity and I let him in, introduced him to Sarah, poured him a wine.

'Thank you,' he said, taking a sip. 'You know, that here in America, if you don't spend money they are going to take it away.'

'Yeah? What you want me to do?'

'Put a payment down on a house.'

'Huh?'

'Mortgage payments are tax deductible.'

'Yeah, what else?'

'Buy a car. Tax deductible.'

'All of it?'

'No, just some. Let me handle that. What we have to do is build you some tax shelters. Look here—'

Vin Marbad opened his briefcase and slipped out many sheets of paper. He stood up and came toward me with the papers.

'Real estate. Here, I've bought some land in Oregon. This

is a tax write-off. There are some acres still available. You can get in now. We look for a 23% appreciation each year. In other words, after four years your money is doubled . . .'

'No, no, please sit back down.'

'What's the matter?'

'I don't want to buy anything that I can't see, I don't want to buy anything that I can't reach out and touch.'

'You mean, you don't trust me?'

'I just met you.'

'I have world-wide recommendations!'

'I always go by my instincts.'

Vin Marbad spun back toward the couch where he had left his coat; he slipped into it and then with briefcase he rushed to the door, opened it, was out, closed it.

'You've hurt his feelings,' said Sarah. 'He's just trying to show you some ways to save money.'

'I have two rules. One is, never trust a man who smokes a pipe. The other is, never trust a man with shiny shoes.'

'He wasn't smoking a pipe.'

'Well, he looks like a pipe smoker.'

'You hurt his feelings.'

'Don't worry, he'll be back . . .'

The door flung open and there was Vin Marbad. He rushed across the room to his original place on the couch, took off his coat again, placed the briefcase at his feet. He looked at me.

'Michael tells me you play the horses.'

'Well, yeah . . .'

'My first job when I came here from India was at Hollywood Park. I was a janitor there. You know the brooms they use to sweep up the discarded tickets?'

'Yeah.'

'Ever notice how wide they are?'

'Yeah.'

'Well, that was *my* idea. Those brooms used to be regular size. I designed the new broom. I went to Operations with it and they put it to use. I moved up into Operations and I've been moving up ever since.'

I poured him another wine. He took a sip.

'Listen, do you drink when you write?'

'Yes, quite a bit.'

'That's part of your inspiration. I'll make that tax deductible.'

'Can you do that?'

'Of course. You know, I was the one who began making deductions for gasoline use in the automobile. That was my idea.'

'Son of a bitch,' I said.

'Very interesting,' said Sarah.

'I'll fix it so you won't have to pay any taxes at all and it will all be legal.'

'Sounds nice.'

'Michael Huntington doesn't pay taxes. Ask him.'

'I believe you. Let's not pay taxes.'

'All right, but you must do what I tell you. First, you put a down payment on a house, then on a car. Get started. Get a good car. Get a new BMW.'

'All right.'

'What do you type on? A manual?'

'Yes.'

'Get an electric. It's tax deductible.'

'I don't know if I can write on an electric.'

'You can pick it up in a couple of days.'

'I mean, I don't know if I can *create* on an electric.'

'You mean, you're afraid to change?'

'Yes, he is,' said Sarah. 'Take the writers of past centuries, they used quill pens. Back then, he would have held on to that quill pen, he would have fought any change.'

'I worry too much about my god damned soul.'

'You change your brands of booze, don't you?' asked Vin.

'Yeah . . .'

'O.K., then . . .'

Vin lifted his glass, drained it.

I poured the wine around.

'What we want to do is to make you a Corporation, so you get all the tax breaks.'

'It sounds awful.'

'I told you, if you don't want to pay taxes you must do as I say.'

'All I want to do is type, I don't want to carry around a big load.'

'All you do is to appoint a Board of Directors, a Secretary, Treasurer, so forth . . . It's easy.'

'It sounds horrible. Listen, all this sounds like pure shit. Maybe I'd be better off just paying taxes. I just don't want anybody bothering me. I don't want a tax man knocking on my door at midnight. I'll even pay extra just to make sure they leave me alone.'

'That's stupid,' said Vin, 'nobody should *ever* pay taxes.'

'Why don't you give Vin a chance? He's just trying to help you,' said Sarah.

'Look, I'll mail you the Corporation papers. Just read them over and then sign them. You'll see that there's nothing to fear.'

'All this stuff, you see, it gets in the way. I'm working on this screenplay and I need a clear mind.'

'A screenplay, huh? What's it about?'

'A drunk.'

'Ah, you, huh?'

'Well, there are others.'

'I've got him drinking wine now,' said Sarah. 'He was about dead when I met him. Scotch, beer, vodka, gin, ale . . .'

'I've been a consultant for Darby Evans for some years now. You heard of him, he's a screenwriter.'

'I don't go to movies.'

'He wrote *The Bunny That Hopped Into Heaven; Waffles with Lulu; Terror in the Zoo*. He's easily into six figures. And, he's a Corporation.'

I didn't answer.

'He hasn't paid a dime in taxes. And, it's all legal . . .'

'Give Vin a chance,' said Sarah.

I lifted my glass.

'All right. Shit. Here's to it!'

'Atta boy,' said Vin.

I drained my glass and got up and found another bottle. I got the cork out and poured all around.

I let my mind go along with it: you're a wheeler dealer. You're slick. Why pay for bombs that mangle helpless children? Drive a BMW. Have a view of the harbor. Vote Republican.

Then another thought came to my mind:

Are you becoming what you've always hated?

And then the answer came:

Shit, you don't have any real money anyhow. Why not play around with this thing for laughs?

We went on drinking, celebrating something.

Chapter Nine

SO, THERE I was over 65 years old, looking for my first house. I remembered how my father had virtually mortgaged his whole life to buy a house. He had told me, 'Look, I'll pay for one house in my lifetime and when I die you'll get that house and then in your lifetime you'll pay for a house and when you die you'll leave those houses to your son. That'll make two houses. Then your son will . . .'

The whole process seemed terribly slow to me: house by house, death by death. Ten generations, ten houses. Then it would take just one person to gamble all those houses away, or burn them down with a match and then run down the street with his balls in a fruit-picker's pail.

Now I was looking for a house I really didn't want and I was going to write a screenplay I really didn't want to write. I was beginning to lose control and I realized it but I seemed unable to reverse the process.

The first realtor we stopped at was in Santa Monica. It was called TwentySecond Century Housing. Now, that was modern.

Sarah and I got out of the car and walked in. There was a young fellow at the desk, bow tie, nice striped shirt, red suspenders. He looked hip. He was shuffling papers at his desk. He stopped and looked up.

'Can I help you?'

'We want to buy a house,' I said.

The young fellow just turned his head to one side and kept looking away. A minute went past. Two minutes.

'Let's go,' I said to Sarah.

We got back into the car and I started the engine.

'What was all that about?' Sarah asked.

'He didn't want to do business with us. He took a reading and he thought we were indigent, worthless. He thought we would waste his time.'

'But it's not true.'

'Maybe not, but the whole thing made me feel as if I was covered with slime.'

I drove the car along, hardly knowing where I was going. Somehow, that had hurt. Of course, I was hungover and I needed a shave and I always wore clothing that somehow didn't seem to fit me quite right and maybe all the years of poverty had just given me a certain look. But I didn't think it was wise to judge a man from the outside like that. I would much rather judge a man on the way he acted and spoke.

'Christ,' I laughed, 'maybe nobody will sell us a house!'

'The man was a fool,' said Sarah.

'TwentySecond Century Housing is one of the largest real estate chains in the state.'

'The man was a fool,' Sarah repeated.

I still felt diminished. Maybe I *was* a jerk-off of some kind. All I knew how to do was to type – sometimes.

Then we were in a hilly area driving along.

'Where are we?' I asked.

'Topanga Canyon,' Sarah answered.

'This place looks fucked.'

'It's all right except for floods and fires and burned-out-neohippy types.'

Then I saw the sign: APES HAVEN. It was a bar. I pulled

up alongside and we got out. There was a cluster of bikes outside. Sometimes called hogs.

We went in. It was damn near full. Fellows in leather jackets. Fellows wearing dirty scarfs. Some of the fellows had scabs on their faces. Others had beards that didn't grow quite right. Most of the eyes were pale blue and round and listless. They sat very still as if they had been there for weeks.

We found a couple of stools.

'Two beers,' I said, 'anything in a bottle.'

The barkeep trotted off.

The beers came back and Sarah and I had a hit.

Then I noticed a face thrust forward along the bar looking at us. It was a very fat round face, a touch imbecilic. It was a young man and his hair and his beard were a dirty red, but his eyebrows were pure white. His lower lip hung down as if an invisible weight were pulling at it, the lip was twisted and you saw the inner lip and it was wet and it shimmered.

'Chinaski,' he said, 'son of a bitch, it's CHINASKI!'

I gave a small wave, then looked straight ahead.

'One of my readers,' I said to Sarah.

'Oh oh,' she said.

'Chinaski,' I heard a voice to my right.

'Chinaski,' I heard another voice.

A whiskey appeared before me. I lifted it, 'Thank you, fellows!' and I knocked it off.

'Go easy,' said Sarah, 'you know how you are. We'll never get out of here.'

The bartender brought another whiskey. He was a little guy with dark red blotches all over his face. He looked meaner than anybody in there. He just stood there, staring at me.

'Chinaski,' he said, 'the world's greatest writer.'

'If you insist,' I said and raised the glass of whiskey. Then I passed it to Sarah who knocked it off.

She gave a little cough and set the glass down.

'I only drank that to help save you.'

Then there was a little group gathering slowly behind us.

'Chinaski. Chinaski . . . Motherfuck . . . I've read all your books, ALL YOUR BOOKS! . . . I can kick your ass, Chinaski . . . Hey, Chinaski, can you still get it up? . . . Chinaski, Chinaski, can I read you one of my poems?'

I paid the barkeep and we backed off our stools and moved toward the door. Again I noticed the leather jackets and the *blandness* of the faces and the feeling that there wasn't much joy or daring in any of them. There was something totally missing in the poor fellows and something in me wrenched, for just a moment, and I felt like throwing my arms around them, consoling and embracing them like some Dostoyevsky, but I knew that would finally lead nowhere except to ridicule and humiliation, for myself and for them. The world had somehow gone too far, and spontaneous kindness could never be so easy. It was something we would all have to work for once again.

And they followed us out. 'Chinaski, Chinaski . . . Who's your beautiful lady? You don't deserve her, man! . . . Chinaski, come on, stay and drink with us! Be a good guy! Be like your writing, Chinaski! Don't be a prick!'

They were right, of course. We got in the car and I started the engine and we drove slowly through them as they crowded around us, slowly giving way, some of them blowing kisses, some of them giving me the finger, a few beating on the windows. We got through.

We made it to the road and drove along.

'So,' said Sarah, 'those are your readers?'

'That's most of them, I think.'

'Don't any intelligent people read you?'

'I hope so.'

We kept driving along not saying anything. Then Sarah asked, 'What are you thinking about?'

'Dennis Body.'

'Dennis Body? Who's that?'

'He was my only friend in grammar school. I wonder whatever happened to him.'

Chapter Ten

AS WE DROVE along, I saw it: Rainbow Realty.

I pulled up in front. The parking area was not paved and there were large potholes and ruts everywhere. I located the flattest surface, then parked. We got out and walked to the office. The door was open and a fat dirty white chicken sat there. I nudged it with my foot. It stood up, emitted a bit of matter and walked into the office, found a place in the corner and sat down again.

There was a lady at the desk, mid-forties, thin, with straight mud-colored hair embossed with a paper flower, red. She was drinking a beer and smoking a Pall Mall.

'Shit, howdy!' she greeted us, 'looking for a place, round-abouts?'

'You might say,' I answered.

'Well, *say* it then! Ha, ha, ha!'

She knocked her beer off, handed me a card:

> RAINBOW REALTY
> Indeed, I got what you
> need.
>
> Lila Gant,
> at your service

Lila stood up.

'Follow me . . .'

She didn't lock the office. She got into her car. It was a '62 Comet. I knew because I once had a '62 Comet. In fact, it looked like the same one I had sold for junk.

We followed her up a rural winding dirt road. We drove for some minutes. I noted the absence of street lights. Also, on each side of the road were deep canyons. I made a note that driving along there at night with a few drinks in you could be hazardous.

Finally, we pulled up in front of an unpainted wooden house. Well, it had been painted, once, a long time ago but the weather had worn away almost all the paint that had been a henshit white to begin with. The house seemed to sag forward and to the left – our left, as we got out of the car. It was a big house, looked homey, earthy.

All of this, I thought, because I've accepted an advance to write a screenplay and because I've got a tax consultant.

We walked up on the porch and the boards, of course, sagged under our weight. I scaled in at 228, most of it fat instead of muscle. My fighting days were over. To think I had once weighed 144 pounds on a 6-foot frame: the grand old starving days when I was writing the good stuff.

Lila beat on the front door.

'Darlene, honey? You decent? You better be because our butts are a-comin' in! Got some folks who wanna see your castle! Ha, ha, ha!'

Lila pushed the door open and we walked in.

It was dark inside and it smelled like there was a turkey burning in the oven. Also, there was the feeling of shadowy winged creatures floating about. A light bulb hung down from a cord. The insulation had peeled away and you could see the bare wire. I felt something like a cold wind at the back of my neck. Then I realized it was only a rush of fear. I shook that idea off with the thought, this place has got to be really cheap.

Then Darlene emerged from the darkness. Big lipstick mouth. Hair in all directions. Eyes gushing kindness to cover up years of waste. She was fat in blue jeans and faded flower blouse. Two earrings like eyeballs, they hung there swinging a bit, those blue irises. She was holding a rolled joint. She rushed forward.

'Lila, you chippy! What's hangin'?'

Lila took the joint from Darlene's hand, took a drag, handed it back.

'How's your ol' peg-legged-fool-of-a-brother, Willy?'

'Oh, shit, he just got thrown in county jail. He's scared shitless they're gonna get him in the ass!'

'Don't worry, honey, he's too hog-ugly.'

'You really think so?'

'Really.'

'I hope so!'

Then we were introduced around. Then there was silence. We stood there as if we had lost all power of thought, of what we were about. I rather liked it. I thought, well, this is all right, I can stand around here as long as anybody. I concentrated on the twisted wire of the light bulb cord.

A tall thin man slowly entered. He walked toward us, one stiff leg at a time. He put one leg forward and then deliberately followed it with the other. He was like a blind man without a cane. He came toward us. His face was a mass of beard and the thick hair was twisted, tangled. But he had beautiful eyes, a dark dark green. Emeralds for eyes. The sucker was worth something. And he had a *big smile*. He walked closer. Stopped and kept *smiling, smiling*.

'This is my husband,' said Darlene, 'this is Double Quartet.'

He nodded. Sarah and I nodded back.

Lila leaned toward me, whispered, 'They both usta be in the movie business.'

Sarah was getting tired of the time all this took.

'Well, let's have a look at the place!'

'Why, *sure*, honey, you all bring your ass and folla me . . .'

We followed Lila into the other room and as we did I glanced back. I saw Double Quartet take the joint from Darlene and have a drag.

Jesus, he had such great eyes; eyes are truly the reflection of the soul. But, damn, that *big big smile* ruined it all.

We were evidently in the dining room or the front room. There was no furniture. There was an empty water bed nailed to one of the walls and across the water bed, scrawled in red paint was:

THE SPIDER SINGS ALONE

'Looka this,' Lila said, 'look at that yard. Some nice *land*!'

We looked out of the window. The yard was like the road, only more so: large potholes, neglected mounds of dirt and rock. And out there, sitting all by itself, upright, was a lone, discarded toilet. The lid was missing.

'That's nice,' I said, 'kind of odd.'

'These here people are ARTISTS,' said our realtor.

We stepped back. I touched the curtain that covered the window. Where I touched it a piece of the curtain dropped away.

'These here people are *deep* inside,' said Lila. 'They just don't bother with the *ordinaries*, you know.'

We went upstairs and the stairway was solid, strangely so. It was good and true, and I felt a little better then, walking up there.

All that there was in the bedroom was a waterbed but this

one was full. It sat in the far corner, lonely by itself. One strange thing, there was a large swelling at one edge. It gave the impression of an explosion to come.

The bathroom was tiled but the floor had gone unwashed for so long that the tiles had almost disappeared in the smear of dirt and footprints.

The toilet was brown-crusted, forever. No ever changing that. There was crust upon crust upon crust. It was worse than any toilet I had ever seen in any dive, in any bar I had ever been in, and I began to gag at the memory of all those crappers and at the thought of this one here. I walked out for a moment, steadied myself, inhaled, made up my mind not to think about any of it, and then re-entered the bathroom.

'Sorry,' I said.

Lila understood. 'Shit, pard,' she said. 'It's all right . . .'

I didn't look *in* the bathtub but did note that somebody had scrawled with various colored paints on the wall over the bathtub:

IF TIM LEARY AIN'T GOD,
THEN GOD IS DEAD.

MY FATHER DIED IN THE
ABRAHAM LINCOLN BRIGADE
AND THE DEVIL HAS A
PUSSY

CHARLES LINDBERG WAS
A
COCKSUCKER

There were a few other messages painted here and there but they were smeared and garbled and difficult to read.

'I'm gonna let you two wander about, you know, so you can get the feel. Buying a home is a real head-shaker. I don't want to rush you none.'

Then Lila left. We heard her going down the stairway. Sarah and I stepped out into the hallway. Hanging near us, from a frayed rope, was an old rusted coffeepot.

'Oh my god,' Sarah said suddenly, 'my god!'

'What is it?'

'I've seen photos of this house before! I remember now! I *thought* it looked familiar!'

'What? What is it?'

'This is one of the houses where *Charles Manson* killed somebody!'

'Are you sure?'

'Yes, yes!'

'Let's get out of here . . .'

We went on down the stairway. They were waiting for us down there: Lila, Darlene and Double Quartet.

'Well,' asked Lila, 'what do you think?'

'I've got your card with your phone number,' I told her, 'We can get in touch.'

'If you people are artists,' said Darlene, 'we can knock some off the price. We like artists. Are you artists?'

'No,' I said. 'Well, I'm not, anyhow.'

'I can show you some more places,' said Lila.

'No, no,' said Sarah, 'we've seen enough today. We have to rest up.'

We had to push past them, and all the time Double Quartet just kept *smiling, smiling* . . .

Chapter Eleven

BACK AT MY place there were two envelopes. While Sarah got a bottle of wine I opened one of the envelopes. It was a manuscript of some sort, with a covering note:

Chinaski! Piss on you! You were once a great writer! Now you suck! You've sold out! My grandmother writes better shit than you do! You've had your head up your asshole too long! I sent my stuff to your publisher and he sent back a letter. He said 'Thank you for submitting but we are overstocked.' The prick, I'll overstock his butthole! He gobbles shit for breakfast!

The great poets are ignored. They are afraid of the great poets! You were once a great poet but now you are only a band-aid covering a pus-hole! You gobble your own weenie under a sky of vomit! You've sold your balls to the butcher! You've killed the baby of your love! You are monkey stink! Forever and ever and ever!

I enclose some of my latest work . . .

He signed his name with a leaping downward stroke to the right, making a long curving line after the last letter of his name, and below that, what appeared to be a drawing of a face.

It was an envelope full of poems, none of them typewritten. They were hastily printed in blue ink on yellow paper with thin blue lines.

Sarah brought the wine bottle and corkscrew, opened it herself and poured two glasses.

'Charles Manson,' she said, 'no wonder they wanted to let that place go cheap.'

'I'm glad you remembered the photographs.'

Sarah opened the *Herald Examiner* and I began on the first poem:

THE POET
they slay the poet
they burn the poet
they ignore the poet
they hate the poet

but the moon knows
the poet
and the prostitutes
know
the agony of the
poet
and they give it to him
for free
they lick the hair
of his balls in
holy prayer

the poet will not
die

even in death
he sits inside the
moon
and gives the finger

to the
universe!

THE POET AT PLAY:
I suck her strawberry
tits.
I suck the hairs of
her ass.
I eat her vanilla
come.
at dawn she sucks
my toes.
I sneeze through my
ass.
she laughs.
we
sleep.

I didn't feel inclined to read the remainder of the manuscript. I knew what the remaining poems would be about: THE
POET.

Sarah looked up from the *Herald Examiner*.

'Somebody send you some more poems to read?'

'Yes, it happens 3 or 4 times a month.'

'You're not a publisher. Why do they do it?'

'It's a hate-love relationship they feel toward me.'

'How are his poems?'

'He's not as good as he thinks he is, but then most of us feel
that way.'

'You get poems from women too, right?'

'Yeah. Some of them with nude photos and come-ons. They
think I can get them published. Or they want a blurb for the
cover of some small press book.'

'Those dirty cunts!'

'Right!'

We clicked our glasses, drained them, then I poured two more. I opened the other envelope. It was from Vin Marbad:

ARTICLES OF INCORPORATION . . .

I began reading. The jargon was Corporate Lawyer. I tried to break it down into plain English and a part I disliked immediately said:

If the President of the Corporation is judged insane by a court-appointed psychiatrist the other members of said Corporation may by a majority vote divide all the assets of said Corporation equally among themselves.

I took my pen and crossed this passage out with heavy dark lines. Then I poured another drink after emptying my glass and read on:

If the President of said Corporation is judged incapable to carry out his duties because of the use of drugs or intoxicating beverages, or if he is deemed sexually overactive detrimental to the common good of Society or the Corporation, then after a majority vote of said members, the President of said Corporation will be placed in a role of diminished authority and all assets of said Corporation will be divided equally among the remaining members.

I took my pen and heavily marked out this section. Then read further:

If the President of the Corporation is judged senile . . .

I crossed out this passage.

If the President of the Corporation is addicted to gambling . . .

Cross out.

The President of the Corporation is allowed one vote equal to the vote of each member, all votes counting the same . . .

Cross out.

I read on and on. It was horrifying, it seemed barbaric. It was terrifying. I crossed out passage after passage. There must have been 17 or 18 pages. When I finished, the pages were a mass of black lines.

Sarah brought another bottle. I pushed the pages away.

'God Almighty, God Almighty, this has made me sick! This is wretched and pitiful stuff! I can't believe it!'

'Don't sign that crap then,' said Sarah.

'Never,' I said.

I found a piece of paper, then wrote on it;

'Vin:
I can't do it. This is a nightmare in hell!'

Then I jammed everything into the stamped return envelope and pushed it away to mail later.

'It's been a long day,' said Sarah.

'And Charles Manson is not the only killer,' I added.

'You know,' she said, 'he bumped them right off. The others do it from a distance and seldom get caught.'

'Let's drink a while,' I said, 'and readjust to our own reality.'

'Let's drink until the sun comes up.'

'Really?'

'Sure, why not?'

'You're on,' I said, already feeling much better.

Chapter Twelve

THE PLACE I was living in at that time did have some qualities. One of the finest was the bedroom which was painted a dark, dark blue. That dark dark blue had provided a haven for many a hangover, some of them brutal enough to almost kill a man, especially at a time when I was popping pills which people would give me without my bothering to ask what they were. Some nights I knew that if I slept I would die. I would walk around alone all night, from the bedroom to the bathroom and from the bathroom through the front room and into the kitchen. I opened and closed the refrigerator, time and time again. I turned the faucets on and off. Then I went to the bathroom and turned the faucets on and off. I flushed the toilet. I pulled at my ears. I inhaled and exhaled. Then, when the sun came up, I knew I was safe. Then I would sleep with the dark dark blue walls, healing.

Another feature of that place were the knocks of unsavory women at 3 or 4 a.m. They certainly weren't ladies of great charm, but having a foolish turn of mind, I felt that somehow they brought me adventure. The real fact of the matter was that many of them had no place else to go. And they liked the fact that there was drink and that I didn't work too hard trying to bed down with them.

Of course, after I met Sarah, this part of my lifestyle changed quite a bit.

That neighborhood around Carlton Way near Western

Avenue was changing too. It had been almost all lower-class white, but political troubles in Central America and other parts of the world had brought a new type of individual to the neighborhood. The male usually was small, a dark or light brown, usually young. There were wives, children, brothers, cousins, friends. They began filling up the apartments and courts. They lived many to an apartment and I was one of the few whites left in the court complex.

The children ran up and down, up and down the court walkway. They all seemed to be between two and seven years old. They had no bikes or toys. The wives were seldom seen. They remained inside, hidden. Many of the men also remained inside. It was not wise to let the landlord know how many people were living in a single unit. The few men seen outside were the legal renters. At least they paid the rent. How they survived was unknown. The men were small, thin, silent, unsmiling. Most sat on the porch steps in their undershirts, slumped forward a bit, occasionally smoking a cigarette. They sat on the porch steps for hours, motionless. Sometimes they purchased very old junk automobiles and the men drove them *slowly* about the neighborhood. They had no auto insurance or driver's licenses and they drove with expired license plates. Most of the cars had defective brakes. The men almost never stopped at the corner stop sign and often failed to heed red lights, but there were few accidents. Something was watching over them.

After a while the cars would break down but my new neighbors wouldn't leave them on the street. They would drive them up the walkways and park them directly outside their door. First they would work on the engine. They would take off the hood and the engine would rust in the rain. Then they would put the car on blocks and remove the wheels. They took the wheels inside and kept them there so they wouldn't be stolen at night.

While I was living there, there were two rows of cars lined up in the court, just sitting there on blocks. The men sat motionless on their porches in their undershirts. Sometimes I would nod or wave to them. They never responded. Apparently they couldn't understand or read the eviction notices and they tore them up, but I did see them studying the daily L.A. papers. They were stoic and durable because compared to where they had come from, things were now easy.

Well, no matter. My tax consultant had suggested I purchase a house, and so for me it wasn't really a matter of 'white flight.' Although, who knows? I had noticed that each time I had moved in Los Angeles over the years, each move had always been to the North and to the West.

Finally, after a few weeks of house hunting, we found the one. After the down payment the monthly payments came to $789.81. There was a huge hedge in front on the street and the yard was also in front so the house sat way back on the lot. It looked like a damned good place to hide. There was even a stairway, an *upstairs* with a bedroom, bathroom and what was to become my typing room. And there was an old desk left in there, a huge ugly old thing. Now, after decades, I was a writer with a desk. Yes, I felt the fear, the fear of becoming like *them*. Worse, I had an assignment to write a screenplay. Was I doomed and damned, was I about to be sucked dry? I didn't feel it would be that way. But does anybody, ever?

Sarah and I moved our few possessions in.

The big moment came. I sat the typewriter down on the desk and I put a piece of paper in there and I hit the keys. The typewriter still worked. And there was plenty of room for an ashtray, the radio and the bottle. Don't let anybody tell you different. Life begins at 65.

Chapter Thirteen

DOWN AT THE Marina del Rey times were getting hard. For transportation Jon Pinchot was driving a green 1968 Pontiac convertible and François Racine drove a brown 1958 Ford. They also had two Kawasaki motorcycles, a 750 and a 1000.

Wenner Zergog had borrowed the 1958 Ford and by driving the car without putting water in the radiator had cracked the engine block.

'He's a genius,' Jon told me. 'He doesn't know about such things.'

The motorcycles were the first to go. The 1958 was used for shorter trips.

Then François Racine packed off for France. Jon sold the 1958 Ford.

And then, of course, the day came when the phone rang and there was Jon.

'I've got to move. They are going to tear this place down and build a hotel or something. Shit, I don't know where to go. I'd like to stay in town and work out a deal for your screenplay. How's that thing coming along?'

'Oh, it's coming . . .'

'I'm close to a deal. And if it falls through I've got a guy in Canada. But I've got to move. The bulldozers are on the way.'

'Listen, Jon, you can stay at our place. We've got a downstairs bedroom.'

'You mean that?'

'Sure . . .'

'I'll be out most of the time. You won't know I'm there.'

'You still have that 1968 Pontiac?'

'Yes . . .'

'Then put your stuff in and come on over . . .'

I walked downstairs and told Sarah. 'Jon is moving in for a while.'

'What?'

'Jon Pinchot. They're going to bulldoze his place. He'll be staying here a while.'

'Hank, you know you can't stand living with people. It will drive you crazy.'

'It will just be for a little while . . .'

'You'll be upstairs typing and he'll be downstairs listening. It won't work.'

'I'll make it work. Jon has paid me money to write this thing.'

'Good luck,' she said, then turned and walked into the kitchen.

The first two nights weren't bad: Jon and Sarah and I just drank and talked. Jon told some stories, mostly about problems with actors and what he had had to do to get them to perform. There was one fellow, halfway through a shooting, who suddenly refused to talk. He would rehearse the scenes but he wouldn't speak. He was demanding that a certain scene be shot as he wished. They were in the middle of a jungle somewhere and running out of time and money. Finally Jon told the actor, 'Shit, have it your way!' And the actor acted out the scene his way, with dialog. Only he didn't know that there wasn't any film in the camera. After that, there were no problems.

It was on the second night that the wine really flowed. I did some talking myself, mostly repeat stuff, stuff that I had already typed up long ago. It was early in the a.m. when Jon said, 'Giselle has fallen in love with a director with one ball . . .'

Giselle was Jon's girlfriend in Paris.

'I'm sorry,' I said.

'Only it's worse now. Cancer. They have cut out the other ball too. Giselle is very very distraught.'

'It sure seems like bad luck.'

'Yes, yes, I write her, I phone her . . . I do all I can to help. And there they are in the middle of a shooting . . .'

(Everything always happened in the middle of a shooting.)

Giselle was a famous actress in France. She shared an apartment with Jon in Paris.

We attempted to cheer Jon up about his girlfriend's bad luck. He unpeeled a long cigar, licked it, bit off the end, lit up, inhaled and let out the first plume of exotic smoke.

'You know, Hank, I always knew that you would write a screenplay for me. There are things that a man knows instinctively. I've known this for a long time. And I've been searching for the money to do this for a long time, long before I contacted you.'

'Maybe I'll write a very bad screenplay.'

'You won't. I've read everything you've written.'

'That's past. In the writing profession there are more has-beens than anything else.'

'This does not apply to you.'

'I believe he's right, Hank,' said Sarah, 'you're just a natural-ass writer.'

'But a *screenplay*! Shit, it's like I've been roller skating and now you put me on an ice rink!'

'You'll do it. I know you'll do it, I knew you would do it when I was in Russia.'

'Russia?'

'Yes, before I met you I went to Russia looking for the money to produce your future screenplay.'

'Which I didn't know anything about yet.'

'Exactly. Only I knew. Anyhow, I heard from a reliable source that there was a woman in Russia who had $80 million in a Swiss account.'

'Sounds like a cheap tv thriller.'

'Yes, I know. But I checked. I have sources for this kind of thing that are very good. I can't tell you too much about them.'

'We don't want to know,' said Sarah.

'So I found out the lady's address. And then began the long slow process. I began writing the lady letters . . .'

'What did you do?' asked Sarah, 'put in frontal nude photos?'

'Or anal nudes?' I asked.

'Not at first. At first the letters were quite formal. I told her that I had come upon her address in the strangest way, that I had found it scribbled on a tiny piece of paper in a shoe box in a closet in Paris. I suggested that we might be destined. Oh, you have no idea how hard I worked on those letters!'

'You'd do all this to get money to produce a movie?'

'More than that!'

'Would you kill?'

'Please don't ask me that. Anyway, I sent letter after letter, gradually turning them into love letters.'

'I didn't know you knew Russian,' said Sarah.

'I wrote the letters in French. The lady had an interpreter. The lady responded in Russian and then my interpreter put them into the French.'

'They wouldn't use that even in a cheap tv thriller,' I said.

'I know. But I thought about her $80 million in that Swiss account and my letters to her got better and better. Love letters. Red hot.'

'Have some more wine,' I said refilling Jon's glass.

'Well, she finally asked me to come see her. And suddenly like that, I was in the snows of Moscow . . .'

'The snows of Moscow . . .'

'I got a room that I think was bugged by the KGB. I think they even had the toilet bugged. They could hear my shit dropping.'

'I think I hear it dropping too . . .'

'No, no, listen to me . . . I finally made an appointment to see the lady. I went to her place, I knocked. The door opened and there stood this *beautiful* girl! Never have I seen such a *beautiful* girl!'

'Ah, god, Jon, *please* . . .'

'Only it wasn't the *lady*, it was the interpreter!'

'Jon,' Sarah asked, 'what are you drinking beside this wine?'

'Nothing! Nothing! It's *true*! I walked into the room and there was an old hag sitting there dressed in black. She had no teeth but many warts. I walked forward, bent down, took her hand, closed my eyes and kissed it. The interpreter sat in a chair and watched us. I turned to the interpreter.

'"I'd like to be alone with *you*," I said.

'She spoke to the old woman. Then she turned to me and said, "Metra desires to be alone with you. But in a church. Metra is very religious."

'"I believe that I am in love with you," I told the interpreter.

'She spoke to the old woman. The old woman spoke back to her. Then the interpreter spoke to me: "Metra says that love is possible but first she wants you to go to church with her."

'I nodded yes and the old lady got up slowly from her chair, and we left the room together, leaving the beautiful young girl behind . . .'

'This fucking thing could win an Academy Award,' I said.

'Please. Remember, I am trying to get the money for your future screenplay.'

'Yes, please go on, Jon. Tell me the rest . . .'

'All right, we got to the church. We kneeled in the pews. I am not religious. We kneeled for some time in silence. Then she tugged at me. We rose and went forward to an altar full of candles. Some were lit. Many weren't. She started lighting many of the unlit candles. It excited her. Her mouth trembled and little streams of saliva came down out of each corner of her mouth. It ran down and disappeared into her wrinkles. Please believe me, I have nothing, nothing against old age! But why is it that some people age so much worse than others?'

'I dunno,' I said, 'but I have an idea that people who don't think too much tend to look young longer.'

'I don't think this one thought too much . . . anyhow, after lighting many candles she became excited again. She took my hand and squeezed it. She was strong, a strong old lady. She pulled me over to a statue of Christ . . .'

'Yes . . .'

'She let go of me and kneeled and started kissing the feet of this Christ. She went at it. The toes were wet with her saliva. She was in a grand passion. She was quivering. Then she stood up, took my hand, pointed to the feet. I smiled. She pointed again. I smiled again. Then she grabbed me and started pushing me down to the feet. Shit, I thought, and then I thought of $80 million and I kneeled down and kissed the feet. You know, they don't clean those feet well in Russia. Metra's saliva . . . and the dust . . . it was only with great will that I was able to kiss. Then I stood up. Metra led me back to the pew. We knelt again. Suddenly she grabbed me and her mouth was on mine. Please understand, I have nothing against the old, the aged, but it was like kissing a sewer hole. I pulled away.

Something turned in my stomach and I went to the confessional booth, pulled back the curtains, entered, kneeled and puked. Then I rose and we left the church together. I left her at her doorway. Then I got a bottle of vodka and went back to my room.

'You know, if I wrote a screenplay like that they'd run me out of town.'

'I know. But wait. This thing is not over. Drinking the vodka, I thought it all over. No need to back off. The old lady was evidently crazy. One doesn't kiss in church, does one? Maybe at a wedding. So there I was . . .'

'Kiss and get married, huh?' I asked.

'Well, I wanted to be sure of the $80 million. After finishing the vodka, I began a long love letter to Metra, only all the time I was thinking of the interpreter. It was some love letter. And in between the love talk I explained to her that I wanted to make a film about the two of us and that I had heard of her money in Switzerland, only that had *nothing* to do with my being there, except that I was without funds and I wanted dearly to bring our love story to the screen and to the public and to the lovers of Christ.'

'All this to get money to produce a screenplay that Hank didn't even know about and hadn't written?' asked Sarah.

'Absolutely,' said Jon.

'You're crazy,' I suggested.

'Maybe. Anyhow, the old lady got my love letter and I believed she had agreed to go to Switzerland with me to pick up the money. We made arrangements. Meanwhile there were two more trips, to kiss the feet of Christ and to light many candles plus some of the other kiss-kiss bit. Then . . . I got a call from my source. The woman who had the $80 million in Switzerland had the same exact name, was the same age of my old woman, but had been born in a different city of different parents. It was a stupid coincidence and it was over for me. I had been tricked. I'd have to get the money elsewhere . . .'

'That's one of the saddest fucking stories I've ever heard,' I said.

'I'm sorry,' said Jon, 'But it's true.'

'Why do you suffer like this just for the business of making movies?' asked Sarah.

'Because I love it,' answered Jon.

Chapter Fourteen

A COUPLE OF days later we were back down at Danny Server's studio in Venice.

'Another guy has written a movie about skid row and drinking,' said Jon, 'so why don't you check it out?'

So we went there, Jon, Sarah and I. The people were already in their seats. But the bar was closed.

'The bar is closed,' I said to Jon.

'Yes,' he said.

'Listen, we've got to get something to drink . . .'

'There's a liquor store about a block away, toward the water, on the other side of the street.'

'We'll be right back . . .'

We made it down there, got 2 bottles of red and a corkscrew. On the way back we were stopped twice for handouts. Then we were outside the studio. I pushed the door open and we entered. It was dark. The movie was rolling.

'Shit,' I said, 'I can't see! I can't see a fucking thing!'

Somebody hissed at me.

'Same to you,' I said.

'Will you *please be quiet!*' a woman said.

'Let's try the first row of seats,' said Sarah, 'I think I see a couple of seats but I'm not sure.'

We worked our way down front. I tripped over some feet.

'You bastard,' I heard a man say softly.

'Blow it,' I told him.

We finally located 2 seats and sat down. Sarah got out the cigarettes and the lighter while I corkscrewed open a bottle. We had no drinking glasses, so I took a pull and passed the bottle to Sarah. She took a pull and handed it back. Then she lit up 2 cigarettes for us.

The man who had written the movie, *Back From Hades*, had once had a series running on tv, one of those family shows. Pat Sellers. Well, the series had gone on and on but Pat lost the battle with the bottle and soon the series was doomed. Divorce. Loss of family, home. Pat was on skid row. Now Pat was making a comeback. Made this movie. He's dry. And on the lecture tour, helping others.

I took another hit of the wine, passed it to Sarah.

I watched the movie. They were down on skid row. It was night and they had built a little fire. The men and women looked fairly well-dressed for skid row. They really didn't look like bums. They looked like people who worked in Hollywood films, they looked like tv actors. And they each had a shopping cart in which they stored their earthly possessions. Only the shopping carts were brand new. They sparkled in the firelight. I had never seen shopping carts that new in any supermarket. Evidently they had been purchased for the movie itself.

'Gimme the bottle,' I said to Sarah.

I lifted it high and took a good hit. I heard the hissing sound again, followed by another hissing sound.

'These people are ugly,' I said to Sarah. 'What the hell's wrong with them?'

'I don't know.'

Back to the movie and the people in the firelight with their shopping carts. There was a man talking. The others listened.

'. . . I'd wake up and I wouldn't recognize the bed I was in, I wouldn't know where I was . . . I'd get dressed and go out and look for my car. I never knew where my car was. Sometimes it took hours to find it . . .'

'Hey, that's good,' I said to Sarah, 'that's happened to me plenty of times!'

There was another hissing sound.

'. . . I was in drunktank after drunktank . . . I often lost my wallet . . . I had my teeth kicked in . . . I was a lost soul . . . lost . . . lost . . . Then my drinking buddy, Mike, he got killed in a drunken car crash . . . that did it . . .'

Sarah took a hit.

'Now I am at peace . . . I sleep well . . . I'm beginning to feel like a functional human being again . . . And Christ is my high, greater than any drink the devil has put upon this earth!'

Tears were in the fellow's eyes.

I took another hit.

Then he recited a poem:

> I am found again.
> I am made over by ten.
> I have lost the yen.
> I am brother to my kin.
> I am found again.

He bowed his head and the others applauded.

Then a woman began to speak. She had, she said, begun drinking at parties. And it had gone on from there. She began to drink alone at home. The plants died because she didn't water them. During an argument she slashed her daughter with a paring knife. Her husband began drinking also. Lost his job. Stayed at home. They drank together. Then she slashed *him* with a paring knife. One day she just got in her car and drove off with her suitcase and her credit cards. Drank in motels. Smoked and drank and watched tv. Vodka. She loved vodka.

One night she set her bed on fire. A fire engine came to the motel. She was drunk in her nightie. One of the firemen squeezed her buttocks. She jumped into her car in just her nightie with only her purse. She drove and drove, in a daze. About noon the next day she was at 4th and Broadway. Two of the tires had gone flat as she was driving along. The tires had ripped off and she was driving on the rims, leaving deep grooves in the asphalt. A cop stopped her. She was taken in – for observation. The days went by. Her husband didn't come by or her daughter. She was alone. She was sitting with the shrink one day and the shrink asked her, 'Why do you insist upon destroying yourself?' And when he asked her this it was no longer the face of the shrink looking at her but the face of Christ. That did it . . .

'How did she know it was the face of Christ?' I asked aloud.

'Who *is* that man?' I heard somebody ask.

My bottle of wine was empty. I corkscrewed open a new one.

Then another fellow told *his* story. The campfire just kept on burning and burning. Nobody had to add fuel to it. And no other bums came by and bothered them. When the fellow finished his story he reached into his shopping cart and pulled out a very expensive guitar.

I took a hit and passed the red to Sarah.

The fellow tuned his guitar, then began playing it and singing. He was right in tune, voice-trained. He sang away.

The camera panned around, capturing the look on all the faces. The faces were enthralled, some of them were crying, others had gentle, beautiful smiles. Then the singer finished and there was hearty and joyful applause.

'I never saw a skid row like that one,' I told Sarah.

The movie continued. Other actors spoke. Some others had expensive guitars. It was guitar night. Then the grand finale came. There was a shooting star. It arched high above the upturned faces. There was a small silence. Then a man began singing. Soon he was joined by a woman. Other voices joined. They all knew the words. Many guitars came out. It was an uplifting chorus of hope and unity. Then it was over. The movie was finished. The lights came on. There was a little stage. Pat Sellers mounted the stage. There was applause.

Pat Sellers looked awful. He looked sleepy, lifeless, dead. His eyes were blank. He began to speak.

'I have not had a drink in five hundred and ninety-five days . . .'

There was wild applause.

Sellers went on: 'I am a recovering alcoholic . . . We are *all* recovering alcoholics . . .'

'Let's get out of here!' I said to Sarah.

We had finished the wine. We rose and moved toward the exit. We walked to our car.

'Son of a bitch,' I said, 'where's Jon? Why isn't he here?'

'Oh, I'm sure he'd seen the movie,' said Sarah.

'He set us up. It's kind of funny when you think about it.'

'Those were all A.A. members in there . . .'

We got in the car and headed toward the freeway.

My idea about the whole thing was that most people *weren't* alcoholics, they only *thought* that they were. It was something that couldn't be rushed. It took at least twenty years to become a bonafide alcoholic. I was on my 45th year and didn't regret any of it.

We got on the freeway and headed back toward reality.

Chapter Fifteen

I STILL HAD the screenplay to write. I was upstairs sitting in front of the IBM. Sarah was in the bedroom beyond the wall to my right. Jon was downstairs watching tv.

I was just sitting there. A half a bottle of wine was gone. I had never had trouble before. In decades, I had never had a writer's block. Writing had always been easy for me. The words just rolled out as I drank and listened to the radio.

I knew that Jon was just listening for the sound of the typer. I had to type something. I began a letter to a fellow who taught English at Cal State Long Beach. We had been exchanging letters for a couple of decades.

I began:

Hello Harry:

How's it hanging? They've been running good. Badly hungover other day, got to track for 2nd race, got ten win on a 10-to-one-shot. I no longer use the Racing Form. *I see everybody reading it and almost everybody loses. I've got a new system, of course, which I can't tell you about. You know, if the writing goes to hell, I think I can make it at the track. Shit. I'll tell you my system, why shouldn't I? O.K. I buy a newspaper, any newspaper. I try to buy a different newspaper every day, just to shake up the gods. Then out of that newspaper I'll choose any handicapper. Then I'll line up his selections in order. Say there's an 8* horse race. On my program I will mark next to each horse the order of his selection. Example:

horse 1. 7

horse 2. 3

horse 3. 5

horse 4. 1

horse 5. 2

horse 6. 4

horse 7. 8

horse 8. 6

The system? Well, you take the horse's odds that go off below *the number of the handicapper's selection*. If more than one set of odds goes off below, then take the greatest drop. For example, horse 1, selection 7 going off at 4-to-one is better than horse 6, selection 4 going off at 3-to-one. There is one exception to this system. If horse 4 goes off at below 1, that is 4/5 or below, then pass the race if there is nothing working against it. That is because plays on nothing but odds-on-favorites always show a loss.

The way I came up with this system was that when I was in highschool I was in the R.O.T.C. and we had to read the Manual of Arms *and in this fat book there was a little bit about the Artillery. Now, remember this was 1936, long before radar and all the homing-in devices. In fact, the book was probably written for World War I, although it might have been compiled some time later, I'm not sure. Anyway, the way they figured how to lob an artillery shell was to take a consensus. The Captain would ask, 'O.K., Larry, how far away do you think the enemy is?'*

'625 yards, sir.'

'Mike?'

'400 yards, sir.'

'Barney?'

'100 yards, sir.'

'Slim?'

'800 yards, sir.'

'Bill?'

'300 yards.'

Then the Captain would add up the yards and divide by the number of men asked. In this case, the answer would be 445 yards. They'd log the shell and generally blow up a large proportion of the enemy.

Decades later I was sitting at the track one day and the Manual of Arms *came back to me and I thought, why not apply the Artillery system to the horses? This system has worked for me most of the time, but the problem was and is human nature: one gets bored with the routine and sets off in another direction. I must have at least 25 systems all based on some kind of crazy logic. I like to move around.*

Now you ask, how the hell did I land on a 10-to-one shot in the 2nd race the other day. Well, it's like this, I write down the handicapper's selections before scratches. *This horse happened to be selection #16 before scratches. When it went off at 10-to-one, curiously, it was the largest drop from the handicapper's selections. A rarity, true, but there it was. And when such things occur, they make one feel very odd indeed. Like maybe there's a chance sometimes. Well, I hope you're O.K. and that your young lady students don't give you a hard-on, or maybe I should hope that they do.*

Listen, is it true that Celine and Hemingway died on the same day?

Hope you're all right . . .

Keep 'em crying,

   yrs,
   Henry Chinaski

I took the sheet out of the typer, folded it, hand-printed the address on an envelope, stuck it inside, found a stamp, and there it was: my writing for the night. I sat there, finished the rest of the wine bottle, opened another one and walked downstairs.

Jon had turned off the tv and was sitting there. I brought two glasses and sat down next to him. I poured them around.

'The typer sounds hot,' Jon said.

'Jon, I was writing a letter.'

'A letter?'

'Have a drink.'

'All right.'

We both had one.

'Jon, you've paid me to write this fucking screenplay . . .'

'But, of course . . .'

'I can't write it. I'm up there trying to write the thing and you're down here listening for the sound of the typer. It's hard . . .'

'I could go some place at night.'

'No, listen, you are going to have to move! I can't go on this way! I'm sorry, man, I'm a dog, a heel, I'm the heel of a dog! Do dogs have heels? Anyhow, you're going to have to find a place to live. I can't write this way, I'm not man enough.'

'I understand.'

'Do you?'

'Of course. But I was going to have to move anyhow.'

'What?'

'François is coming back. His business in France is done.

We are going to have to find a place together. I am looking now. In fact, today I think I found a place. I just didn't want to bother you with all this.'

'But are you guys able to . . . ?'

'We have money. We are consolidating our resources.'

'Christ, then will you forgive me for wanting to throw you into the street?'

'There's nothing to forgive. I was only worried about how to tell you that I had to move out.'

'You wouldn't bullshit an old drunk, would you?'

'No. But have you written anything?'

'A smidge . . .'

'Can I see it?'

'Sure, buddy.'

I went upstairs, brought down the pages, put them on the coffee table. Then I went back upstairs, went into the bedroom.

'Come on, Sarah, we're going to celebrate!'

'Celebrate what?'

'Jon's moving out. I'm going to be able to write again!'

'Did you hurt his feelings?'

'I don't think so. You see, François is coming back, they have to find a place together.'

We went downstairs. Sarah got another glass. Jon was into the screenplay.

He laughed when he saw me.

'This stuff is fucking great! I knew that it would be!'

'You wouldn't bullshit an old drunk, would you?'

'No. Never.'

Sarah sat down and we had a quiet drink together.

Jon spoke. 'I used Wenner Zergog's phone to call François. I found out François fucked up. He got canned. He got a few days' pay, then got canned. Same old thing . . .'

'Like what?' asked Sarah.

'He's a great actor but now and then he goes crazy. He'll just forget the script and the scene he's supposed to be doing and do his thing. It's a sickness, I think. He must have done it again. He got canned.'

'What does he do?' I asked.

'It's always the same. He does all right for a while. Then he fails to follow direction. I will tell him, 'You walk over there and say your line.' He won't do it. He'll walk somewhere else and say some other line. And I'll ask him, 'Why do you do this?' and he'll answer, 'I don't know. I have no idea.' Once we were shooting and he walked away and pulled down his pants and bent over. He wasn't wearing shorts.'

'God damn,' I said.

'Or, he will say things like, "We must hasten the natural process of death." Or, "All men's lives diminish me."'

'Sounds like a hell of a guy.'

'Ah, he is . . .'

We drank into the early morning, far into the early morning.

I awakened about noon and went downstairs and knocked at Jon's door. There was no answer. I opened the door. Jon was gone. There was a note.

Dear Hank and Sarah:

Thanks much for all the drinks and everything. I felt like an honored guest.

Hank, your screenplay is a justification of my belief in you. It is even better than that. Please continue it.

I will phone you soon with my location and phone number.

This is a wonderful day. It's Mozart's birthday. There will be beautiful music all day . . .

yrs,
Jon

The note made me feel terrible and good at the same time, which was the way I felt most of the time anyhow. I went upstairs, pissed, brushed my teeth and got back into bed with Sarah.

Chapter Sixteen

THAT NIGHT WITHOUT Jon listening downstairs, the screenplay began to move. I was writing about a young man who wanted to write and drink but most of his success was with the bottle. The young man had been me. While the time had not been an unhappy time, it had been mostly a time of void and waiting. As I typed along, the characters in a certain bar returned to me. I saw each face again, the bodies, heard the voices, the conversations. There was one particular bar that had a certain deathly charm. I focused on that, relived the barroom fights with the bartender. I had not been a good fighter. To begin with my hands were too small and I was underfed, grossly underfed. But I had a certain amount of guts and I took a punch very well. My main problem during a fight was that I couldn't truly get angry, even when it seemed my life was at stake. It was all play-acting with me. It mattered and it didn't. Fighting the bartender was something to do and it pleased the patrons who were a clubby little group. I was the outsider. There is something to be said for drinking – all those fights would have killed me had I been sober but being drunk it was as if the body turned to rubber and the head to cement. Sprained wrists, puffed lips and battered kneecaps were about all I came up with the next day. Also, knots on the head from falling. How all this could become a screenplay, I didn't know. I only knew that it was the only part of my life I hadn't written much about. I believe that I was sane at that time, as sane as anybody. And

I knew that there was a whole civilization of lost souls that lived in and off bars, daily, nightly and forever, until they died. I had never read about this civilization so I decided to write about it, the way I remembered it. The good old typer clicked along.

The next day about noon the phone rang. It was Jon.

'I have found a place. François is with me. It's beautiful, it has *two* kitchens and the rent is nothing, really nothing . . .'

'Where are you located?'

'We're in the ghetto in Venice. Brooks Avenue. All blacks. The streets are war and destruction. It's beautiful!'

'Oh?'

'You must come see the place!'

'When?'

'Today!'

'I don't know.'

'Oh, you wouldn't want to miss this! There are people living under our house. We can hear them under there, talking and playing their radio! There are gangs everywhere! There's a large hotel somebody built down here. But nobody paid their rent. They boarded the place up, cut off the electricity, the water, the gas. But people still live there. THIS IS A WAR ZONE! The police do not come in here, it's like a separate state with its own rules. I love it! You must visit us!'

'How do I get there?'

Jon gave me the instructions, then hung up.

I found Sarah.

'Listen, I've got to go see Jon and François.'

'Hey, I'm coming too!'

'No, you can't. It's in the ghetto in Venice.'

'Oh, the ghetto! I wouldn't miss that for anything!'

'Look, do me a favor: please *don't* come along!'

'What? Do you think I would let you go down there all by *yourself*?'

I got my blade, put my money in my shoes. 'O.K.,' I said . . .

We drove slowly into the Venice ghetto. It was not true that it was all black. There were some Latinos on the outskirts. I noted a group of 7 or 8 young Mexican men standing around and leaning against an old car. Most of the men were in their under-shirts or had their shirts off. I drove slowly past, not staring, just taking it in. They didn't seem to be doing much. Just waiting. Ready and waiting. Actually, they were probably just bored. They looked like fine fellows. And they didn't look worried worth a shit.

Then we got to black turf. Right away, the streets were clut-tered: a left shoe, an orange shirt, an old purse . . . a rotted grapefruit . . . another left shoe . . . a pair of bluejeans . . . a rubber tire . . .

I had to steer through the stuff. Two young blacks about eleven years old stared at us from bicycles. It was pure, perfect hate. I could feel it. Poor blacks hated. Poor whites hated. It was only when blacks got money and whites got money that they mixed. Some whites loved blacks. Very few, if any, blacks loved whites. They were still getting even. Maybe they never would. In a capitalistic society the losers slaved for the winners and you have to have more losers than winners. What did I think? I knew politics would never solve it and there wasn't enough time left to get lucky.

We drove on until we found the address, parked the car, got out, knocked.

A little window slid open and there was an eye looking at us.

'Ah, Hank and Sarah!'

The door opened, shut, and we were inside.

I walked to the window and looked out.

'What are you doing?' asked Jon.

'Just want to check the car now and then . . .'

'Oh, yes, come look, I'll show you the two kitchens!'

Sure enough there were two kitchens, a stove in each, a refrigerator in each, a sink in each.

'This used to be two places. It's been turned into one.'

'Nice,' said Sarah, 'you can cook in one kitchen and François can cook in the other . . .'

'Right now we are living mostly on eggs. We have chickens, they lay many eggs . . .'

'Christ, Jon, is it that bad?'

'No, not really. We figure we are here for a long stand. We need most of our money for wine and cigars. How's the screenplay coming?'

'I'm happy to say that there are quite a few pages. Only sometimes I don't know about CAMERA, ZOOM IN, PAN IN . . . all that crap . . .'

'Don't worry, I'll take care of that.'

'Where's François?' asked Sarah.

'Ah, he's in the other room . . . come . . .'

We went in and there was François spinning his little roulette wheel. When he drank his nose became very red, like a cartoon drunk. Also, the more he drank the more depressed he became. He was sucking on a wet half-finished cigar. He managed a few sad puffs. There was an almost empty bottle of wine nearby.

'Shit,' he said, 'I am now 60 thousand dollars in the hole and I am drinking this cheap wine of Jon's which he claims is good stuff but it is pure crap. He pays a dollar and 35 cents a bottle. My stomach is like a balloon full of piss! I am 60 thousand dollars in the hole and I have no visible means of employment. I must . . . kill . . . myself . . .'

'Come on, François,' said Jon, 'let's show our friends the chickens . . .'

'The chickens! HEGGS! All the time we eat HEGGS! Nothing but HEGGS! Poop, poop, poop! The chickens poop HEGGS! All day, all night long my job is to save the chickens from the young black boys! All the time the young black boys climb the fence and run at the chicken coop! I hit them with a long stick, I say, "You muthafuckas you stay away from my chickens which poop the HEGGS!" I cannot think, I cannot think of my own life or my own death, I am always chasing these young black boys with the long stick! Jon, I need more wine, another cigar!'

He gave the wheel another spin.

It was more bad news. The system was failing.

'You see, in France they only have one zero for the house! Here in America they have a zero and a double zero for the house! THEY TAKE BOTH YOUR BALLS! WHY? Come on, I'll show you the chickens . . .'

We walked into the yard and there were the chickens and the chicken coop. François had built it himself. He was good that way. He had a real talent for that. Only he hadn't used chicken wire. There were bars. And locks on each door.

'I give roll call each night. "Cecile, you there?" "Cluck, cluck," she answers. "Bernadette, you there?" "Cluck, cluck" she answers. And so on. "Nicole?" I asked one night. She did not cluck. Can you believe it, through all the bars and all the locks they got Nicole! They have taken her out already! Nicole is gone, gone forever! Jon, Jon, I need more wine!'

We went back in and sat down and the new wine poured. Jon gave François a new cigar.

'If I can have my cigar when I want it,' said François, 'I can live.'

We drank a while, then Sarah asked, 'Listen, Jon is your landlord black?'

'Oh, yes . . .'

'Didn't he ask why you were renting here?'

'Yes . . .'

'And what did you tell him?'

'I told him that we were filmmakers and actors from France.'

'And he said?'

'He said, "oh."'

'Anything else?'

'Yes, he said, "well it's *your* ass!"'

We drank for some time making small talk.

Now and then I got up and went to the window to see if the car was still there.

As we drank on I began to feel guilty about the whole thing.

'Listen, Jon, let me give you the screenplay money back. I've driven you to the wall. This is terrible . . .'

'No, I want you to do this screenplay. It *will* become a movie, I promise you . . .'

'All right, god damn it . . .'

We drank a bit more.

Then Jon said, 'Look . . .'

Through a hole in the wall where we were sitting could be seen a hand, a black hand. It was wriggling through the broken plaster, fingers gripping, moving. It was like a small dark animal.

'GO AWAY,' yelled François. 'GO AWAY MURDERER OF NICOLE! YOU HAVE LEFT A HOLE IN MY HEART FOREVER! GO AWAY!'

The hand did not go away.

François walked over to the wall and the hand.

'I tell you now, go away. I only wish to smoke my cigar and drink my wine in peace. You disturb my sight! I cannot feel right with you grabbing and looking at me through your poor black fingers!'

The hand did not go away.

'ALL RIGHT THEN!'

The stick was right there. With one demonic move François picked up the long stick and began whacking it against the wall, again and again and again . . .

'CHICKEN KILLER, YOU HAVE WOUNDED MY HEART FOREVER!'

The sound was deafening. Then François stopped.

The hand was gone.

François sat back down.

'Shit, Jon, my cigar is out! Why don't you buy better cigars, Jon?'

'Listen, Jon,' I said, 'we've got to be going now . . .'

'Oh, come now . . . please . . . the night is just *beginning*! You've seen nothing yet . . .'

'We've got to be going . . . I have more work to do on the screenplay . . .'

'Oh . . . in that case . . .'

Back at the house I went upstairs and did work on the screenplay but strangely or maybe not so strangely my past life hardly seemed as strange or wild or as mad as what was occurring now.

Chapter Seventeen

THE SCREENPLAY WENT well. Writing was never work for me. It had been the same for as long as I could remember: turn on the radio to a classical music station, light a cigarette or a cigar, open the bottle. The typer did the rest. All I had to do was be there. The whole process allowed me to continue when life itself offered very little, when life itself was a horror show. There was always the typer to soothe me, to talk to me, to entertain me, to save my ass. Basically, that's why I wrote: to save my ass, to save my ass from the madhouse, from the streets, from myself.

One of my past ladies had screamed at me, 'You drink to escape reality!'

'Of course, my dear,' I had answered her.

I had the bottle *and* the typer. I liked a bird in each hand, to hell with the bush.

Anyhow, the screenplay went well. Unlike the novel or the short story or the poem where I would take a night or two off from time to time, I worked on the screenplay each night. And then it was finished.

I phoned Jon. 'Well, I don't know what we have but it's finished.'

'Great! I'd come to get it but we're having kind of a lunch party down here. Drinks, food, guests. François is the chef. Can you drive the screenplay down?'

'I'd like to but I'm afraid to drive it down there.'

'Oh, shit, Hank, nobody is going to steal that old Volks.'

'Jon, I just bought a new BMW.'

'What?'

'The day before yesterday. My tax accountant says it's tax deductible.'

'Tax deductible? That doesn't seem possible . . .'

'That's what he told me. He said that in America you have to spend your money or they'll take it away. Now they can't take mine away: I don't have any.'

'But I've got to see that screenplay! With something to show the producers I can really get going.'

'All right, you know the Ralph's Market just outside the ghetto?'

'Yes.'

'I'll park in the parking lot and phone you from there. Then you come get me, all right?'

'Good, I'll do it . . .'

Sarah and I were waiting by our black 320i BMW when Jon pulled up. We climbed in and moved toward the ghetto.

'What are your readers and the critics going to say when they find out about the BMW?'

'As always those fuckers will have to judge me on how well I write.'

'They don't always do that.'

'That's their problem.'

'You have the screenplay with you?'

'I've got it right here,' said Sarah.

'My secretary.'

'He wrote it right out,' said Sarah.

'I'm a 320i genius,' I said.

We rolled up to Jon's place. A number of automobiles were parked outside. It was still daytime. Maybe about 1:30 p.m. We walked through the house and into the backyard.

The luncheon party had been going on for some time. Empty bottles sat about on wooden tables. Half-eaten watermelon slices looked sad in the sun. The flies lit upon them, then left. The guests looked as if they had been there for at least 3 hours. It was one of those splintered parties: clusters of 3 or 4 people here, ignoring clusters of 3 or 4 people there. There was an admixture of European and Hollywood types plus some others. The others had no special character, they were just there and they were damned determined to stay there. I felt hatred in the air but didn't know what to do about it. Jon knew: he opened a few fresh bottles of wine.

We walked over to François. He was working the grill. He was slobbering drunk and totally depressed. He was turning chicken parts on the grill. The chicken parts were already done, getting black, but François was still turning them.

François looked terrible. He had on one of those large white chef's hats, only it had evidently fallen from his head several times and there were mud smears on it. He saw us.

'AH! I'VE BEEN WAITING FOR YOU! YOU'RE LATE! WHAT HAPPENED? I CANNOT UNDERSTAND THIS!'

'I'm sorry, François, we had to park at Ralph's.'

'I HAVE BEEN SAVING SOME CHICKEN FOR YOU! HAVE SOME CHICKEN!'

He gathered two paper plates and flung a bit of chicken upon each.

'Thank you, François.'

Sarah and I found a table and sat down. Jon sat with us.

'François is upset. He thinks I killed one of the chickens. There was no chicken ever born with this many legs, breasts and wings. I've counted the chickens with him over and over. It's a full count. But he gets to drinking and he thinks I killed one of the chickens. I got the parts at Ralph's.'

'François is very sensitive,' said Sarah.

'And how,' said Jon. 'And to make things worse, now he prides himself upon guarding us against theft. He has little wires and signals set up everywhere. All types of crazy alarms. Very sensitive. I farted and one of them went off.'

'Come on, Jon . . .'

'No, it's true. So, to make matters worse, the other day François went out to start the car. It started. He shifted it into reverse and nothing happened. He thought the reverse gear was finished. He got out of the car and found that the 2 rear wheels were *missing* . . .'

'Unbelievable . . .'

'It happened. The rear of the car was sitting on a pile of rocks and the wheels were missing . . .'

'They left the front wheels?'

'Yes.'

'Where'd you get new wheels and tires?' Sarah asked.

'We bought them back from the crooks.'

'What?' I said. 'May we have another drink?'

Jon poured.

'They knocked on the door. They said, "You want your wheels? We have your wheels." I told them to come in. "I WILL KILL YOU!" François shouted. I told him to be still. We drank wine with them and haggled over the price. It took much haggling and much wine, but we finally reached an agreement and they brought the wheels and tires in and dumped them on the floor. That was it.'

'How much did it cost you?' Sarah asked.

'$33. It seemed a good deal for 2 wheels and 2 tires.'

'Not bad,' I said.

'Well, actually, it came to $38. We had to pay them $5 to promise not to steal the wheels again.'

'But suppose somebody else steals the wheels?'

'They said the $5 would guarantee that *nobody* would ever

touch the wheels. But they said the $5 applied *only* to the wheels and not to anything else on the car.'

'Were there any more agreements?'

'No, then they left. But we noticed that our radio was gone. We had been watching them all the time and yet the radio was gone. I have no idea how they did it. It's a standard size radio. How could they hide it? How did they get it out the door? I don't understand. It is something to be admired.'

'Yes.'

Jon stood up. He had the screenplay.

'I must now hide this. I have a very special place. And I thank you for your work on this, Hank.'

'It was nothing. Easy money.'

Jon left with the screenplay. I looked down at my chicken.

'Jesus, I can't eat this . . . it's burned damn near rock-hard . . .'

'I can't eat mine either . . .'

'There's a trash can by the fence there. Let's try to sneak this stuff . . .'

We went over to the trash can. All along the top of the fence were these little eyes looking out of little black faces.

'Hey, let's have some chicken!'

'Give me a wing, motherfucker . . .'

I walked over to the fence.

'This stuff is burned . . . nobody can eat it . . .'

A little hand shot out and the piece of chicken was gone. Another hand shot out and Sarah's piece of burnt chicken was gone also.

The two little guys ran off screaming followed by a bunch of other little guys screaming.

'Sometimes I hate being white,' said Sarah.

'There are white ghettos too. And rich blacks.'

'It's not comparable.'

'No, but I don't know what to do about it.'

'Start somewhere . . .'

'I don't have the guts. I'm too worried about my own white ass. Let's join this jolly group here and have some more to drink.'

'That's your answer to everything: drink.'

'No, that's my answer to nothing.'

It was still splinter-group time. Even in that broken down backyard there were ghetto areas and Malibu areas and Beverly Hills areas. For example, the best-dressed ones with designer clothes hung together. Each type recognized its counterpart and showed no inclination to mix. I was surprised that some of them had been willing to come to a black ghetto in Venice. Chic, they thought, maybe. Of course, what made the whole thing smell was that many of the rich and the famous were actually dumb cunts and bastards. They had simply fallen into a big pay-off somewhere. Or they were enriched by the stupidity of the general public. They usually were talentless, eyeless, soulless, they were walking pieces of dung, but to the public they were god-like, beautiful, and revered. Bad taste creates many more millionaires than good taste. It finally boiled down to a matter of who got the most votes. In the land of the moles a mole was king. So, who deserved anything? Nobody deserved anything . . .

François was sitting at a table and we went and sat with him. But he was saddened, completely out of it. He hardly recognized us. A wet and broken cigar was in his mouth and he stared down into his drink. He still had on his dirty chef's hat. He had always had a bit of style even at his worst moments. Now it was all gone. It was terrible.

'WHY WERE YOU LATE? I DO NOT UNDERSTAND! I HELD BACK THE LUNCH AND WAITED FOR YOU! WHY WERE YOU LATE?'

'Look, friend, why don't you sleep this one off? Tomorrow will look better . . .'

'TOMORROW ALWAYS LOOKS THE SAME! THAT'S THE PROBLEM!'

Jon walked up.

'I'll take care of him. He'll be all right. Come on, let me introduce you to some of the guests.'

'No, we've got to go . . .'

'So soon?'

'Yes, I'm worried about the 320i.'

'I'll drive you over . . .'

It was still there. We got in and waved to Jon as he drove off back to the ghetto and the party and poor François.

Soon we were on the freeway.

'Well, you've written the screenplay,' said Sarah, 'at least there's that.'

'At least . . .'

'Do you think it will ever become a movie?'

'It's about the life of a drunk. Who cares about the life of a drunk?'

'I do. Who would you like to play the lead?'

'François.'

'François?'

'Yes.'

'Do we have anything to drink at home?'

'Half a case of gamay beaujolais.'

'That ought to do it . . .'

I pushed down on the gas pedal and we moved toward it.

Chapter Eighteen

JON GOT BUSY. Copies of the screenplay were made, mailed to producers, agents, actors. I went back to fiddling with the poem. I also came up with a new system for the racetrack. The racetrack was important to me because it allowed me to forget that I was supposed to be a writer. Writing was strange. I needed to write, it was like a disease, a drug, a heavy compulsion, yet I didn't like to think of myself as a writer. Maybe I had met too many writers. They took more time disparaging each other than they did doing their work. They were fidgets, gossips, old maids; they bitched and knifed and they were full of vanity. Were these our creators? Was it always thus? Probably so. Maybe writing was a form of bitching. Some just bitched better than others.

Anyhow, the screenplay went around and there weren't any takers. Some said it was interesting but the main complaint was that there wouldn't be an audience for that type of film. It was all right to show how a person who had once been great or unusual was destroyed by drink. But just to focus on a bum drinking or a bunch of bums drinking, that didn't make sense. Who cared? Who cared how they lived or died?

But I did get a phone call from Jon: 'Listen, Mack Austin got hold of the screenplay and he likes it. He wants to direct it and he wants the same guy I want to play the lead.'

'Who's that?'

'Tom Pell.'

'Yeah, he'd make a good drunk . . .'

'Pell is crazy for the screenplay. He's crazy about your writing, he's read all your stuff. He's so crazy about the screenplay he says he'll do the acting for a dollar.'

'Jesus . . .'

'Only he *insists* that Mack Austin directs. I do not like this Mack Austin. He is my enemy.'

'Why?'

'Oh, we've had some problems.'

'Why don't you guys kiss and make up?'

'NEVER! MACK AUSTIN WILL NEVER DIRECT MY FILM!'

'All right, Jon, then let's forget it.'

'No, wait, I want to arrange a meeting at your house between Mack Austin, Tom Pell and myself. And you, of course. Maybe you can get Tom Pell to change his mind and do the film without Austin. He's a great actor, you know.'

'I know. So have them come over. Is he going to bring Ramona?'

'No.'

Tom had married Ramona, the famed pop singer.

'Well, when would be a good time?'

'They've agreed to tomorrow night at 8:30 if it's all right with you.'

'You move fast.'

'In this game you move fast or you die.'

'It's not like chess?'

'More like a checker game between idiots.'

'One idiot wins?'

'And one idiot loses.'

I found out a little more about the Jon Pinchot and Mack Austin affair. Although Jon had made most of his films in

Europe, and Austin's films were American, the film crowd hung out in the same places in Hollywood. Jon and Mack Austin were in the same fancy eatery. I am not quite sure who was drinking and who wasn't but it seems that some bickering started between these two directors from tables not too close together. Shoptalk, you know. Technique. Background. Training. Insight, etc.

It went back and forth between the tables before a goodly audience of people in the 'industry.'

Finally, Mack rose and shouted at Jon:

'YOU CALL YOURSELF A DIRECTOR? YOU CAN'T DIRECT TRAFFIC!'

Well, I don't know. Directing traffic is a job that takes great skill.

Anyway, some other people had once accused Mack in public of not being able to direct traffic. Now he was passing on the compliment. All's fair in hate and Hollywood.

I later heard some other half-documented accounts of run-ins between Mack and Jon.

Anyhow, the meeting was on . . .

INTERIOR. WRITER'S HOME. 8:15 p.m.
Jon had arrived a little early.

'Wait until you see this Austin,' he said. 'He's off drugs and booze. He's like a flat tire, an empty stocking . . .'

'I think it's great,' said Sarah, 'that he has gotten himself cleaned up. That takes courage.'

'O.K.,' said Jon.

They arrived about 8:35 p.m. Tom in leather jacket. Mack in a calfskin jacket with a leather fringe. He had on a half dozen gold chains. Introductions over, I poured Tom a wine. We hunkered around the coffee table.

Tom started it off.

'I've seen the screenplay. I love it. I want to sink my bicuspids into the fucker. I can taste it already. It's my kind of part.'

'Thank you, my man. Yours is the only nibble we've gotten.'

'Tom and I even have a backer. We're ready to roll,' said Mack.

'You sure you don't want a drink, Mack?' I asked.

'No, thanks.'

'I'll get you a soda,' said Sarah. 'Or would you rather have tea?'

'A soda would be fine.'

Sarah went off to get Mack something to make him comfortable. We had health food sodas. The best.

I drank my drink right off, poured another. I was beginning to sense a futility about any sort of compromise or agreement.

'I need Mack for a director. I know his work, I trust him,' Tom said.

'You don't trust me?' asked Jon.

'It's not that. It's only that I feel that I could work closer with Mack.'

'I am the only one who will direct this movie,' said Jon.

'Listen,' said Tom, 'I know this movie means a lot to you. We can create a position for you. You'll be paid well and you'll be allowed plenty of control. Please accept this. I want this thing to roll. Please try to understand.'

Sarah was back with Mack's soda.

'I know that I can work well with Tom,' said Mack.

'You can't,' Jon began . . .

'. . . direct traffic,' Mack finished it.

The discussion went on and on. For hours. Sarah, Jon and

I kept drinking. Tom kept drinking. And Mack kept working on the health food sodas.

'You're all bullheads,' said Sarah. 'Surely something can be worked out.'

But everything was just as it was in the beginning. Nobody gave way. And I had no ideas. I couldn't break the deadlock.

We even began talking about other things. We told various funny stories in turn. The drinks went round and round.

Toward the end, I don't remember who was telling the story, but it got to Mack Austin. It struck him, health food sodas and all. He fell backwards laughing loudly. His gold chains bounced up and down.

Then he pulled himself together.

Soon after that, it was time to part. Tom and Mack had to leave. We said our goodbyes. After their car backed down the drive Jon looked at me:

'Did you hear that fake laugh? Did you see how those fucking gold chains bounced up and down on his neck? What was he laughing about? Did you see all those fucking gold chains?'

'Yeah, I saw them,' I said.

'He was nervous,' said Sarah. 'He was the only one who wasn't drinking. Have you ever been in a roomful of drunks when you aren't drinking?'

'No,' I said.

'Listen,' Jon asked me, 'can I use your phone?'

'Sure . . .'

'I must phone *Paris*! *Now*!'

'What?'

'Don't worry, I will call collect. I want to talk to my lawyer. It's about an addition to my will . . .'

'Go ahead.'

Jon walked to the phone and began making arrangements

for a connection. I walked over and refilled his glass. Then I came back.

'It's awful,' said Sarah, 'there goes the movie.'

'Well, almost something is better than nothing.'

'Is it?'

'Come to think of it, I'm not so sure . . .'

Then Jon had his connection. He'd had more than a few drinks and was excited. He was easily heard:

'PAUL! YES, IT'S JON PINCHOT! YES, IT IS URGENT! I WANT AN ADDITION TO MY WILL! ARE YOU READY? YES, I'LL WAIT!'

Jon looked over at us.

'This is very important . . .'

Then:

'YES, PAUL! THERE IS THIS MOVIE. I HAVE CONTROL. IT IS CALLED *THE DANCE OF JIM BEAM*, WRITTEN BY HENRY CHINASKI! VERY WELL, GET THIS DOWN! IN CASE OF MY DEATH THIS MOVIE IS NEVER TO BE DIRECTED BY MACK AUSTIN! THIS MOVIE CAN BE DIRECTED BY ANYBODY ON THIS EARTH EXCEPT MACK AUSTIN! DO YOU HAVE THAT, PAUL? YES, THANK YOU VERY MUCH, PAUL. YES, I AM WELL. HOW IS YOUR HEALTH? ALL RIGHT, ANYBODY BUT MACK AUSTIN! THANK YOU SO MUCH, PAUL! GOOD-NIGHT, GOODNIGHT!'

After that, we had one more drink together. Then Jon had to go. He stopped at the door.

'Did you hear that fake laugh? Did you see those gold chains bounce?'

'Yes, Jon . . .'

Then he was gone and that night was over. We went out

to call the cats. We had 5 cats and we couldn't sleep until all 5 cats were in the house.

The neighbors heard us calling those cats late each night or early in the morning. We had nice neighbors. And those 5 cats each took their damned time coming in.

Chapter Nineteen

3 OR 4 days later Jon was on the phone.

'Jack Bledsoe has read the screenplay and he likes it, he wants to act in it. I've been trying to get him to come see you but he claims he doesn't want to be overwhelmed by you. He says you must come see him.'

'Will that overwhelm him less?'

'I guess that's what he thinks.'

'You think he can play the part?'

'Oh yes, he's from the *streets*! He once sold chestnuts in the streets! He's from New York!'

'I've seen some of his films . . .'

'Well, what do you think?'

'Maybe . . . Listen, he's got to stop *smiling* all the time when he doesn't know what else to do. And he's got to stop beating refrigerators with his fists. And he's got to stop that New York strut where they walk like they've got a banana up their ass.'

'He used to be a boxer, this Jack Bledsoe . . .'

'Shit, we *all* used to be boxers . . .'

'He can do the part, trust me . . .'

'Jon, he can't be *New York*. This main character is a California boy. California boys are laid back, in the woodwork. They don't come rushing out, they cool it and figure their next move. Less panic. And under all this, they have the ability to kill. But they don't blow a lot of smoke first.'

'You tell him this . . .'

'All right, when and where?'

It was 8 p.m. in North Hollywood. We were about 5 minutes late. We were walking up various dark paths looking for the apartment.

'I hope he has something to drink. We should have brought something.'

'I'm sure he'll have something,' Sarah said.

It was hard to make out the numbers. Then there was Jon standing on a balcony.

'Up here . . .'

I went up the stairway and followed Jon. It was one of Jack's little hideaways.

Jon pushed the door open and we walked in. They were sitting on an old couch. Jack Bledsoe and his buddy Lenny Fidelo. Fidelo acted bit parts. Jack Bledsoe looked exactly like Jack Bledsoe. Lenny was a big guy, wide, a little too heavy. He was marked by life, he'd been rubbed in it. I liked him. Big sad eyes. Large hands. Looked tired, lonely, O.K.

Introductions went around.

'Who's this guy?' I asked Jack, nodding at Lenny. 'Your bodyguard?'

'Yeah,' said Jack.

Jon just stood there smiling as if the thing was a meeting of great souls. But, you never knew.

'Got anything to drink?' I asked.

'All we've got is beer. Beer all right?'

'All right,' I said.

Lenny went off into another room for the beer. I was sorry for Sarah, she wasn't nutty for beer.

There were boxing posters all over the wall. I walked around looking at them. Great. Some of them went way back. I began to feel macho just looking at them.

There were springs sticking out of the sofa and there were pillows on the floor, shoes, magazines, paper bags.

'This is a real male hangout,' Sarah laughed.

'Yeah, yeah, I like it,' I said. 'I've lived in some real wrecked places but never anything like this.'

'We like it,' said Jack.

Lenny was back with the beer. Cans. We cracked them and sat there having a hit or two.

'So, you read the script?' I asked Jack.

'Yeah. Was that guy you?'

'Me, long ago.'

'You got your ass kicked,' said Lenny.

'Mostly.'

'You really ran errands for sandwiches?' Jack asked.

'Mostly.'

The beer was good. There was a silence.

'Well, what do you think?' Jon asked.

'You mean Jack?'

'Yes.'

'He'll do. We may have to beat him up a bit.'

'Lemme see your fighting style,' said Jack.

I got up and sparred.

'Quick hands,' said Sarah.

I sat down again. 'I could take a punch fine. But I lacked a certain desire. I wasn't sure what I was doing. You got another beer?'

'Oh sure,' said Lenny, then he got up to get one for me.

It was known in Hollywood that Jack Bledsoe didn't like Tom Pell. He liked to lay it on Tom in almost all his interviews: 'Tom comes from Malibu. I come from the streets.' It didn't matter to me where an actor came from as long as he could act. Both of them could act. And there was no need for either of them to act the way writers acted.

Lenny was back with the beer.

'It's the last beer,' he said.

'Oh shit, no,' I said.

'I'll be right back,' Jon said.

Then he was out the door. Beer-run. I liked Jon.

'You like this Jon Pinchot as a director?' Jack asked.

'You ever seen his documentary on Lido Mamin?'

'No.'

'Pinchot has no fear. He loves fucking with death.'

'He's got a hard-on for death, huh?'

'Seems so. But he's done other stuff besides the Mamin film. I trust him as a director all the way. He hasn't been diluted by Hollywood, although some day he might be.'

'How about you?'

'How about me, what?'

'Will Hollywood get your balls?'

'No way.'

'Famous last words?'

'No, famous first words.'

'Hank hates movies,' said Sarah. 'The last movie he liked was *The Lost Weekend* and you know how many years ago that was.'

'Ray Milland's only bit of acting. But it was aces,' I said.

Then I had to piss, asked directions to the crapper.

I went back there, opened the door, went in, did my bit.

Then I turned to the sink to wash my hands.

What the fuck was that?

Pushed down in the sink was this white towel. One end of it was stuffed into the drain and the remainder of it hung out over the sink and dropped to the floor. It didn't look good. And it was soaking wet, just soaked through. What was it for? What did it mean? Left over after some orgy? It didn't make sense to me. I knew it must mean something. I was just an old guy. Was the world passing me by? I'd lived through some shitty nights and days, plenty of them full of anti-meaning, yet I couldn't figure out that giant soaking white towel.

And worse, Jack knew that I was coming by. Why would he leave that thing in there like that? Was it a message?

I walked back out.

Now, if I had been a New Yorker I would have said, 'Hey, what's that fucking white dripping towel doing in that fucking sink, huh?'

But I was a California boy. I just walked out and sat down, saying nothing, figuring that what they did was up to them and I didn't want any part of it.

Jon was back with more beer and there was an open can where I was sitting. I went for it. Life was good again.

'I want Francine Bowers for the female lead,' said Jack. 'I think I can get her.'

'I know Francine,' said Jon, 'I think I can get her too.'

'Why don't you both work on it?' Sarah asked.

Lenny went for more beer. He looked like a beer-o. My kind of guy.

'Hey, you think there's a part for me in this movie?' he asked. I looked at Jon.

'I like Lenny in my flicks,' said Jack.

'I think there's a part for you. I promise,' said Jon, 'we'll work you in.'

'I read the script,' said Lenny, 'I think I could play the part of the bartender.'

'Come on,' I said, 'you wouldn't want to beat up your buddy Jack here, would you?'

'No problem,' said Lenny.

'Yeah,' said Jack, 'he already did it once. Knocked one of my teeth out.'

'Really?' Sarah asked.

'And how,' said Jack.

We drank the beer. Mostly it was small talk, about the many exploits of Lenny. He'd not only paid his dues, he could recollect them.

When the beer was about gone, I figured it was about time to leave.

I made one more bathroom run, then Sarah and I were at the door. Jon was evidently staying behind to talk over something or other.

Then at the door, something strange happened. I asked Jack, 'Hey, man, what the fuck is that big sopping wet dripping-ass towel doing hanging out of your bathroom sink?'

'What big sopping wet dripping-ass towel?' Jack asked.

And that was the end of that particular night.

Chapter Twenty

3 OR 4 weeks went by.

The phone rang one night. It was Jon.

'How are you? How is Sarah?'

'We're all right. Are you alive?'

'Yes. And so is *The Dance of Jim Beam*. Francine Bowers read the script and loved it. She even took a cut from her usual salary to do it. Jack did too, but don't tell anybody.'

'No, but why these cuts?'

'We're dealing with Firepower Productions, Harry Friedman and Nate Fischman. They cut a hard deal but everything's signed. There was a snag because Jack's agent demanded a "Play or pay" clause in the contract.'

'What's that?'

'That means Jack must get paid whether the film is made or not. Most big stars have "Play or pay" in their contracts.'

'It's hard to believe there's going to be a movie.'

'Tom Pell had a lot to do with it when he offered to do the thing for a dollar. It gave the project some credibility.'

'I wish we had Tom . . .'

'Well, he helped. When Jack heard Tom wanted to do it for a dollar, then he got interested. Firepower got interested. We got lucky.'

'You know what Lippy Leo Durocher said?'

'Who's that?'

'An old-time baseball player. He said, "I'd rather be lucky than good."'

'I think we're lucky *and* good.'

'Maybe. But who are those Firepower guys?'

'They're new in Hollywood. They're outcasts. Nobody knows what to make of them. They used to make exploitation films in E urope. They arrived overnight and began making movies by the score, one after the other. They are hated by everyone. But they deal, although they deal hard.'

'At least they took *Jim Beam*.'

'Yes, when nobody else would. They have this big building in North Hollywood. I walked into the office and there was Harry Friedman sitting there. "You got Bledsoe and Bowers?" he asked. "Yes," I told him. "All right," he said, "We've got a movie." "But don't you want to read the script?" I asked him. "No," he said.'

'Interesting man.'

'Hollywood hates him.'

'Too bad . . .'

'You should see him. A very heavy man. By the way, he's having a birthday party at this place Thursday night. You and Sarah should come. His partner Nate Fischman will be there too.'

'We'll be there. Give me the directions . . .'

Within ten minutes the phone rang again.

'Hank, this is Tim Ruddy, I'm one of the producers of *Jim Beam*.'

'You work for Firepower?'

'No, I work with Jon. We are co-producers. Me and Lance Edwards.'

'Oh . . .'

'Anyhow, do you know Victor Norman?'

'I've read his books.'

'Well, he's read you too. He's writing and directing a film for Firepower. And he's going to the party. Wants to know if you'll drop off at the Chateau Marmont to meet him, then you can go together.'

'What's his suite number . . . ?'

That Thursday we drove up to the Chateau Marmont. The valet took our car and we moved toward the entrance. A smiling, partly bald man was waiting. It was Tim Ruddy. Introductions went around and then we followed him in. Victor Norman answered our knock. I liked his eyes. He looked calm and knowing.

Introductions. Sarah was looking fine. Norman beamed at her.

I shook hands with him, said, 'The barfly meets the champ.'

He liked that.

Victor Norman was perhaps the best known novelist in America. He appeared on tv constantly. He was glib and deft with the word. What I liked best about him was that he had no fear of the Feminists. He was one of the last defenders of maleness and balls in the U.S. That took guts. I wasn't always pleased with his literary output but I wasn't always pleased with mine either.

'They gave me the largest suite in the place at a cut-rate. Good advertising, they said. But anyhow Firepower's picking up the tab.'

We followed him out on the balcony. A hell of a view of a hell of a town.

It was chilly out there.

'Listen, man,' I asked, 'don't you have anything to drink around here?'

We followed Victor back into the vast connecting rooms. In there you felt protected from everything. A fortress of security. Nice, nice.

Victor came out holding a bottle of wine.

'I've got some wine but not an opener around . . .'

'Ah, god,' I sighed. An amateur drunk.

Victor Norman was on the phone: 'We need an opener. A corkscrew . . . Some more wine . . . A few bottles of . . .'

He looked at us.

It took the wine some time to arrive.

'I'm making two movies for Firepower. I'm writing and directing one. I'm *acting* in the other. Jon-Luc Modard is directing. I hope I can get along with him.'

'Good luck,' I said.

There was some minor conversation. Then Victor told us how he met Charlie Chaplin. It was a good, wild and funny story.

The wine arrived and we sat down. Sarah and Tim Ruddy got to talking. Sarah sensed that Tim Ruddy was feeling left out and was trying to cheer him up. Sarah was good at that. I wasn't so good at that.

Victor looked at me. 'You doing anything now?'

'Fucking with the poem.'

Victor looked a touch sad.

'They gave me a million dollars to write my next novel. That was a year ago. I haven't written a page and the money's gone.'

'Jesus.'

'Jesus won't help.'

'I've heard about your alimony, all those x-wives . . .'

'Yeah.'

I moved my glass toward him. It was empty. He refilled it.

'I've heard about your drinking . . .'

'Yeah.'

'What's those things you're smoking?'

'Beedi's. From India. The lepers roll them.'

'Really?'

The wine poured and time passed.

'Well, I guess we better head for the party,' said Victor Norman.

'We can take my car,' I said to Victor.

'O.K.'

We went downstairs. Tim Ruddy wanted to take his own car.

The valet brought my car around. I tipped him and Victor and Sarah got in. I pulled out and around and headed for Harry Friedman's birthday party.

'I've got a black BMW too,' said Victor Norman.

'Tough guys drive black BMWs,' I said.

Chapter Twenty-one

WE WERE A little late for the party but there still weren't very many people there. Victor Norman was seated a few tables away from ours. After Sarah and I were seated the waiter came with our wine. White wine. Well, it was free.

I drained my glass and nodded the waiter over for a refill.

I noticed Victor peering at me.

People were gradually arriving. I saw the famous actor with the perpetual tan. I'd heard that he went to almost every Hollywood party, everywhere.

Then Sarah gave me the elbow. It was Jim Serry, the old drug guru of the 60s. He too went to many of the parties. He looked tired, sad, drained. I felt sorry for him. He went from table to table. Then he was at ours. Sarah gave a delighted laugh. She was a child of the 60s. I shook hands with him.

'Hi, baby,' I said.

Quickly it began to get crowded. I didn't know most of the people. I kept waving the waiter in for more wine. He then brought a full bottle, plopped it down.

'When you finish that, I'll bring another.'

'Thank you, buster . . .'

Sarah had wrapped a little present for Harry Friedman. I had it in my lap.

Jon arrived and sat at our table.

'I'm glad you and Sarah could make it,' he said. 'Look, it's filling up, this place is full of gangsters and killers, the worst!'

Jon loved it. He had some imagination. It helped get him through the days and the nights.

Then a very important looking man walked in. I heard some applause.

I leaped up with the birthday gift. I moved toward him.

'Mr Friedman, happy . . .'

Jon rushed up and grabbed me from behind. He pulled me back to the table.

'No! No! That isn't Friedman! That's Fischman!'

'Oh . . .'

I sat back down.

I noticed Victor Norman staring at me. I figured he would let up in a while. When I looked again, Victor was still staring. He was looking at me as if he couldn't believe his eyes.

'All right, Victor,' I said loudly, 'so I shit my pants! Want to make a World War out of it?'

He glanced away.

I got up and looked for the men's room.

Coming out I got lost and went into the kitchen. There was a busboy there smoking a cigarette. I reached into my wallet and got a ten. I gave him the ten. I put it in his shirt pocket.

'I can't take this, sir.'

'Why not?'

'I just can't.'

'Everybody else gets tipped. Why not the busboy? I always wanted to be a busboy.'

I walked off, found the main room again and the table.

When I sat down Sarah leaned over and whispered, 'Victor Norman came over while you were gone. He says that it's very nice of you that you haven't said anything about his writing.'

'I've been good, haven't I, Sarah?'

'Yes.'

'Haven't I been a good boy?'

'Yes.'

I looked over at Victor Norman, got his attention. I gave a little nod, winked.

Just then the real Harry Friedman walked in. Some rose to their feet and applauded. Others looked bored.

Friedman sat down at his table and the food was served. Pasta. The pasta came around. Harry Friedman got his and went right in. He looked like an eater. He was wide, yes. He was in an old suit, his shoes were scuffed. He had a large head, big cheeks. He shoved that pasta into those cheeks. He had large round eyes and the eyes were sad and full of suspicion. Alas, to live in the world! There was a button missing from his wrinkled white shirt, near his belly, and the belly pushed out. He looked like a big baby who had somehow gotten loose, grown real fast, and almost turned into a man. There was charm there but it could be dangerous to believe in it – it would be used against you. No necktie. Happy birthday, Harry Friedman!

A young lady came in dressed as a cop. She walked right up to Friedman's table.

'YOU ARE UNDER ARREST!' she screamed.

Harry Friedman stopped eating and smiled. His lips were wet from the pasta.

Then the lady cop took off her coat and then her blouse. She had huge breasts. She shook her breasts under Harry Friedman's nose.

'YOU ARE UNDER ARREST!' she screamed.

Everybody applauded. I don't know why they applauded.

Then Friedman motioned the lady cop to bend over. She bent close and he whispered something into her ear. Nobody knew what it was.

You take me to your place. We'll see what happens?

You forgot your club. I'll take care of that?

You come see me. I'll get you in the movies?

The lady cop put her blouse back on, her coat back on, and then she was gone.

People came up to Friedman's table and said little things to him. He looked at them as if he didn't know who they were. Soon he was finished eating and was drinking wine. He did well with the wine. I liked that.

He really went for the wine. After a while he went around from table to table, bending over, talking to people.

'Christ,' I said to Sarah, 'look at that!'

'What?'

'He's got a little piece of pasta hanging out of one side of his mouth and nobody is telling him about it. It's just *hanging* there!'

'I see it! I see it!' said Jon.

Harry Friedman kept walking from table to table, bending over, talking. Nobody told him.

Finally, he got closer. He was a table or so away from ours when I stood up and walked over to him.

'Mr Friedman,' I said.

He looked at me from that big monster baby face.

'Yes?'

'Hold still!'

I reached out, got hold of the end of the pasta and yanked. It came away.

'You been walkin' around with that danglin'. I couldn't stand it anymore.'

'Thank you,' he said.

I went back to our table.

'Well, well,' asked Jon, 'what do you think of him?'

'I think he's delightful.'

'I told you. I haven't met anybody like him since Lido Mamin.'

'Anyhow,' said Sarah, 'it was nice of you to clean that pasta off his face since nobody else had the nerve to. It was very nice of you.'

'Thank you, I am a very nice guy, really.'

'Oh yes? What else have you done that is nice lately?'

Our wine bottle was empty. I got the attention of the waiter. He scowled at me and moved forward with another bottle.

And I couldn't think of anything nice that I had done. Lately.

Chapter Twenty-two

PRE-PRODUCTION HAD BEGUN.

Things seemed to go well.

Then the phone rang. It was Jon.

'We're in trouble . . .'

'What is it?'

'Friedman and Fischman . . .'

'Yes?'

'They want to get rid of my co-producers, Tim Ruddy and Lance Edwards . . .'

'I met Ruddy, not Edwards . . . What goes?'

'These guys have been working with me a long time on this film. They've put in time and money. Now Friedman and Fischman want to dump them. I'm being pressured from all directions. Everybody has taken a pay cut. And Firepower is in real trouble. The SEC is investigating them. Their stock was up to 40, now it's selling at 4 . . .'

'Uh huh.'

'"Get rid of those guys," they tell me. "We don't need them!" "But," I tell them, "I need them . . ." "Why do you need them?" they ask me, "Aren't we as good as they are?" "But they are in the contract," I tell them. "You signed the contract." "You know what a contract is?" they ask me and then they tell me, "A contract only is something to be *renegotiated*!"'

'Jesus . . .'

'These guys are squeezing and pressuring, squeezing and

pressuring . . . And they are going to squeeze until there's nothing left to squeeze . . . Already I've agreed to shoot the movie in 32 days instead of 34. The budget has been cut again and again . . . They don't like my sound man . . . They don't like my cameraman . . . They want somebody cheaper. "And you must get rid of these producers," they tell me, "we don't need them . . ."'

'What are you going to do?'

'Well, I can't abandon Tim and Lance . . . We have a plan. Tomorrow Tim and I are having lunch with this lawyer. This lawyer is known all over Hollywood. Just the mention of his name puts fear in the hearts of everybody. He is real, total power. And he owes Tim a favor. So, after lunch we are going to drop in on Friedman and Fischman and we are going to have the lawyer with us. Now it would be good if you were there too. Can you?'

'Sure . . . What's the time and place?'

Lunch was at Musso's. We had the big table in the corner. We had drinks and lunch. A number of people stopped by to say a few words to the big lawyer. It was true, they were all in awe of him. The big lawyer was very genteel and he wore a very expensive suit.

The lawyer, Lance and Jon planned their strategy regarding Friedman and Fischman. I didn't pay much attention. The lawyer laid it out: you say this, I'll say that. Don't you say that. Leave it to me.

Lawyers, doctors, plumbers, they made all the money. Writers? Writers starved. Writers suicided. Writers went mad.

Lunch did end and we went to our respective cars and made our way to the big green building where Friedman and Fischman were waiting. We were to meet at the entrance.

The secretary escorted us into Harry Friedman's office and as we walked in Friedman stood up behind his desk and began right away: 'I am sorry but this company has no money and there is nothing that can be done. These other producers must go. We cannot pay them. We have no money!'

We found chairs about the room and sat down.

Jon said, 'Mr Friedman, I need these men, they are essential to the production.'

Friedman remained standing. He put his knuckles down on top of his desk.

'NOBODY IS NEEDED! LEAST OF ALL, THESE MEN. WHAT DO WE NEED THEM FOR? TELL ME, FOR WHAT DO WE NEED THEM?'

'They are my co-producers, Mr Friedman . . .'

'I AM A PRODUCER! I AM BETTER THAN THEY ARE! I DO NOT NEED THESE MEN! THESE MEN ARE BLOODSUCKERS! BLOODSUCKERS!'

A door opened behind Friedman's desk and out came Fischman. Fischman was not as heavy as Friedman. He ran in a little circle around Friedman's desk. Fischman moved well. As he ran in his little circle he yelled:

'BLOODSUCKERS! BLOODSUCKERS! BLOOD-SUCKERS!'

Then he ran back through the door, which evidently led to his office.

Friedman sat down behind his desk. It was evident that he knew who the big lawyer was.

He sat behind his desk and said quietly, 'We need nobody.'

The big lawyer coughed, then spoke: 'Please pardon me, but there is . . . a contract . . .'

Friedman leaped up from behind his desk:

'YOU SHUT UP, YOU WISE-ASS!'

'I will be in touch with you,' said the big lawyer.

'YES! YOU BE IN TOUCH! YOU GO AHEAD, BE IN TOUCH, YOU WISE-ASS! YOU ARE NOTHING TO ME!'

We got up and huddled near the door. Some words were whispered back and forth, then Tim and the big lawyer left. Jon said he wanted to talk further with Friedman. I remained.

We sat back down.

'I cannot pay these men,' said Friedman.

Jon leaned forward, gestured with a hand. 'But, Harry, you just can't ask those men to work for you for . . . *nothing*!'

'I LOVE it when men work for NOTHING! I LOVE IT!'

'But . . . this is not *right* . . . those men have worked for *months!* You must give them *something!*'

'All right, I'll give them 15 thousand . . .'

'Only 30 thousand, for all those months of work?'

'No, the 15 thousand is for *both* of them . . .'

'But this is impossible . . .'

'Nothing is impossible . . .' He looked at me: 'Who's this guy?'

'He's the writer.'

'He's an old guy. He won't live long. I cut him 10 thousand . . .'

'No, he's paid through me . . .'

'Then I cut you ten and you cut him ten.'

'Harry, stop it, please . . .'

Friedman got up from his chair and walked over to a leather sofa against the wall. He threw himself full length upon the sofa. He looked ceilingward. He remained silent. Then there seemed to be a slight sobbing. Liquid was forming in Harry Friedman's eyes.

'We have no money. We have no money. I don't know what to do. Help me, help me!'

He was silent a good two minutes. Jon lit a cigarette and waited.

Then Friedman spoke, still looking up at the ceiling.

'This could be called an Art Film, couldn't it?'

'Well, yes,' said Jon.

Harry Friedman leaped up from his couch, ran over to Jon:

'AN ART FILM! AN ART FILM! THEN *YOU* WILL WORK FOR NOTHING!'

Jon stood up. 'Mr Friedman, we have to go . . .'

We moved toward the door.

'Jon,' Friedman said, '*those bloodsuckers* will have to go.'

'Bloodsuckers,' we heard Fischman's voice again from behind the door.

We headed toward the boulevard.

Chapter Twenty-three

SARAH AND I decided to visit the ghetto again. Since we still had the old Volks I decided to drive over in that.

Once there, it looked about the same except somebody had left an old mattress in the middle of the street and we had to circle around it.

The whole place had the look of a bombed-out village. On that day there was nobody in sight. It was as if at some signal everybody had gone into hiding. But I could feel a hundred eyes upon us. Or so I imagined.

I parked and Sarah and I got out, knocked on the door. The door had 5 bullet holes in it. Something new.

I knocked again.

'Yes?' I heard Jon's voice.

'It's Hank and Sarah. We phoned. We're here.'

'Oh . . .'

The door opened. 'Come in, please . . .'

François Racine was at a table with his wine bottle.

'Life is for nothing,' he said.

Jon put the chains on the door. Sarah ran her fingers through the bullet holes.

'I see you've had some termites . . .'

Jon laughed. 'Oh, yes . . . sit down . . .'

He got some glasses and we sat down. He poured the wine.

'The other day they raped a girl on the hood of my car. There were 5 or 6 of them. We objected. They became very angry. A couple of days went by, then one night we are sitting here and bang, bang, bang, bang, bang, the bullets came through the door. Then it was quiet . . .'

'We are still alive,' said François. 'We sit and drink wine.'

'It is just a ploy,' said Jon. 'They want us to move. I refuse to move.'

'Someday we will never be able to move,' said François.

'They have more guns than the police,' said Jon, 'and they shoot them more often.'

'You ought to move out of here,' said Sarah.

'Are you kidding? We leased this place for 3 months in advance. We'd lose all the money.'

'Better we lose our lives?' said François taking a big hit.

'Can you sleep at night?' I asked.

'We have to drink to sleep. And then you can never be sure. Those bars on the windows might not mean much. My neighbor has them. The other night he's eating dinner alone and then there's a man standing behind him with a gun. Somehow he got in through the roof. There's some kind of passageway up there. They are under the house and in the roof. They can hear everything we say. They are listening now.'

Four loud taps came up through the floorboards.

'See?'

François jumped up and stamped on the floor.

'BE QUIET! BE QUIET! WHAT KIND OF DEVIL MEN ARE YOU?'

It was silent down there. I guess they just wanted us to know that they were there. They had no desire to get chummy about the whole thing.

François sat back.

'This whole thing is terrifying,' said Sarah.

'I know it,' said Jon. 'They stole our tv but we don't need a tv around here.'

'I thought this was just a black ghetto,' I said, 'but I saw some Hispanics last time . . .'

'Oh yeah,' said Jon, 'we have one of the toughest Mexican gangs here, the V-66. To be a member you must have killed somebody.'

There was a long pause.

'How's the movie going?' I asked, mostly to break the silence.

'Pre-production is rolling. I'm there every day, many hours working with people. We'll soon be shooting. As each day goes by, as Firepower invests more and more money, the *film* becomes more of a reality. But there are fuck-ups of every sort every day . . .'

'Like?' Sarah asked.

'Well, we went to rent a camera . . .'

'You rent a camera?'

'Yes. So we went to rent a camera and the company said they couldn't rent it to us.'

'Why?' I asked, walking to the window and looking out to check on the Volks.

'Firepower hadn't paid for the *last* rental. The company insisted that Firepower furnish them with a certified check for the use of the last camera and for the rental of the one we wanted to use.'

'Did they?' I asked.

'Yes.'

François got up.

'I am going to count the chickens,' he said, then left.

'Isn't François afraid of this kind of living?' Sarah asked.

'No,' said Jon, 'he is crazy. The other day he was sitting here alone and he looked up and there were two guys standing there. One of them had a knife. "Give us your money!" said the guy. "No," said François, "you give me *your* money!" He was drunk and he got his stick and he started hitting both of them with his stick. They ran out of the house and François chased them down the street beating them with his stick yelling, "YOU STAY OUT OF MY HOME! GO TO SOMEBODY ELSE'S HOME! AND DON'T STEAL MY CHICKENS!" He ran after them all the way down the street.'

'They could have killed him.'

'He's too crazy to realize that.'

'He's lucky to be alive,' said Sarah.

'Yes. But I think being French instead of an American helps. It confuses them as they don't have quite the same hatred as for an American. They sense that he is crazy and not *all* these guys are killers. Some of them are only human and just trying to get by.'

'Aren't they *all* human?' Sarah asked.

'All too human,' Jon answered.

François walked in.

'I counted my chickens. They are all still there. I talked to them. I talked to my chickens.'

François sat down. Jon filled his glass.

'I want a castle,' François said, 'I want 6 children and a big fat wife.'

'Why do you want all those things?' I asked.

'So when I lose at gambling somebody will talk to me. Now when I lose at gambling nobody talks to me.'

I wanted to suggest that when he lost at gambling maybe a fat wife and 6 children might not talk to him either. But I didn't. François was suffering enough.

Instead I said, 'We must go to the racetrack together sometime.'

'WHEN?' he asked.

'We'll do it soon.'

'I have a new system.'

'We all have.'

Then the phone rang. Jon got it after the 3rd ring.

'Allo . . .'

'Yes . . . yes, this is Jon . . .'

'What? But this can't be!'

He looked at us, still holding the phone.

'He hung up . . .'

'Who?'

Jon put the phone down. He stood there.

'It was Harry Friedman . . .'

'And?' I asked.

'And the movie has been cancelled,' he answered.

Chapter Twenty-four

SEVERAL DAYS PASSED. I wasn't doing much, just going to the track, coming in and playing with the poem. I worked in 3 areas: the poem, the short story and the novel. Now, it was 4 with the screenplay. Or was it 4? Without the movie was I a screenplay writer? Jim Beam wasn't dancing.

Then Jon phoned. 'How are the horses?'

'They are all right. Hey, how are you, anyhow?'

'I'm all right . . . just wanted to let you know what's happening . . .'

'Yes? . . .'

'Well, after the cancellation, first thing François and I did was to get drunk for two days and nights . . .'

'A cleansing, right?'

'Yes. So, after that I went down to the Firepower building in an attempt to see Friedman and find out why he cancelled the movie. It was a shocker to me.'

'Me too . . .'

'So, I went down there. The guard wouldn't let me in. Evidently Friedman had given orders for me not to see him.'

'Son of a bitch.'

'Yes, he is sometimes. Anyhow, I went to the other entrance, there are two entrances . . .'

'Yes, I know.'

'I know the lawyer there. So I told the guard that I wanted to see the lawyer and he let me in. But I didn't go see the lawyer,

I went down to Friedman's office and I walked right in there.'

'Good . . .'

'Friedman looked up and saw me. He said, "Why, hello, Jon, how are you?" I told him that I was fine. I decided not to ask him why he had cancelled the movie. That was his business, anyhow. So I told him, "Now we are going to get somebody else for this movie." And he asked, "Have you gotten anybody else?" and I told him that I hadn't. Then I said, "Now we are going to get somebody. And when we do, I want your word on something." "Like what?" he asked. "Well, when we get somebody we are going to have them pay you all your expenses up to date on your pre-production costs." "Good," he said. "But," I told him, "I want your word that you will allow the movie to go forward under those conditions and that Firepower will not ask for additional monies." "Fine," Friedman told me, "go ahead. Get somebody else. I agree to the terms. And good luck to you."'

'And that was it?'

'Yes, we shook hands and I left. I believe that he was delighted with the possibility of recovering pre-production costs.'

'Now all we gotta do is find somebody.'

'We have . . .'

'What?'

'You see, all the time we have been dealing with Firepower, even after they signed to do the movie we have been secretly seeking other backers. We never quite trusted Firepower. So when one of the other backers found out the movie had been cancelled he jumped right in.'

'Oh? Who are these people?'

'It's Edleman, a *big* real estate operator in the east. His west coast man is Sorenson. We've checked everything out. The money is there, it's real. And they say, "Yes, we have the money. Yes, we want to do the movie. Let's do it."'

'Are you sure these guys are all right?'

'The money is there. They are established. We are better off than with Firepower. And they love the screenplay and the actors. They are ready to roll. The papers are being drawn up. We sign Thursday afternoon.'

'Beautiful, Jon. I'm happy for you. For me too.'

'The movie would have been made anyhow. I was determined about that. But now we can do it right away.'

'I'm proud of you, Jon.'

'I'll keep you up to the moment. Goodbye.'

'Do that. Goodbye, Jon . . .'

The next phone call was a couple of days later.

'Son of a bitch!' Jon said.

'What is it?'

'Firepower has backed down! They know about Edleman and Sorenson. NOW THEY ARE DEMANDING BETWEEN $500,000 AND $750,000 EXTRA!'

'WHAT?'

'Friedman went back on his word. I got him on the phone, I said, "But you told me you wouldn't ask for anything more! You gave me your word!"'

'What did he say?'

'He didn't say anything. He hung up. Now I can't contact him. He won't take calls from me. I'm going on a HUNGER STRIKE!'

'What?'

'A HUNGER STRIKE! I've got my bottle of water and a little low-back chair and I'm going to sit out in front of Firepower and starve myself!'

'Now?'

'Yes, I'll be down there in ten minutes!'

'You don't mean it . . .'

'Of course, I mean it!'

When I drove down, there was Jon Pinchot sitting out in front of the building in his little low-back chair. There was the bottle of water. And a crudely made sign:

HUNGER STRIKE!
FIREPOWER IS
LIAR POWER!

I parked and went around to where Jon was. There were 4 or 5 people staring at him. I knelt down by him.

'Look, Jon. Let's forget the fucking film. I'll give you your money back. I don't need it this bad. Let's knock this shit off and go get stinko somewhere, huh?'

Jon reached into his coat pocket and handed me a piece of paper.

'I arranged to have this delivered by messenger to Harry Friedman. He got it. This is a copy.' And, he pulled out another paper, 'Here is the release agreement.'

I read the first paper he had handed me:

Dear Harry:

Here are the two alternatives I told you on the phone. As you can see they are both acceptable to me. Believe me, when I suggest a solution where I get no money it is not only to save the project but also because I love you, much more than you can imagine.

O.K., now you decide. Please do so quickly because I have Edleman who is ready to take over the film and all obligations in all contracts. If Edleman who is ready to take over the film right away does not have this piece of paper (Solution #1 enclosed) signed by you by Thursday afternoon he will not be able to start production on the 19th. Ten important people will have to be hired before then. This leaves us only

Tuesday and Wednesday for the takeover of the film by
Edleman. If this is not done we will lose Jack Bledsoe as our
lead in the film and you will lose around a million dollars.
This is suicide for everybody, financially, at any rate. But I
must go a step further, as follows: if my movie is not freed
by you by tomorrow morning at 9 a.m. like you promised
me, Solution #2 is that I will start cutting parts off my body
and sending them to you in envelopes every day. I am serious.
You cannot afford to wait one more day. It Is a Matter of
Life or Death for the Movie.

love,

Jon

The other piece of paper was called Solution #1 and was
headed:

AMENDMENT TO LOAN-OUT AGREEMENT
FOR DIRECTING SERVICES OF JON PINCHOT

And having been written by a lawyer was almost unread-
able, but it seemed to call for Friedman to release the film to
Edleman and to keep the money that was coming to Jon.

I handed the papers back to Jon.

'What is Solution #2?'

'The cutting off of the parts.'

'You call that a solution?'

'I guess it should be called a resolution.'

'You aren't going to do it?'

'Yes, I am. It's all I know.'

'You're crazy.'

'No. No. But come with me. I must prepare.'

'Prepare?'

'Yes.'

We were in Jon's car. 'I have the first part I need. The pain-killer. You see I had to go to a doctor for an ingrown toenail. He operated. Then he gave me a pain-killer afterwards. It worked great . . .'

'Where are we going?'

'You'll see. Anyhow, I had to go back to get the toe checked. I said to the doctor, "That pain-killer was great, it lasted ten hours. Tell me about it." He told me about it. Then I asked him, "Can I see it?" And he took me to this medicine cabinet and pointed it out. "Very interesting," I said. We talked a bit more, then I left. But I had a bag with me, a small traveling bag. I left it by the medicine cabinet. Then I left the office, came back. "Oh," I told the receptionist, "I left my bag." I went to get the bag and there was nobody around. I opened the cabinet and took the pain-killer.'

'You can't do this,' I told Jon.

'I must,' he answered.

We were in a hardware store.

'Yes?' the clerk asked.

'I need a saw,' Jon said, 'an electric chainsaw.'

The clerk walked over to a wall display and came back with this orange job.

'This is a Black and Decker, one of our finest.'

'Where does the blade go?' asked Jon. 'How do you put it in?'

'Oh, it's quite easy,' said the clerk. He got a blade and fitted it.

Jon looked at it. The blade had very large teeth.

'Umm,' Jon said, 'that isn't quite the blade I was looking for.'

'What kind of blade do you want?' the clerk asked.

Jon thought a moment. Then said, 'Something to cut small pieces of wood with. A hard wood.'

'Oh,' said the clerk, 'how about this?'

He attached a new blade. It had fine teeth, very close together, sharp.

'Yes,' said Jon, 'that's what I want. That will do.'

'Cash or credit card?' the clerk asked.

Back in the car and driving back to resume the hunger strike I asked Jon, 'You're not really going to do this, are you?'

'Of course, I am going to start with the little finger of the left hand. What good is it anyhow?'

'That's what you use to hit the "a" key on the typewriter.'

'I'll type without using "a"s.'

'Listen, friend, isn't there any way to turn this whole thing around and just forget it?'

'No. Not at all.'

'And you're going to be there at 9 a.m.?'

'In his lawyer's office. I will plug it in. I will do it unless the film gets released.'

I believed him. It was the way he said it: a simple statement of fact without melodramatic overtones.

'Will you wait for me before you walk into the lawyer's office?'

'Yes, but you must be on time. Will you be there on time?'

'I'll be there on time,' I said.

We drove back toward Firepower.

Chapter Twenty-five

I WAS THERE at 8:50 a.m. I parked and waited for Jon. He rolled up at 8:55 a.m. I got out and walked over to Jon's car.

'Good morning, Jon . . .'

'Hello, Hank . . . How are you?'

'Fine. Listen, what happened to the hunger strike?'

'Oh, I am still on that. But more important is the cutting off of the parts.'

Jon had the Black and Decker with him. It was wrapped in a dark green towel. We walked into the Firepower building together. The elevator took us up to the lawyer's office. Neeli Zutnick. The receptionist was expecting our arrival. 'Please go right in,' she said.

Neeli Zutnick was waiting. He rose from behind his desk and shook hands with us. Then he returned, sat down behind his desk. 'Would you gentleman care for some coffee?' he asked.

'No,' said Jon.

'I'll have some,' I said.

Zutnick hit the intercom button. 'Rose? Rose, my dear . . . one coffee, please . . .' He looked at me, 'Cream and sugar?'

'Black.'

'Black. Thank you, Rose . . . Now, gentlemen . . .'

'Where's Friedman?' Jon asked.

'Mr Friedman has given me full instructions. Now . . .'

'Where's your plug?' Jon asked.

'Plug?'

'For this . . .' Jon pulled the towel away revealing the Black and Decker.

'Please, Mr Pinchot . . .'

'Where's the plug? Never mind, I see it . . .'

Jon walked over and plugged the Black and Decker into the wall.

'You must understand,' said Zutnick, 'that if I had known you were going to bring that instrument I would have arranged to turn off the electricity.'

'That's all right,' said Jon.

'There's no need for that instrument,' said Zutnick.

'I hope not. It's just . . . in case . . .'

Rose entered with my coffee. Jon pressed the button on the Black and Decker. The blade sprang into action and began to hum.

Rose nervously tilted the coffee cup just a bit . . . just enough to spill a touch of it on her dress. It was a nice red dress and Rose, a heavy girl, filled it nicely.

'Wow! That *scared* me!'

'I'm sorry,' Jon said, 'I was just . . . testing . . .'

'Who gets the coffee?'

'I do,' I told her, 'thank you.'

Rose brought the coffee over to me. I needed it.

Rose exited, giving us a worried look over her shoulder.

'Both Mr Friedman and Mr Fischman have expressed dismay at your present state of mind . . .'

'Cut the shit, Zutnick! Either I get the release or the first piece of my flesh will be deposited . . . *there*!'

Jon tapped the center of Zutnick's desk with the end of the Black and Decker.

'Now, Mr Pinchot, there is no need . . .'

'THERE IS A NEED! AND YOU'RE RUNNING OUT OF TIME! I WANT THAT RELEASE! NOW!'

Zutnick looked at me. 'How is your coffee, Mr Chinaski?'

Jon squeezed the trigger of the Black and Decker and held up his left hand, little finger extended. He waved the Black and Decker about as the blade furiously worked away.

'NOW!'

'VERY WELL!' yelled Zutnick.

Jon took his finger off the trigger.

Zutnick opened the top drawer of his desk and pulled out two legal-sized sheets of paper. He slid them toward Jon. Jon walked over, picked them up, sat back down, began reading.

'Mr Zutnick,' I asked, 'can I have another cup of coffee?'

Zutnick glared at me, hit the intercom.

'Another cup of coffee, Rose. Black . . .'

'Like in Black and Decker,' I said.

'Mr Chinaski, that isn't funny.'

Jon continued to read.

My coffee arrived.

'Thank you, Rose . . .'

Jon continued to read as we waited. The Black and Decker lay across his lap.

Then Jon said, 'No, this won't do . . .'

'WHAT?' said Zutnick. 'THAT IS A COMPLETE RELEASE!'

'All of clause "e" must be deleted. It contains too many ambiguities.'

'May I see those papers?' asked Zutnick.

'Certainly . . .'

Jon placed them on the blade of the Black and Decker and passed them over to Zutnick. Zutnick took them off the blade with some disgust. He began reading clause "e".

'I see nothing wrong here . . .'

'Delete it . . .'

'Do you really intend to cut off one of your fingers?'

'Yes. I may even cut off one of yours.'

'Is that a threat? Are you threatening me?'

'Consider this: I have nothing to lose here. Only you have.'

'A contract signed under these conditions can be considered invalid.'

'You are making me sick, Zutnick! Eliminate clause "e" or my finger goes! NOW!'

Jon hit the button. The Black and Decker sprang into action again. Jon Pinchot stuck out his little finger, left hand.

'STOP!' screamed Zutnick.

Jon stopped.

Zutnick was on the intercom. 'ROSE! I need you . . .'

Rose entered. 'More coffee for the gentleman?'

'No, Rose. I want this entire contract revised and run out again, but eliminate clause "e", then return it to me.'

'Yes, Mr Zutnick.'

We all just sat a while then.

Then Zutnick said, 'You can unplug that thing now.'

'Not yet,' said Jon. 'Not until everything is finalized . . .'

'Do you really have another producer for this thing?'

'Of course . . .'

'Do you mind telling me who?'

'Of course not. Hal Edleman. Friedman knows that.'

Zutnick blinked. Edleman was money. He knew the name.

'I've read the screenplay. It seems very . . . crude . . . to me.'

'Have you read any other of Mr Chinaski's works?' Jon asked.

'No. But my daughter has. She read his book of stories, *Cesspool Dreams*.'

'And?'

'She hated it.'

Rose was back with the new contract. She handed it to Zutnick. Zutnick gave it a glance, stood up and walked it over to Jon.

Jon reread the whole thing.

'Very well.'

He walked it over to the desk, bent over, signed it. Zutnick signed for Friedman and Fischman. It was done. One copy each.

Then Zutnick laughed. He looked relieved.

'The practice of law gets stranger all the time . . .'

Jon unplugged the Black and Decker. Zutnick walked to a small cabinet on the wall, opened it, pulled out a bottle, 3 glasses. He sat them on his desk, poured around.

'To the deal, gentlemen . . .'

'To the deal . . .' said Jon.

'To the deal,' the writer chimed in.

We drank them down. It was brandy. And we had the movie again.

I walked Jon to his car. He threw the Black and Decker into the back seat, then climbed into the front.

'Jon,' I asked from the sidewalk, 'can I try you with the big question?'

'Sure.'

'You can tell me the truth about the Black and Decker. It will never get further than this. Were you really going to do it?'

'Of course . . .'

'But the other parts to follow? The other pieces. Were you going to do that?'

'Of course. Once you begin such a thing there is no stopping.'

'You've got guts, my man . . .'

'It is nothing. Now I am hungry.'

'Can I buy you breakfast?'

'Well, all right . . . I know just the place . . . Get into your car and follow me . . .'

'All right.'

I followed Jon through Hollywood, the light and the shadows of Alfred Hitchcock, Laurel and Hardy, Clark Gable, Gloria Swanson, Mickey Mouse and Humphrey Bogart, falling all around us.

Chapter Twenty-six

THERE WASN'T MUCH for a week or so. I was playing with one of the cats on the rug when the phone rang. Sarah got it.

'Yes? Oh, hello Jon. Yes, he's here. There's no racing on Mondays or Tuesdays. What? Oh god, what a mess . . . Look, I'll get Hank . . .'

I got up off the rug and took the phone.

'Hello, Jon . . .'

'Hank, it fell through . . .'

'What?'

'The Edleman thing. They were going around trying to sell *The Dance of Jim Beam* for 7 million behind our back. The people I had hired to go around secretly to find another backer when we were with Firepower have just told me that the Edleman group offered to sell *them* the rights to the movie for 7 million.'

'But they don't have the rights, yet . . .'

'They claimed that they did. They presented the package: the screenplay, the actors, the budget. For the right to produce the film they were asking 7 million. They were going to buy the rights from us for less after they had made a deal in secret . . .'

'Jesus . . .'

'We are once again the victim of another bunch of crooks. So that's out. The Edleman thing is finished. So we are now going to try to get another producer. I didn't want to bother you with all this but I thought I'd better let you know.'

'Of course. So, how's it going?'

'We get people on the phone. We present it to them on the phone and they all say, "Fine, fine, we'll do it." Then when they see the screenplay they say, "No." The whole *town* says, "No." The moment they see the screenplay they say, "No." Here's a film with 2 great actors and a budget so low that there is no way this film isn't going to make money. Yet the whole town says "No." It's unheard of.'

'They don't like the screenplay,' I said.

'They don't like it.'

'And I don't like them. I don't like them at all.'

'Well, we are going to keep working. There must be some people somewhere that we haven't tried.'

'It sounds dark.'

'Somehow we are going to do this thing.'

'I like your faith.'

'Don't worry.'

'All right . . .'

I got back down on the rug and played with the cat. The cat liked to chase this piece of string.

'The movie's back to nowhere,' I told Sarah. 'Nobody likes the screenplay.'

'Do you like it?'

'I think it's better than most of the screenplays I've seen but maybe I'm wrong. Mostly I'm sorry for Jon.'

The cat missed the string but sunk a claw into the top of my hand. The blood came. I walked to the bathroom and doused the wound with hydrogen peroxide. There was my face in the mirror: just an old man who had written a screenplay. Shit. I walked out of there.

When the horses were running I never got any bad news because I wasn't home and nobody could find me.

Well, the track did come around again and I went every day, did all right, came in, as was my wont, ate, watched a bit of tv with Sarah, went upstairs to the wine bottle and the typer. I was working on the poem. There wasn't much money in the poem but it sure was a big playground to flounder around in.

Within a couple of weeks after his last phone call there was another from Jon.

'Everything is hell again,' he said. 'We are worse off than ever!'

'What?'

'Listen, we found a producer, he said all right, he liked everything, even the screenplay. He told me, "All right, we'll do it. Bring the papers, I'll sign them and we'll get right into production." So a time was set for the signing but before I could get over there he phoned me. He said, "I can't do the film." Apparently there is a well known director who claims he has the dramatic rights to all the works about Henry Chinaski. "There is nothing I can do," he told me. "The deal is off."'

Henry Chinaski was the name I had used for my main character in my various novels. I had used the name again in the screenplay.

'What is this bullshit?' I asked.

'It's not bullshit. You have sold the rights to the Henry Chinaski character.'

'There's no truth in this,' I said, 'but even if it were true, all we would have to do is to change the name.'

'No, the contract says that he owns the *character* no matter what name you use. Forever!'

'This can't be true . . .'

'I am afraid when you sold your novel *Shipping Clerk* to the director Hector Blackford, you also sold those dramatic rights.'

'Yes, I sold the movie rights. It was only 2 thousand dollars. I was starving. It looked like a lot of money to me at the time. Blackford never made a movie out of *Shipping Clerk*.'

'It doesn't matter. It says in the contract that he owns the character forever.'

'Listen, how did you hear all this?'

'Well, there's this lawyer, Fletcher Jaystone. He's in bed with a lady film editor. They've completed their business and the lawyer sees the screenplay on the side table. He reaches over. It's *The Dance of Jim Beam*. He flips through it, puts the screenplay back down and says, 'HENRY CHINASKI! MY CLIENT OWNS THIS GUY! I DREW UP THE CONTRACT MYSELF!' And right from there the word goes around town. *The Dance of Jim Beam* is dead. Now nobody will touch it because Blackford and his lawyer *own* Henry Chinaski.'

'That's not true, Jon. I wouldn't sell these rights into perpetuity for a lousy 2 grand. That wouldn't make any sense.'

'But it's in the contract!'

'I read the contract before I signed it. I never saw anything like that.'

'See section VI.'

'I don't believe it.'

'I phoned this lawyer. He is a tough guy. "We own Henry Chinaski," he told me. "I invested 15 thousand of my own money at the time and it was lot of money then. It's *still* a lot of money." I started to get excited, I started to scream at him. "Wait," he said, "don't talk to me like that. Don't you talk to me like that." I couldn't get anywhere with him. I don't know if he wants a lot of money or what but right now *Jim Beam* is dead, deader than anything around. It's finished.'

'Jon, I'll phone you back.'

I looked up the contract and checked section VI. To my mind I could see no implied or direct sale of the rights to the character. I read section VI again and again but couldn't see it.

I phoned Jon.

'There's nothing in section VI that says anything about handing over the character forever. What kind of sickness is this? Has everybody gone crazy?'

'No, but that's what it means.'

'What means?'

'Section VI.'

'Do you have the contract there, Jon?'

'Yes.'

'Will you read me where it states that this guy owns Henry Chinaski.'

'Well, it infers it.'

'This is SICK! I don't even see an *inference*!'

'If we have to go to court it will take 3, 4, 5 years . . . And meanwhile, *Jim Beam* will be dead. Nobody will touch it!'

'IS EVERYBODY IN THIS TOWN THAT FRIGHT-ENED? THERE IS NOTHING IN SECTION VI THAT STATES ANYTHING IN THE VAGUEST WAY ABOUT SELLING THE CHINASKI CHARACTER TO THESE PEOPLE!'

'You have signed away the rights to Henry Chinaski forever,' said Jon.

He was sick too. I hung up.

I found Hector Blackford's phone number. It was listed in the phone book as it had always been. I had known Hector since he had come out of filmmaking school at USC. One of his first films had been a documentary about me. It played on PBS one night. The next morning 50 people phoned in and cancelled their subscriptions.

Hector and I had been drunk together a few times. He had shown some interest in doing *Shipping Clerk* and he had even handed me a screenplay but it was so badly done that I told him to forget it. Meanwhile, he went his way and I went mine. And *he* became rich and famous, directing a number of big hits. I played with the poem and forgot about *Shipping Clerk*.

The phone rang and he was there.

'Hector, this is Hank . . .'

'Oh, hello Hank. How's it going?'

'Not well.'

'What is it?'

'It's about *Jim Beam*. There's a guy going around town who claims you and he own Henry Chinaski. You know him.'

'Fletcher Jaystone?'

'Yes. Now, Hector, you know I wouldn't sell my ass and soul for a lousy 2 thousand bucks.'

'Fletcher says that you have . . .'

'It's not in section VI.'

'He says it is.'

'Have you read it?'

'Yes.'

'Is it?'

'I don't know.'

'Listen, baby, you're not going to yank my balls off because of some vague wordage that nobody can understand, are you?'

'What do you mean?'

'I mean, we've got a movie under way and this is going

to kill it off forever. Don't you remember all those nights we got drunk together and talked all that good talk?'

'Yes, those were good nights.'

'Then talk to your man and get him off our ass. We only want to inhale and exhale. That's all.'

'Hank, I'll call you back.'

I sat by the phone and waited. I waited 15 minutes.

It rang.

It was Hector. 'All right, Jaystone is going to relent.'

'Thank you, man, I know you've got a good heart. The business hasn't killed you yet.'

'Jaystone is going to send you a release, immediately.'

'Great! Great! Hector, you're beautiful!'

'And Hank . . .'

'Yes?'

'I'm still going to make a movie out of *Shipping Clerk* some day.'

'All right, baby! Hello to your wife!'

'Hello to Sarah,' said Hector.

Nine-tenths of this kind of action is resolved over the telephone; the other tenth is the signing of the papers.

I phoned Jon.

'Hector is calling your man Jaystone off. Jaystone is sending a release.'

'Great! Great! Now we can go ahead! Hector was your buddy, wasn't he?'

'Well, I think he's proved that.'

'As soon as we get the release I'll go back to our new producer . . . By the way, instead of waiting on the mail why don't I just go to Jaystone's office and pick up the release?'

'Sure, phone him and set it up.'

'Well, we're back in the movie business,' said Jon.

'Sure. Maybe we ought to have lunch at Musso's.'

'When?'

'Tomorrow. One-thirty.'

'See you there,' said Jon.

'See you,' I answered.

Chapter Twenty-seven

SO THERE I was sitting around typing up poems and sending them out to the little magazines. For some reason the short story wasn't arriving on the typer and I didn't like that but I couldn't force it, so there I was playing with the poem. It was my release and my feast. Maybe the short story would come back some day. I certainly hoped so. The horses ran, the wine still poured and Sarah did some beautiful work in the garden.

I didn't hear from Jon for about a week, then one night the phone rang.

'You know that new producer we got the release from Blackford for?'

'Yes, is he ready to go?'

'He's backed out. Says he doesn't want to do the film.'

'Why?'

'He said that while he was waiting for the release papers he was offered another property he preferred. A screenplay about twin orphans who become the Doubles Champions of the Tennis World.'

'Sounds great. Wish I had thought of that.'

'But there's some good news too.'

'Like?'

'Firepower has decided to go ahead with the movie.'

'What? Why?'

'I think they got scared that somebody else was going to do

it. I think they smell money there. After all, the budget is pared to the bone. Everybody took a cut. And that was their doing, their artwork. I don't think they wanted anybody else to benefit from that. Harry Friedman phoned me. "I want that god damned movie," he said. "All right," I told him, "you've got it." "And if this movie doesn't make money, I will personally cut off *all* of your fingers!"'

'So, it's on again . . . ?'

'It's on again.'

Then three or four nights later the phone rang. It was Jon.

'All right if I come over? There is something we must talk about.'

'Sure, Jon . . .'

Thirty minutes later he was at the door. The bottle and the glasses waited on the coffee table.

'Come on in, Jon . . .'

'Where's Sarah?'

'Acting class.'

'Oh . . .'

Jon walked around and found his favorite seat near the fireplace. I filled his glass.

'All right, tell me.'

'Well, we are all set to start shooting, the schedule is set. Then Francine Bowers, she's in Boston, she falls ill. There must be an operation. She won't be ready for two weeks . . .'

'What happens?'

'We shoot around her. We shoot Jack Bledsoe, everything else. We will shoot her last. We get set to shoot the first scene with Jack and he refuses!'

'Why?'

'He demands a Rolls-Royce convertible to bring him to the set before he will do any acting.'

'How the hell can he do that?'

'It's in his contract. We find him one. No good. It's the wrong color. We shoot some scenes without Jack or Francine. Then we find the right color Rolls convertible and Jack is back and ready to go to work.'

I refill the drinks.

'He wants you down there watching him,' said Jon.

'What? Doesn't he know that I have to go to the racetrack?'

'He says that they don't run every day.'

'That's true.'

'Listen, Hank, he wants you to write a scene just for him.'

'Oh yeah?'

'He wants to do a scene in front of a mirror, he wants to say something in front of a mirror. Maybe a poem . . .'

'That could ruin everything, Jon.'

'These actors can be very difficult. If they get unhappy in the beginning, they can kill the whole film.'

Here I go, I thought, selling my ass down the river . . .

'All right,' I said, 'I'll write a poem in the mirror.'

'Also, Francine wants a scene where she can show off her legs. She has great legs, you know.'

'All right, I'll write in a leg scene . . .'

'Thank you. You know, you have another payment coming. You were supposed to get it when the shooting started but Firepower has held off paying us. But we'll get it and when we do you'll be paid.'

'All right, Jon.'

'I wish you'd come down and see the bar and the hotel where we're shooting. We're using real barflies, you know. They live in that hotel. You'll like them.'

'We'll be down there Monday . . .'

'I had some other little problems with Jack . . .'

'Like?'

'He wanted to get a tan, wear a little fedora and a pig-tail . . .'

'I don't believe that . . .'

'It's true. It took me hours to talk him out of it. And look what he wanted to wear in the movie!'

Jon reached down into his briefcase and pulled out a pair of dark shades. He put them on. They were huge. And the frame was shaped into green plastic palm trees.

'Is this guy crazy?' I asked. 'There isn't a man in the state of California who'd wear those things.'

'I told him that. He insisted that he be allowed to wear the glasses *somewhere* in the movie, if only for a moment. "OTHER-WISE," he screamed at me, "YOU'LL BE TAKING MY BALLS AWAY!"'

'Well,' I said, 'I don't want to take his balls away. I'll figure out a scene somewhere where he can put the glasses on.'

'You'll get this stuff to me as soon as you write it?'

'I'll do it tonight.'

I poured another round of drinks.

'How's François?'

'You know that 60 thousand he got behind on that practice roulette wheel?'

'Yes.'

'Well, he worked his way out of that. He's now six thousand ahead and a much happier man.'

'Good.'

Three things a man needed: faith, practice, and luck.

Chapter Twenty-eight

THE SHOOTING WAS to start in Culver City. The bar was there and the hotel with my room. The next part of the shooting was to be done in the Alvarado Street district, where the apartment of the female lead was located.

Then there was a bar to be used near 6th Street and Vermont. But the first shots were to be in Culver City.

Jon took us up to see the hotel. It looked authentic. The barflies lived there. The bar was downstairs. We stood and looked at it.

'How do you like it?' Jon asked.

'It's great. But I've lived in worse places.'

'I know,' said Sarah, 'I've seen them.'

Then we walked up to the room.

'Here it is. Look familiar?'

It was painted grey as so many of those places were. The torn shades. The table and the chair. The refrigerator thick with coats of dirt. And the poor sagging bed.

'It's perfect, Jon. It's *the* room.'

I was a little sad that I wasn't young and doing it all over again, drinking and fighting and playing with words. When you're young you can really take a battering. Food didn't matter. What mattered was drinking and sitting at the machine. I must have been crazy but there are many kinds of crazy and some are quite delightful. I starved so that I could have time to write. That just isn't done much anymore. Looking at that table I saw myself sitting there again. I'd been crazy and I knew it and I didn't care.

'Let's go down and check the bar again . . .'

We went down. The barflies who were to be in the movie were sitting there. They were drinking.

'Come on, Sarah, let's grab a stool. See you later, Jon . . .'

The bartender introduced us to the barflies. There was Big Monster and Little Monster, The Creeper, Buffo, Doghead, Lady Lila, Freestroke, Clara and others.

Sarah asked The Creeper what he was drinking. 'It looks good,' she said.

'This is a Cape Cod, cranberry juice and vodka.'

'I'll have a Cape Cod,' Sarah told the barkeep, Cowboy Cal.

'Vodka 7,' I told the Cowboy.

We had a few. Big Monster told me a story about how they had all got in a fight with the cops. Quite interesting. And I knew by the way he told it that it was the truth.

Then there was lunch call for the actors and crew. The barflies just stayed in there.

'We'd better eat,' said Sarah.

We went out behind and to the east of the hotel. A large bench was set up. The extras, technicians, hands and so forth were already eating. The food looked good. Jon met us out there. We got our servings at the wagon and followed Jon down to the end of the table. As we walked along, Jon paused. There was a man eating by himself. Jon introduced us.

'This is Lance Edwards . . .'

Edwards gave a slight nod and went back to his steak.

We sat down at the end of the table. Edwards was one of the co-producers.

'This Edwards acts like a prick,' I said.

'Oh,' said Jon, 'he's very bashful. He's one of the guys that Friedman was trying to get rid of.'

'Maybe Friedman was right.'

'Hank,' said Sarah, 'you don't even know the man.'

I was working at my beer.

'Eat your food,' said Sarah.

Sarah was going to add ten years to my life, for better or worse.

'We are going to shoot a scene with Jack in the room. You ought to come watch it.'

'After we finish eating we're going back to the bar. When you're ready to shoot, have somebody come get us.'

'All right,' said Jon.

After we ate we walked around the other side of the hotel, checking it out. Jon was with us. There were several trailers parked along the street. We saw Jack's Rolls-Royce. And next to it was a large silver trailer. There was a sign on the door: JACK BLEDSOE.

'Look,' said Jon, 'he has a periscope sticking out of the roof so he can see who's coming . . .'

'Jesus . . .'

'Listen, I've got to set things up . . .'

'All right . . . See you . . .'

Funny thing about Jon. His French accent was slipping away as he spoke only English here in America. It was a little sad.

Then the door of Jack's trailer opened. It was Jack.

'Hey, come on in!'

We went up the steps. There was a tv on. A young girl was lying in a bunk watching the tv.

'This is Cleo. I bought her a bike. We ride together.'

There was a fellow sitting at the end.

'This is my brother, Doug . . .'

I moved toward Doug, did a little shadow boxing in front

of him. He didn't say anything. He just stared. Cool number. Good. I liked cool numbers.

'Got anything to drink?' I asked Jack.

'Sure . . .'

Jack found some whiskey, poured me a whiskey and water.

'Thanks . . .'

'You care for some?' he asked Sarah.

'Thanks,' she said, 'I don't like to mix drinks.'

'She's on Cape Cods,' I said.

'Oh . . .'

Sarah and I sat down. The whiskey was good.

'I like this place,' I said.

'Stay as long as you like,' said Jack.

'Maybe we'll stay forever . . .'

Jack gave me his famous smile.

'Your brother doesn't say much, does he?'

'No, he doesn't.'

'A cool number.'

'Yeah.'

'Well, Jack, you memorized your lines?'

'I never look at my lines until right before the shooting.'

'Great. Well, listen, we've got to be going.'

'I know you can do it, Jack,' said Sarah, 'we're glad you got the lead.'

'Thanks . . .'

Back at the bar the barflies were still there and they didn't look any drunker. It took a lot to buzz a pro.

Sarah had another Cape Cod. I went back to the Vodka 7.

We drank and there were more stories. I even told one. Maybe an hour went by. Then I looked up and there was Jack standing looking over the swinging doors in the entrance. I could just see his head.

'Hey, Jack,' I yelled, 'come on in and have a drink!'

'No, Hank, we're going to shoot now. Why don't you come up and watch?'

'Be right there, baby . . .'

We ordered up another pair of drinks. We were working on them when Jon walked in.

'We're going to shoot now,' he said.

'All right,' said Sarah.

'All right,' I said.

We finished our drinks and I got a couple of bottles of beer to take with us.

We followed Jon up the stairway and into the room. Cables everywhere. Technicians were moving about.

'I'll bet they could shoot a movie with about one-third of these fucking people.'

'That's what Friedman says.'

'Friedman is sometimes right.'

'All right,' said Jon, 'we're just about ready. We've had a few dry runs. Now we shoot. You,' he said to me, 'stand in this corner. You can watch from here and not be in the scene.'

Sarah moved back there with me.

'SILENCE!' screamed Jon's assistant director, 'WE'RE GETTING READY TO ROLL!'

It became very quiet.

Then from Jon: 'CAMERA! ACTION!'

The door to the room opened and Jack Bledsoe weaved in. Shit, it was the young Chinaski! It was me! I felt a tender aching within me. Youth, you son of a bitch, where did you go?

I wanted to be the young drunk again. I wanted to be Jack Bledsoe. But I was just the old guy in the corner, sucking on a beer.

Bledsoe weaved to the window by the table. He pulled up the tattered shade. He did a little shadow boxing, a smile on his face. Then he sat down at the table, found a pencil and a piece of paper. He sat there a while, then pulled the cork from a wine bottle, had a hit, lit a cigarette. He turned on the radio and lucked into Mozart.

He began writing on that piece of paper with the pencil as the scene faded . . .

He had it. He had it the way it was, whether it meant anything or not, he had it the way it was.

I walked up to Jack, shook his hand.

'Did I get it?' he asked.

'You got it,' I said . . .

Down at the bar, the barflies were still at it and they looked about the same.

Sarah went back to her Cape Cods and I went the Vodka 7 route. We heard more stories which were very very good. But there was a sadness in the air because after the movie was shot the bar and hotel were going to be torn down to further some commercial purpose. Some of the regulars had lived in the hotel for decades. Others lived in a deserted train station nearby and action was being taken to remove them from there. So it was heavy sad drinking.

Sarah said finally, 'We've got to get home and feed the cats.'

Drinking could wait.

Hollywood could wait.

The cats could not wait.

I agreed.

We said our goodbyes to the barflies and made it to the car. I wasn't worried about driving. Something about seeing young Chinaski in that old hotel room had steadied me. Son of a bitch, I had been a hell of a young bull. Really a top-notch fuck-up.

Sarah was worried about the future of the barflies. I didn't like it either. On the other hand I couldn't see them sitting around our front room, drinking and telling their stories. Sometimes charm lessens when it gets too close to reality. And how many brothers can you keep?

I drove on in. We got there.

The cats were waiting.

Sarah got down and cleaned their bowls and I opened the cans.

Simplicity, that's what was needed.

We went upstairs, washed, changed, made ready for bed.

'What are those poor people going to do?' asked Sarah.

'I know. I know . . .'

Then it was time for sleep. I went downstairs for a last look, came back up. Sarah was asleep. I turned out the light. We slept. Having seen the movie made that afternoon we were now somehow different, we would never think or talk quite the same. We now knew something more but what it was seemed very vague and even perhaps a bit disagreeable.

Chapter Twenty-nine

JON PINCHOT HAD escaped from the ghetto. In his contract it stated that he would be supplied with an apartment to be paid for by Firepower. Jon found an apartment near the Firepower building. Each night, from his bed, Jon could see the lit sign at the top of the building, Firepower, and it shone through his window and upon his face as he slept.

François Racine remained in the ghetto. He began a garden, growing vegetables. He spun his roulette wheel, tended his garden and fed the chickens. He was one of the strangest men I had ever met.

'I cannot leave my chickens,' he told me. 'I will die in this strange land here with my chickens, here among the blacks.'

I went to the track on the days that the horses were running and the movie continued shooting.

The phone rang every day. People wanted to interview the writer. I never realized that there were so many movie magazines or magazines interested in the movies. It was a sickness: this great interest in a medium that relentlessly and consistently failed, time after time after time, to produce anything at all. People became so used to seeing shit on film that they no longer realized it *was* shit.

The racetrack was another waste of human life and effort. The people marched up to the windows with their money which they exchanged for pieces of numbered paper. Almost all of the numbers weren't good. In addition the track and the state took 18% off the top of each dollar, which they roughly divided. The biggest damn fools went to the movies and the racetracks. I was a damn fool who went to the racetrack. But I did better than most because after decades of race-going I had learned a minor trick or two. With me, it was a hobby and I never went wild with my money. Once you have been poor a long time you gain a certain respect for money. You never again want to be without any of it at all. That's for saints and fools. One of my successes in life was that in spite of all the crazy things I had done, I was perfectly normal: I chose to do those things, they didn't choose me.

Anyhow, one night the phone rang. It was Jon Pinchot.

'I don't know what to do,' he said.

'Did Friedman cancel the movie again?'

'No, it's not that . . . I don't know how this guy got my phone number . . .'

'What guy?'

'He just phoned me . . .'

'What did he say?'

'He said, "YOU MOTHERFUCKER, YOU KILLED MY BROTHER! YOU KILLED MY BROTHER! NOW I AM COMING TO KILL YOU! I AM COMING TO KILL YOU TONIGHT!"'

'God . . .'

'He was sobbing, he seemed out of his mind, it seemed very real. Maybe it is. In this town, you never know . . .'

'Did you phone the police?'

'Yes.'

'What did they say?'

'They said, "Call us when he gets there."'

'You can stay over here . . .'

'No, thanks, it's all right . . . but I'm sure I won't sleep well tonight . . .'

'Do you have a gun?'

'No, tomorrow I will get one, but then it may be too late.'

'Go to a motel . . .'

'No, he may be watching . . .'

'What can I do?'

'Nothing. I just wanted to let you know and to thank you for writing the screenplay.'

'It's all right.'

'Goodnight, Hank . . .'

'Goodnight, Jon . . .'

He hung up.

I knew how he felt. A guy phoned me once and told me he was going to kill me because I had fucked his wife. He called me by my last name and told me he was on the way over. He didn't make it. He must have been killed in a traffic accident.

I decided to phone François Racine to see how he was doing.

I got his answering machine:

'DO NOT SPEAK TO ME, SPEAK TO THIS MACHINE. I DO NOT WISH TO SPEAK. SPEAK TO THIS MACHINE. I AM NOWHERE AND YOU ARE ALSO NOWHERE. DEATH COMES WITH HIS LITTLE HANDS TO GRIP US. I DO NOT WISH TO SPEAK. SPEAK TO THE MACHINE.'

The beep sounded.

'François, you fuck-head . . .'

'Oh, it's you, Hank . . .'

'Yeah, babe . . .'

'There has been a fire . . . a fire . . . FIRE . . .'

'What?'

'Yes, I buy this cheap black and white tv . . . I leave it on while I am going somewhere . . . I want to fool them . . . Make them think there is somebody inside . . . I guess while I was gone the tv caught on fire or exploded . . . When I drive up I see all the smoke . . . The fire department does not come down here . . . This whole block could be in flames, they would not come . . . I walk through the smoke . . . There are flames . . . The blacks are in there . . . The killers and the thieves . . . They have buckets of water and they are running back and forth putting out the fire . . . I sit and watch . . . I find a bottle of wine, open it, drink . . . The blacks are running about . . . Soon the fire is out . . . There are embers and much smoke. We cough. "Sorry, man," one of the blacks says. "We got here late. We were having a gang meeting . . . somebody smelled smoke . . ." "Thank you," I told them. One of them had a pint of gin, we passed it around, then they left . . .'

'I'm sorry, François . . . Christ, I don't know what to say . . . Is it still liveable there?'

'I sit in the smoke, I sit in the smoke . . . It is like a fog, a fog . . . Now my hair is white, I am an old man, I sit in the fog . . . There is fog everywhere and my hair is white . . . I am an old man, I sit in the fog . . . Now I am a young boy, I sit in the fog . . . I hear my mother's voice . . . Oh no! She is moaning! She is getting FUCKED! She is getting FUCKED by somebody terrible! I must go back to France, I must help my mother, I must help France!'

'François, you can stay here . . . or I'm sure Jon has room . . . It's not as bad as you think . . . Every dark cloud passes . . .'

'No, no, sometimes there is a dark cloud that never passes. It stays forever!'

'Well, that's death.'

'Each day in life is death! I go back to France! I act again!'

'François, how about the chickens? You love the chickens, remember?'

'Fuck the chickens! Let the blacks have the chickens! Let the black meat and the white meat meet!'

'Meat meet?' I asked.

'I am in the fog. There has been a fire. A fire. I am an old man, my hair is white. I sit in the fog . . . I go now . . .'

François hung up.

I tried him again. All I got was: 'DO NOT SPEAK TO ME, SPEAK TO THIS MACHINE . . .'

I hoped he had a bottle or two of good red wine to get him through the night because it appeared if ever a man needed that it was my friend, François. Unless it was my friend, Jon. Unless it was me. I opened one.

'Care for a glass or two?' I asked Sarah.

'Certainly,' she answered. 'What's new?'

I told her.

Chapter Thirty

THE MAN DIDN'T come to kill Jon the first night. On the second night Jon had a gun and waited. The man didn't come. Sometimes they do, sometimes they don't.

Meanwhile, Francine Bowers had recovered from her operation.

'$50 per diem, plus room and board, that's all I can give her,' Friedman told Jon.

There was also some argument about paying for her flight to California but Firepower finally agreed to do it.

I was to receive a payment upon the first day of shooting and so was Jon but nothing had occurred. Firepower was to pay Jon and then Jon was to pay me. There had been nothing. I had no idea if the other people in the crew were being paid.

Maybe that's why I decided to go to the Distributor's Party. I could ask Friedman where my money was.

The party was on a Friday night at the Lemon Duck, a large dark place with a big bar and many tables. When Sarah and I arrived, most of the tables were filled. These people were the distributors from all over the world. They looked calm and almost bored. They were eating or ordering their meals, not saying much, not drinking much. We found a table off to the corner.

Jon Pinchot walked in and spotted us right away. He came to the table, smiling. 'Surprised to find you here. Distributor's parties are horrible . . . By the way, I have something . . .'

He had the screenplay there in its blue cover and he opened it.

'Now, this scene here, we need to cut a minute and a half. Can you do it?'

'Sure. But listen, could you get Sarah and me a drink?'

'Of course . . .'

'Jon is right,' said Sarah, 'this party doesn't seem to have much life.'

'Maybe we can add something to it,' I said.

'Hank, we don't have to always be the last ones to leave a party.'

'But somehow, we are . . .'

I began crossing out lines. My people talked too much. Everybody talked too much.

Jon was back with the drinks.

'How's it going?'

'My people talk too much . . .'

'They drink too much . . .'

'No, they can't drink too much. There is never enough . . .'

Then there was applause.

'It's Friedman,' said Sarah.

Here he came in an old suit, no necktie, top button missing from his shirt and the shirt was wrinkled. Friedman had his mind on other things besides dress. But he had a fascinating smile and his eyes looked right at people as if he were x-raying them. He had come from hell and he was still in hell and he'd put you in hell too if you gave him the slightest chance. He went from table to table, dropping small and precise sentences.

Then he came to our table. He made some remark on how nice Sarah looked.

'Look,' I pointed to the screenplay on the table, 'this son

of a bitch Pinchot has me WORKING during this party!'

'GOOD!' said Friedman, then turned and walked off toward another table.

I finished the cuts and handed the screenplay to Jon. He read it.

'It's fine,' he said, 'nothing important is left out and I think it reads just as well.'

'Maybe better.'

Then there was more applause. Francine Bowers was making her entrance. She wasn't that old but she was from the old school. She stood very straight (straight as in regal) turning her head slowly to the right and then to the left, smiling, then not smiling, then smiling again. She hesitated and stood there. She stood like a statue for ten seconds, then moved forward gracefully into the room. This earned her more applause. A few flashbulbs popped. Then she relaxed. She stopped at some of the tables for a word or two, then moved on.

God, I thought, what about the writer? The writer was the blood and bones and brains (or lack of same) in these creatures. The writer made their hearts beat, gave them words to speak, made them live or die, anything he wanted. And where was the writer? Who ever photographed the writer? Who applauded? But just as well and damn sure just as well: the writer was where he belonged: in some dark corner, watching.

Then, behold! Francine Bowers approached our table. She smiled at Sarah and Jon, then spoke to me, 'Did you write in that leg scene for me yet?'

'Francine, it's in there. You get to flash them.'

'You'll see. I have great legs!'

'I certainly hope so.'

She leaned over the table toward me, smiled her beautiful

smile, her eyes shone above those famous high cheek bones. 'Don't worry.'

Then she straightened and was gone, off to another table.

'I have to see Friedman about something,' said Jon.

'Yes,' I said, 'ask him about pay day.'

Sarah and I continued to sit and study the crowd. Sarah was good at parties. She pointed people out to me, told me about them. I saw things that I never would have noticed. I had most of humanity pegged on a very low scale and preferred not even to take notice of them. So Sarah made them a bit more interesting, which I appreciated.

The night wore on, and as usual Sarah and I didn't order any food. Eating was hard work and, after 2 or 3 drinks, the food was tasteless. Strangely as the wine got warmer it seemed to taste better. Then, out of nowhere, appeared Jon Pinchot.

'Look,' he pointed to a table, 'over there is one of Friedman's lawyers.'

'Good,' I said, 'I'm going over there. Please join me, Sarah . . .'

We walked over and sat down. The lawyer was well into his cups. Next to him was a very tall, blond lady. She sat tall and rigid, as if frozen. She had a long long neck and the neck stretched and stretched, rigid. It was painful to look at her. She looked frozen.

The lawyer knew us.

'Ah, Chinaski,' he said, 'and Sarah . . .'

'Hello,' said Sarah.

'Hello,' I said.

'This is my wife, Helga . . .'

We said hello to Helga. She didn't answer. She was frozen, sitting tall in her chair.

The lawyer waved in some drinks. Two bottles appeared.

Things looked good. The lawyer, Tommy Henderson, poured.

'Betcha you don't like lawyers,' he said to me.

'Not as a group, no.'

'Well, I'm an all-right lawyer, I'm not a crook. You think because I'm working for Friedman that I'm out to screw everybody?'

'Yes.'

'Well, I'm not . . .'

Tommy drained his wine glass, poured another. I drained mine.

'Take it easy, Hank,' said Sarah, 'we have to drive back.'

'If it gets too bad we'll take a cab back. The lawyer will pay.'

'That's right, I'll pay . . .'

'Well, in that case . . .' Sarah drained her glass right off.

The tall frozen woman was still frozen. Mostly it was painful to look at her. Her neck was so long and stretched that the veins protruded – long hard aching veins. It was truly awful.

'My wife,' said the lawyer, 'has given up drinking.'

'Oh, I see . . .' I said.

'Good for you,' said Sarah, 'that takes courage, especially with people drinking all around you.'

'I couldn't do it,' I said, 'worst thing in the world is being sober around a bunch of damn fool drunks.'

'I woke up alone and naked one morning at 5 a.m. on the sands of Malibu. That did it for me.'

'Good for you,' I said, 'it takes guts to cut it out.'

'Don't let anybody talk you out of it,' said Sarah.

The lawyer, Tommy Henderson, poured fresh drinks for himself, Sarah and me.

'Chinaski doesn't like me,' he said to his wife, Helga. 'He thinks I'm a crook.'

'I don't blame him,' said Helga.

'Oh yeah? Oh yeah?' said the lawyer. He drained most of his drink, then looked at me. He stared deeply. 'You think I'm a crook?'

'Well,' I said, 'probably . . .'

'You think we're not going to pay you?'

'That's the feeling that I have . . .'

'Well, listen, I've read most of your books, what do you think of that? I think you're a great writer. I think you're almost as good as Updike.'

'Thanks.'

'And, listen to this, this morning I mailed out all the checks. You people are going to get paid. You'll have your money in the next mail.'

'It's true,' said Helga, 'I saw him put the checks in the mail.'

'Great,' I said, 'you know, it's only fair . . .'

'Sure, it's fair. We want to be fair. We had a cash flow problem. Now it's solved.'

'It's going to be a good movie,' I said.

'I know it. I've read the script,' said Tommy. 'Now, do you feel better about everything?'

'Hell yes.'

'Do you still think I'm a crook?'

'Well, no, I can't.'

'Let's drink to it!' said Tommy.

He filled the glasses. We raised them in a toast. That is, Tommy, Sarah and I did.

'To an honest world,' I said.

We clicked the glasses and drank them down.

I noticed that the veins in Helga's neck were protruding further than ever. Nevertheless, we drank on.

We made small talk. A lot of it was about how brave Helga was.

We were the last to leave. That is, Helga, Tommy, Sarah and myself. The remaining two waiters gave us very dirty looks as we left. But Sarah and I were used to that. And Tommy most probably was too. Helga walked with us toward the exit, still rigid and suffering. Well, she wouldn't have a hangover in the morning. Then, it would be our turn.

Chapter Thirty-one

WE WENT DOWN to the other set on Alvarado Street on Monday a week later. We parked a couple of blocks away and walked over. As we got closer we could see that there was some activity around Jack Bledsoe's Rolls-Royce.

'They're taking some shots,' said Sarah.

There was Jack Bledsoe standing on the hood of the Rolls and standing up there with him were two of his biker pals. The flashbulbs went off, the bikers laughed, Bledsoe smiled and they all walked around on the hood in their heavy boots, changing positions for more shots.

'I don't think that's too good for the hood,' said Sarah.

Then I saw Jon Pinchot. He walked toward us. There was a tired smile upon his face.

'What the hell's going on here, Jon?'

'We have to keep the children happy.'

Then there was a yell from one of the bikers. Everybody leaped off the hood. The shots were finished. They walked off, laughing and talking.

'Look at those dents on the hood,' said Jon.

'Everywhere. Didn't they notice?'

'They don't know. They live, not knowing.'

'That poor beautiful car,' said Sarah.

(It would later cost $6,000 to get those dents taken out of the hood and to repaint it.)

'You talked to the lawyer at the party, didn't you, Hank?'

'Yes.'

'What did he say?'

'He said the checks had been mailed out.'

'That's true. I got them and deposited them in my account.'

Jon opened his wallet. He took them out. There were two of them. Stamped across the face of each it said: *Insufficient Funds*.

'They are on a Netherlands bank. Rubber.'

'I can't believe this,' I said.

'Why?' Sarah asked. 'Why is Firepower doing this?'

'I don't know. I confronted Friedman this morning. He claimed the checks were good, that the accountant deposited funds in the wrong bank account and that as soon as the funds were transferred back the checks would be good. I told him, "These are drawn on a Netherlands bank. No bank here will touch them when they are marked and stamped as they are. You must write me new checks." Friedman said, "No, I can't do this on my own. I must wait for my accountant to straighten it out."'

'I can't believe it,' I said.

'I told Friedman, "All right, let's get your accountant in here." And he said, "My accountant is at the deathbed of his mother in Chicago. She is dying of cancer." Then he leaned back in his chair and looked out the window.'

'"Mr Friedman," I told him, "this is not right."'

'Then what did the monster say?' Sarah asked.

'He looked at me with those innocent blue eyes and he said, "Remember, baby, nobody else in this town wanted this film. They spit on it. They laughed at it. We took it on, remember that. Work with us, honey-boy, and you'll be in the clover."'

'Then what did you do?'

'Sarah, Hank, please come with me now,' Jon said. 'We are getting ready to shoot the bathtub scene. Remember it?'

'Yes, of course. Are you going to go ahead without pay?'

We walked toward the set.

'The bathtub scene is going to be a good one. I like it,' Jon said.

'Yes,' I said, 'it's all right.'

Jon continued his story. 'Anyhow, after seeing Friedman, I went around the block. I walked around the block twice looking at that green Firepower building. Then I finally had had it. I walked back to Friedman's office . . . Pardon me, Hank, please stand behind me as I sit in this chair . . .'

'Huh?'

There was a photographer standing and waiting. Jon sat in a chair.

'Are you behind me?'

'Yes.'

'Now give a big phoney smile.'

I did.

The flash went off.

'Again,' said Jon.

The flash went off again.

'Good. That's it.'

Jon got up. 'Follow me. We're shooting upstairs . . .'

We began up the stairway.

'Friedman and Fischman had a photo just like that taken last week, Friedman in the chair, Fischman standing behind him, both of them smiling. The photo appeared as a full page ad in *Variety*. And under it were the words, FIREPOWER WILL WIN!'

'Yeah?'

'Wait. Stop here. Let me tell the rest before we enter the set.'

'All right.'

We stood there at the top of the stairway. The shooting was to take place down the hall.

'I went back to his office. I told Friedman that I had seen his ad in *Variety*. I said that you and I were taking out an ad next week. You and I with the same pose. And underneath would also be a picture of the two bounced checks with the caption, FIREPOWER WILL WIN, BUT HOW? I told him that unless we received two *certified checks* within 48 hours that this ad would appear.'

There was an extremely tall man standing at the end of the hall. It was Jon's assistant director, Marsh Edwards.

'We're ready to shoot, Jon. Everything's ready.'

'Wait . . . I'll be right there . . .'

'Maybe you can tell us later?' Sarah asked.

'No, I want to finish. Then I told Friedman, "On the other hand, if we get the *certified checks* within 48 hours, we can still run the ad in *Variety*, minus the Netherland checks, and the caption will say, FIREPOWER, WE WILL HELP YOU WIN!"'

'What'd he say?' I asked.

'He didn't say anything for a while. Then he said, "O.K., you'll have your checks."'

'But those shots you just took of us have big fake smiles. Won't we need better shots for a FIREPOWER, WE WILL HELP YOU WIN! ad?'

'If we get the checks,' said Jon, 'we'll forget the ad. Such an ad would cost $2,000.'

With that we moved along the hall to shoot the bathtub scene.

Chapter Thirty-two

THE BATHTUB SCENE was a simple one. Francine was to sit in the tub and Jack Bledsoe was to sit with his back against it, there on the floor, while Francine sat in the water talking about various things, mainly about a killer who lived there in her building, now on parole. He was shacked up with an old woman and beat her continually. One could hear the killer and his lady ranting and cursing through the walls.

Jon Pinchot had asked me to write the sound of people cursing through the walls and I had given him several pages of dialog. Basically, that had been the most enjoyable part of writing the screenplay.

Oftentimes in those roominghouses and cheap apartments there was nothing to do when you were broke and starving and down to the last bottle. There was nothing to do but listen to those wild arguments. It made you realize that you weren't the only one who was more than discouraged with the world, you weren't the only one moving toward madness.

We couldn't watch the bathtub scene because there just wasn't space enough in there, so Sarah and I waited in the front room of the apartment with its kitchen off to the side. Actually, over 30 years ago I had briefly lived in that same building on Alvarado Street with the lady I was writing the screenplay about. Strange and chilling indeed. 'Everything that goes around comes around.' In one way or another. And after 30 years the place looked just about the same. Only the people I'd known had all died. And the lady had died 3 decades ago and there I was sitting drinking a beer in that same building full of cameras and sound and crew. Well, I'd die too, soon enough. Pour one for me.

They were cooking food in the little kitchen and the refrigerator was full of beers. I made a few trips in there. Sarah found people to talk to. She was lucky. Every time somebody spoke to me I felt like diving out a window or taking the elevator down. People just weren't interesting. Maybe they weren't supposed to be. But animals, birds, even insects were. I couldn't understand it.

Jon Pinchot was still one day ahead of the shooting schedule and I was damned glad for that. It kept Firepower off our backs. The big boys didn't come around. They had their spies, of course. I could pick them out.

Some of the crew had books of mine. They asked for autographs. The books they had were curious ones. That is, I didn't consider them my best. (My best book is always the last one that I have written.) Some of them had a book of my early dirty stories, *Jacking-Off the Devil*. A few had books of poems, *Mozart In the Fig Tree* and *Would You Let This Man Babysit Your 4 Year Old Daughter?* Also, *The Bar Latrine Is My Chapel*.

The day wafted on, peacefully but listlessly.

Some bathtub scene, I thought. Francine must be fully cleansed by now.

Then Jon Pinchot just about ran into the room. He looked undone. Even his zipper was only halfway up. He was uncombed. His eyes looked wild and drained at the same time.

'My god!' he said, 'here you are!'

'How's it going?'

He leaned over and whispered into my ear. 'It's awful, it's maddening! Francine is worried that her tits might show above the water! She keeps asking "Do my tits show?"'

'What's a little titty?'

Jon leaned closer. 'She's not as young as she'd like to be . . . And Hyans hates the lighting . . . He can't abide the lighting and he's drinking more than ever . . .'

Hyans was the cameraman. He'd won damn near every award and prize in the business, one of the best cameramen alive, but like most good souls he liked a drink now and then.

Jon went on, whispering frantically: 'And Jack, he can't get this one line right. We have to cut again and again. There is something about the line that bothers him and he gets this silly smile on his face when he says it.'

'What's the line?'

'The line is, "He must masturbate his parole officer when he comes around."'

'All right, try, "He must jack-off his parole officer when he comes around."'

'Good, thank you! THIS IS GOING TO BE THE 19TH TAKE!'

'My god,' I said.

'Wish me luck . . .'

'Luck . . .'

Jon was out of the room then. Sarah walked over.

'What's wrong?'

'19th take. Francine is afraid to show her tits, Jack can't say his line and Hyans doesn't like the lighting . . .'

'Francine needs a drink,' she said, 'it will loosen her up.'

'Hyans doesn't need a drink.'

'I know. And Jack will be able to say his line when Francine loosens up.'

'Maybe.'

Just then Francine walked into the room. She looked totally lost, completely out of it. She was in a bathrobe, had a towel around her head.

'I'm going to tell her,' Sarah said.

She walked over to Francine and spoke quietly to her. Francine listened. She gave a little nod, then walked into the bedroom off to the left. In a moment Sarah came out of the kitchen with a coffeecup. Well, there was scotch, vodka, whiskey, gin in that kitchen. Sarah had mixed something. The door opened, closed and the coffeecup was gone.

Sarah came over. 'She'll be all right now . . .'

Two or three minutes passed, then the bedroom door flung open. Francine came out, headed for the bathroom and the camera. As she went past, her eyes found Sarah: 'Thank you!'

Well, there was nothing to do but sit about and indulge in more small talk.

I couldn't help but look back into the past. This was the very building I had been thrown out of for having 3 women in my room one night. In those days there was no such thing as Tenants' Rights.

'Mr Chinaski,' the landlady had said, 'we have religious people living here, working people, people with children. Never have I heard such complaints from the other tenants. And I heard you too – all that singing, all that cursing . . . things breaking . . . coarse language and laughter . . . In all my days, never have I heard anything like what went on in your room last night!'

'All right, I'll leave . . .'

'Thank you.'

I must have been mad. Unshaven. Undershirt full of cigarette holes. My only desire was to have more than one bottle on the dresser. I was not fit for the world and the world was not fit for me and I had found some others like myself, and most of them were women, women most men would never want to be in the same room with, but I adored them, they inspired me, I play-acted, swore, pranced about in my underwear telling them how great I was, but only *I* believed that. They just hollered, 'Fuck off! Pour some more booze!' Those ladies from hell, those ladies in hell with me.

Jon Pinchot walked briskly into the room.

'It worked!' he told me. 'Everything worked! What a day! Now, tomorrow we start again!'

'Give Sarah the credit,' I said. 'She knows how to mix a magic drink.'

'What?'

'She loosened up Francine with something in a coffeecup.'

Jon turned to Sarah.

'Thank you very much . . .'

'Any time,' Sarah answered.

'God,' said Jon, 'I've been in this business a long time and never *nineteen* takes!'

'I've heard,' I answered, 'that Chaplin sometimes took a hundred takes before he got it right.'

'That was Chaplin,' said Jon. 'A hundred takes and our whole budget would be used up.'

And that was about all for that day. Except Sarah said, 'Hell, let's go to Musso's.'

Which we did. And we got a table in the Old Room and ordered a couple of drinks while we looked at the menu.

'Remember?' I asked, 'remember in the old days when we used to come here to look at the people at the tables and try to spot the types, the actor types, the producer or director types, the porno types, the agents, the pretenders? And we used to think, "Look at them, talking about their half-assed movie deals or their contracts or their last films." What moles, what misfits . . . better to look away when the swordfish and the sand dabs arrive.'

'We thought they were shit,' said Sarah, 'and now we are.'

'What goes around comes around . . .'

'Right! I think I'll have the sand dabs . . .'

The waiter stood above us, shuffling his feet, scowling, the hairs of his eyebrows falling down into his eyes. Musso's had been there since 1919 and everything was a pain in the ass to him: us, and everybody else in the place. I agreed. Decided on the swordfish. With french fries.

Chapter Thirty-three

THE FILM WAS being shot in 3 locations. Different rooms, different streets and alleys, different bars had to be juggled about.

There was a night scene which was to entail some stealing of corn from a vacant lot and a chase by the police.

The corn had been planted and was ready to steal.

To use the location cost the budget 5 thousand dollars. The vacant lot was now owned by a Rehabilitation Center for Alcoholics. Pinchot had searched everywhere for a cheaper location but finally had to settle for that one, which actually was the *same* vacant lot which my lady had stolen the corn from over 3 decades ago. The new corn had been planted in the exact location where the old corn had been planted. Other things were not quite so exact. The apartment building nearby where the lady had lived, the one I moved into with her, had now been turned into a Home for the Aged.

The large building next to the vacant lot, now being used as a Rehabilitation Center, back then had been a popular ballroom. It was always busy especially on Saturday nights. The entire bottom floor was a ballroom, gigantic, with large globes of light slowly turning in the ceiling as the live band played dance music until early in the a.m. while many fancy cars, some with chauffeurs, waited outside.

We hated that ballroom and those people while we starved and fought with each other and the police and the landlord, as we were taken to and then bailed out of the Lincoln Heights Jail.

Now that building was full of reformed drunks who read the Bible, smoked too many cigarettes and played Bingo in the room that had once been the grand ballroom.

The vacant lot was all that hadn't changed. In all those decades nobody had ever built a structure of any kind there.

Francine and Jack had already had a couple of rehearsals and had vanished into their trailers and we were standing around waiting for the action. I was tilting a beer when there was a tap on my shoulder. It was a nice looking fellow, neatly trimmed beard, nice eyes, nice smile. I had seen him about, but didn't know him, didn't know his position and didn't ask. Actually I guessed that his real job was being a Firepower spy.

'Please,' he said, 'we can't have drinking on the set here.'

'Why not?'

'In the contract we signed with the people here it states that we can shoot on the premises but no drinking will be allowed.'

'Water?'

'You know what I mean.'

'Yes, those x-drunks can't stand to see anybody else have a drink.'

'They don't believe in it.'

'But the whole movie is *about* drinking.'

'We had a very hard time securing these premises. Please don't spoil it.'

'O.K., buddy. But it's for Pinchot, not you . . .'

He walked off with his clipboard, wobbling his soft little ass which had not been kicked often enough.

I turned my back to the building, took another gulp, put the bottle in my coat pocket.

'They can see you,' said Sarah.

'You mean all those x-drunks are hanging out of windows watching me drink this beer?'

'No, but they have people around.'

'All right, I'll go into hiding when I take a hit of my beer.'

'You're acting as spoiled as some of these stars.'

Sarah was correct. I had no right to be spoiled. The leading man was making 750 times as much money as I was.

Then Jon Pinchot found us.

'Hello, Sarah . . . Hello, Hank . . .'

He told me that Friedman had actually sent the new checks, that mine had been made out directly to me and was in the mail. Our scheme had succeeded.

'I've got to go,' said Jon, 'we're about ready to shoot the cornfield scene. You watch it and let me know what you think . . .'

Finally they went into action and Francine ran up the hill to the rows of corn.

'I want some corn!' she screamed.

I remembered Jane going up that same hill while I was carrying the large sack of bottles. Only when she had screamed 'I want some corn!' it had been as if she wanted the whole world back, the world that she had somehow missed out on or the world that had somehow passed her by. The corn was to be her victory, her reward, her revenge, her song.

But when Francine screamed, 'I want some corn!' it sounded petulant, there was a whine in her voice, and it was not the desperate voice of the drunk. It was all right, it was good but it wasn't quite right.

Then when Francine began ripping at the ears I knew that it wasn't the same, that it could never be the same. Francine was an actress. Jane had been a mad drunk. Properly and finally mad. But one doesn't expect perfection from a performance. A good imitation will do.

So Francine ripped the corn, stuffed it in her purse, Jack saying, 'You're drunk . . . That corn is green . . .'

Then the cop car rolled up, flashing its red light and its bright spotlight on them, and Francine and Jack ran toward her place, just as Jane and I had, and they just got to the elevator as the cops shouted over the loudspeaker, 'HALT OR WE'LL FIRE!'

But instead of those cops jumping out of the car and running after Jack and Francine they just sat there. The shot was over.

It took Sarah and me a few minutes to find Jon Pinchot.

He was just standing there, quietly.

'Jon, man, the cops were supposed to get out and chase their ass!'

'I know. The car doors got stuck. They couldn't get out.'

'What?'

'I know. It's unbelievable. We are going to have to fix the car doors and shoot it all over.'

'We're sorry,' said Sarah.

Jon was depressed. He usually laughed when things went wrong.

'I'll get back to you after we re-shoot it.'

We left, walked back across the street. I hated to see Jon deflated that way. He had natural guts. Some people disliked him because he seemed to have too much bravado. But most of it was real. We all played at being brave. I did too. But I didn't like to see Jon lose his bravado.

Francine and Jack and many of the other people returned to their trailers. I hated the long delays between shots. Movies cost a great deal of money because most of the time nobody was doing anything but waiting and waiting and waiting. Until *this* was ready and *that* was ready and the lighting was ready and the camera was ready and the hairdresser had finished pissing and the consultant had been consulted, nothing happened. It was all a deliberate jack-off, a salary for this and a salary for that, and there was only one man who was allowed to put a plug in the wall, and the sound man was pissed-off at the assistant director, and then the actors were not feeling good because that's the way actors were supposed to feel and so forth. It was all waste waste waste. Even on this extremely low budget film, I felt like yelling, 'ALL RIGHT, CUT OUT THE SHIT! THERE'S NOTHING HERE THAT CAN'T BE DONE IN 10 MINUTES AND YOU HAVE BEEN TAKING HOURS PLAYING AROUND WITH IT!'

I didn't have the guts to say it. I was just the writer. A minor expense.

Then I got an ego boost. A television crew came from Italy and one came from Germany. They both wanted interviews with me. The directors were both ladies.

'He promised us first,' said the Italian lady.

'But you'll take all his juice away,' said the German lady.

'I hope so,' said the Italian lady.

I sat down before the Italian lights. We were on camera.

'What do you think of film?'

'Movies?'

'Yes.'

'I stay away from them.'

'What do you do when you're not writing?'

'Horses. Bet them.'

'Do they help your writing?'

'Yes. They help me forget about it.'

'Are you drunk in this movie?'

'Yes.'

'Do you think drinking is brave?'

'No, but nothing else is either.'

'What does your movie mean?'

'Nothing.'

'Nothing?'

'Nothing. Peeking up the ass of death, maybe.'

'Maybe?'

'Maybe means not sure.'

'What do you see when you look up the "ass of death"?'

'The same thing you do.'

'What is your philosophy of life?'

'Think as little as possible.'

'Anything else?'

'When you can't think of anything else to do, be kind.'

'That's nice.'

'Nice is not necessarily kind.'

'All right, Mr Chinaski. What word do you have for the Italian people?'

'Don't shout so much. And read Celine.'

The lights went out on that one.

The German interview was even less interesting.

The lady kept wanting to know how *much* I drank.

'He drinks but not as much as he used to,' Sarah told her.

'I need another drink right now or I'm not going to talk anymore.'

It came immediately. It was in a large white paper cup and I drank it down. Ah, it was good. It suddenly seemed foolish to me that anybody wanted to know what I thought. The best part of a writer is on paper. The other part was usually nonsense.

The German lady was right. The Italian lady had used up all my juice.

I was now a spoiled star. And I was worried about the cornfield shoot.

I needed to talk to Jon, to tell him to make Francine drunker, madder, with one foot in hell, one hand yanking corn from the stalk as death approached, with the nearby buildings having faces out of dreams, looking down on the sadness of existence for us all: the rich, the poor, the beautiful and the ugly, the talented and useless.

'You don't like movies?' the German lady asked.

'No.'

The lights went out. The interview was over.

And the cornfield scene got reshot. Maybe not exactly the way it could have been, but almost.

Chapter Thirty-four

IT WAS TEN a.m. when the phone rang. It was Jon Pinchot.

'The film has been cancelled . . .'

'Jon, I no longer believe such stories. It's just their way of getting more leverage.'

'No, it's true, the film has been cancelled.'

'How can they? They've invested too much, they'd take a huge loss on the project . . .'

'Hank, Firepower just doesn't have any more money. Not only has our film been cancelled, *all* films have been cancelled. I went to their office building this morning. There are only the security guards. There is NOBODY in the building! I walked all through it, screaming, "Hello! Hello! Is anybody here?" There was no answer. The whole building is empty.'

'But, Jon, how about Jack Bledsoe's "Play or Pay" clause?'

'They can't pay *or* play him. All the people at Firepower, including us, are without any more income. Some of them have been working for 2 weeks now without pay. Now there's no more money for anybody . . .'

'What are you going to do?'

'I don't know, Hank, this looks like the end . . .'

'Don't make any hasty moves, Jon. Maybe some other company will take over the film?'

'They won't. Nobody likes the screenplay.'

'Oh, yeah, that's right . . .'

'What are you going to do?'

'Me? I'm going to the track. But if you want to come over for some drinks this evening, I'd be glad to see you.'

'Thanks, Hank, but I've got a date with a couple of lesbians.'

'Good luck.'

'Good luck to you too . . .'

I drove north up the Harbor freeway toward Hollywood Park. I'd been playing the horses over 30 years. It started after my near fatal hemorrhage at the L.A. County Hospital. They told me that if I took another drink that I was dead.

'What'll I do?' I had asked Jane.

'About what?'

'What'll I use as a substitute for drink?'

'Well, there are the horses.'

'Horses? What do you do?'

'Bet on them.'

'Bet on them? Sounds stupid.'

We went and I won handsomely. I began to go on a daily basis. Then, slowly, I began to drink a little again. Then I drank more. And I didn't die. So then I had both drinking *and* the horses. I was hooked all around. In those days there was no Sunday racing, so I would nurse the old car all the way to Agua Caliente and back on Sunday, a few times staying for the dog races after the horses were through, and then hitting the Caliente bars. I was never robbed or rolled and was treated rather kindly by both the Mexican bartenders and the patrons even though sometimes I was the only gringo. The late night drive back was nice and when I got home I didn't care whether Jane was there or not. I had told her that Mexico was simply too dangerous for a lady. She usually wasn't home when I got in. She was in a much more dangerous place: Alvarado Street. But as long as there were 3 or 4 beers waiting for me, it was all right. If she drank those and left the refrigerator empty, then she was in *real* trouble.

As for horses, I became a real student of the game. I had about two dozen systems. They all worked only you couldn't apply them all at one time because they were based on varying factors. My systems had only one common factor: that the Public must always lose. You had to determine what the Public play was and then try to do the opposite.

One of my systems was based on index numbers and post positions. There are certain numbers that the public is reluctant to call. When these numbers get a certain amount of play on the board in relation to their post position you have a high percentage winner. By studying many years of result charts from tracks in Canada, the USA and Mexico I came up with a winning play based solely upon these index numbers. (The index number indicates the track and race where the horse made its last appearance.) The *Racing Form* used to put out big, fat, red result books for $10. I read them over for hours, for weeks. All results have a pattern. If you can find the pattern, you're in. And you can tell your boss to jam it up his ass. I had told this to several bosses, only to have to find new ones. Mostly because I altered or cheated on my own systems. The weakness of human nature is one more thing you must defeat at the track.

I pulled into Hollywood Park and drove through the 'Sticker Lane'. A horse trainer I knew had given me an 'Owner/Trainer' parking sticker and also a pass to the clubhouse. He was a good man and the best thing about him was that he wasn't a writer or an actor.

I walked into the clubhouse, found a table and worked at my figures. I always did that first, then paid a buck to go over to the Cary Grant Pavilion. There weren't many people there and you could think better. About Cary Grant, they have a huge photo of him hanging in the pavilion. He's got on old-fashioned glasses and that smile. Cool. But what a horseplayer he was. He was a two dollar bettor. And when he lost he would run out toward the track screaming, waving his arms and yelling, 'YOU CAN'T DO THIS TO ME!' If you're only going to bet two dollars you might as well stay home and take your money and move it from one pocket to the other.

On the other hand, *my* biggest bet was $20 win. Excessive greed can create errors because very heavy outlays affect your thinking processes. Two more things. Never bet the horse with the highest speed rating off his last race and never bet a big closer.

My day out there was pleasant enough but as always I resented that 30 minute wait between races. It was too long. You can feel your life being pounded to a pulp by the useless waste of time. I mean, you just sit in your chair and hear all the voices talking about who should win and why. It's really sickening. Sometimes you think that you're in a madhouse. And in a way, you are. Each of those jerk-offs thinks he knows more than the other jerk-offs and there they were all together in one place. And there I was, sitting there with them.

I liked the actual action, that time when all your calculations came out correctly at the wire and life had some sense, some rhythm and meaning. But the wait between races was a real horror: sitting with a mumbling, bumbling humanity that would never learn or get better, would only get worse with time. I often threatened my good wife Sarah that I would stay home from the track during the days and write dozens and dozens of immortal poems.

So I managed to get through the afternoon out there and headed back home, winner of a little over $100. Drove back with the working crowd. What a gang they were. Pissed and vicious and broke. In a hurry to get home to fuck if possible, to look at tv, to get to sleep early in order to do the same thing next day all over again.

I pulled into the driveway and Sarah was watering the garden. She was a great gardener. And she put up with my insanities. She fed me healthy food, cut my hair and toenails and generally kept me going in many ways.

I parked the car and went out to the garden, gave her a hello kiss.

'Did you win?' she asked.

'Yeah. Sure. A little.'

'No phone calls,' she said.

'Too bad, all this . . .' I said. 'You know, after Jon threatened to cut off his finger and all that. I really feel sorry for him.'

'Maybe you should have asked him over tonight.'

'I did, but he was tied up.'

'S & M?'

'I don't know. A couple of lesbians. Some sort of relief for him.'

'Did you notice the roses?'

'Yes, they look great. Those reds and whites and yellows. Yellow is my favorite color. I feel like eating yellow.'

Sarah walked with the hose over to the faucet, shut off the water and we walked into the house together. Life was not too bad, sometimes.

Chapter Thirty-five

THEN, JUST LIKE that, the movie was on again. Like most of the news it came over the phone via Jon.

'Yes,' he told me, 'we begin production again tomorrow.'

'I don't understand. I thought the movie was dead.'

'Firepower sold some assets. A film library and some hotels they owned in Europe. On top of that they managed to swing a big loan from an Italian group. It's said that this Italian money is a bit tainted but . . . it's money. Anyhow, I'd like you and Sarah to come to the shooting tomorrow.'

'I don't know . . .'

'It's tomorrow night . . .'

'O.K., fine . . . When and where?'

Sarah and I sat in a booth. It was Friday night and there was a good feel in the air. We were sitting there when Rick Talbot walked in and sat down with us. There he was in our booth. He only wanted a coffee. I had seen him many times on tv reviewing movies with his counterpart, Kirby Hudson. They were very good at what they did and often got emotional about it all. They gave entertaining evaluations and although others had attempted to copy their format, they were far superior to their competitors.

Rick Talbot looked much younger than he did on tv. Also, he appeared to be more withdrawn, almost shy.

'We watch you often,' Sarah said.

'Thank you . . .'

'Listen,' I asked him, 'what bothers you most about Kirby Hudson?'

'It's his finger . . . When he points his finger.'

Then Francine Bowers walked in. She slid into the booth. We greeted her. She knew Rick Talbot. Francine had a little note pad.

'Listen, Hank, I want to know some more about Jane. Indian, right?'

'Half-Indian, half-Irish.'

'Why did she drink?'

'It was a place to hide and also a slow form of suicide.'

'Did you ever take her any place besides a bar?'

'I took her to a baseball game once. To Wrigley Field, back when the L.A. Angels played in the Pacific Coast League.'

'What happened?'

'We both got quite drunk. She got mad at me and ran out of the park. I drove for hours looking for her. When I got back to the room, there she was passed out on the bed.'

'How did she speak? Was she loud?'

'She would be quiet for hours. Then all at once she would go crazy and start yelling, cursing and throwing things. I wouldn't react at first. Then she'd get to me. I'd walk up and down, up and down, yelling and cursing back. This would go on for maybe about 20 minutes, then we'd quiet down, drink some more and begin again. We were continually being evicted. We were thrown out of so many places that we couldn't remember them all. Once, looking for a new place, we knocked on a door. It opened and there stood a landlady who had just gotten rid of us. She saw us, turned white, screamed and slammed the door . . .'

'Is Jane dead now?' asked Rick Talbot.

'Long time dead. They're all dead. All those I drank with.'

'What keeps *you* going?'

'I like to type. It gives me a thrill.'

'And I've got him on vitamins and a low-fat, non-red-meat diet,' Sarah told her.

'Do you still drink?' Rick asked.

'Mostly when I type or when people come around. I'm not happy around people and after I drink enough they seem to vanish.'

'Tell me some more about Jane,' Francine asked.

'Well, she slept with a rosary under her pillow . . .'

'Did she go to church?'

'At strange times she went to what she called "the alka seltzer mass". I believe it began at 8:30 a.m. and ran about an hour. She hated the ten o'clock mass which often ran over two hours.'

'Did she go to Confession?'

'I didn't ask . . .'

'Can you tell me anything about her which would explain her character?'

'Only that in spite of all the seemingly terrible things she did, the cursing, the madness, the love of the bottle, she always did things with a certain style. I'd like to think that I learned a few things about style from her . . .'

'I want to thank you for these things, I think they might help.'

'You're welcome.'

Then Francine and her note pad were gone.

'I don't think I've ever had such a good time on a set,' said Rick Talbot.

'What do you mean, Rick?' Sarah asked.

'It's a feel in the air. Sometimes with low budget films you get that feel, that carnival feel. It's here. But I feel it more here than I ever have . . .'

He meant it. His eyes sparkled, he smiled with real joy.

I called for another round of drinks.

'Just coffee for me,' he said.

The new round came and then Rick said, 'Look! There's Sesteenov!'

'Who?' I asked.

'He did that marvelous film on Pet Cemeteries! Hey, Sesteenov!'

Sesteenov came over.

'Please sit down,' I asked.

Sesteenov slid into the booth.

'Care for anything to drink?' I asked.

'Oh, no . . .'

'Look,' said Rick Talbot, 'there's Illiantovitch!'

I knew Illiantovitch. He had made some crazy dark movies, the main theme being the violence in life overcome by the courage of people. But he did it well, roaring out of the blackness.

He was a very tall man with a crooked neck and crazy eyes. The crazy eyes kept looking at you, looking at you. It was a bit embarrassing.

We slid over to let him in. The booth was full.

'Care for a drink?' I asked him.

'Double vodka,' he said.

I liked that, waved to the barkeep.

'Double vodka,' he told the barkeep while fixing him with his crazy eyes. The barkeep ran off to do his duty.

'This is a great night,' said Rick.

I loved Rick's lack of sophistication. That took guts, when you were on top, to say that you enjoyed what you did, that you were having fun while you did it.

Illiantovitch got his double vodka, slammed it down.

Rick Talbot was asking questions of everybody, including Sarah. There was no feeling of competition or envy in that booth. I felt totally comfortable.

Then Jon Pinchot walked in. He came up to the booth, gave a little bow, grinning, 'We're going to shoot soon, I hope. I will come get everybody then . . .'

'Thank you, Jon . . .'

Then he moved off.

'He's a good director,' said Rick Talbot, 'but I'd like to know why you chose him.'

'He chose me . . .'

'Really?'

'Yes . . . and I can tell you a story about him that will explain why he is a good director and why I like him. But it's off the record . . .'

'Let me hear it,' said Rick.

'Off the record?'

'Of course . . .'

I leaned forward into the booth and told the story about Jon and the electric chainsaw and his little finger.

'That really happen?' Rick asked.

'Yes. Off the record.'

'Of course . . .'

(I knew: nothing is off the record once you tell it.)

Meanwhile, Illiantovitch had finished 2 double vodkas and was sitting looking at another. He kept staring at me. Then he took out his wallet and pulled out a greasy business card. He handed it to me. All 4 corners were worn away and it was limp and dark with grime. It had given up being a business card. Illiantovitch looked like a soiled genius. I admired him for it. He was hardly weighed down by pretense. He grabbed the double vodka and tossed it down his throat.

Then he looked at me, heavily. I stared back. But his dark eyes were entirely too much. I had to look away. I motioned in the barkeep for a refill. Then I looked back at Illiantovitch.

'You're the best man,' I said. 'After you there is nothing.'

'No, not so,' he said, 'YOU are the best! I give you my card! On card is time of SCREENING OF MY NEW MOVIE! YOU MUST BE THERE!'

'Sure, baby,' I said and I took out my wallet and carefully placed the card in there.

'This is a hell of a night,' said Rick Talbot.

There was some more small talk, then Jon Pinchot walked in.

'We're about ready to shoot. Will you please come outside now so that we can find places for you?'

We all got up to follow Jon, except Illiantovitch. He sank into the booth.

'Fuck it! I am going to have more double vodkas! You people go!'

That bastard had stolen a page or two from me. He waved to the barkeep, took out a bent cigarette, stuck it between his lips, flicked his lighter and burnt part of his nose.

That bastard.

We walked out into the night.

Chapter Thirty-six

THEY WERE SET up to shoot in the alley. There was to be an alley fight between the bartender and the barfly. It was cold out there. Almost everything was ready. There was to be a double in the fight scene for both the bartender and Jack Bledsoe. The closeups were to show the faces of Bledsoe and the bartender but the real fight scenes were to be with the doubles.

Bledsoe saw me. 'Hey, Hank, come here!'

I walked over.

'Let them see your fighting style.'

I circled about, shooting out weak left jabs, then now and then I rushed forward throwing lefts and rights. Then I stopped. I explained those fights of long ago.

'It really didn't look very good. At first, there was much circling. Around and around. And then the crowd would get on us and somebody would rush in. I believe that in spite of the drinking the exchanges were very hard and brutal. Then we would back off, size up the situation and charge again, fists pumping. It finally became a matter of outgutting the other guy. Only one could win. And a fight was never over until a man was unconscious. It was a good show and it was free . . .'

It got close to shooting time. We backed out of the alley and took positions out of the way. Just then Harry Friedman strolled in with a Hollywood babe with a wig, false eyelashes, excessive makeup. Her lips were done over to twice the size and her breasts too. Also strolling in was the great director, Manz Loeb, who had directed such films as *The Rat Man* and *Pencilhead*. Along with him was the famous actress Rosalind Bonelli. So we had to go over and be introduced. Loeb and Bonelli smiled nicely and were polite but I got the terrible feeling that they felt superior to us. But that was all right because I felt superior to them. That was just the way it worked.

Then we went back to our vantage points and the big fight began. It looked brutal enough, right from the start. Except in our fights the brutality came near the end when one fighter was helpless (usually me) and the other man would not quit.

Another thing about those fights. If you didn't belong to the Bartender's 'Club', and you lost, you were left out there with the garbage cans and the rats. There were attendant memories. One morning I was awakened by the blaring of a horn and truck headlights shining upon me. It was the garbage truck.

'HEY, MAN, GET THE FUCK OUT OF THE WAY! WE ALMOST RAN YOU OVER!'

'Ohh, oh, I'm sorry . . .'

To get up then, dizzy, sick, beaten, leaning toward the suicide dream with those nice healthy black men only interested in staying on schedule and getting the garbage out of there.

Or it would be a black woman's head coming out of a window: 'HEY, WHITE TRASH, GET THE FUCK AWAY FROM MY BACK DOOR!'

'Yes, ma'am, I'm sorry, ma'am . . .'

And the worst, upon first regaining consciousness, down between the garbage cans, aching too bad to move but knowing you are going to have to, the worst of all was the thought, I'll bet my wallet is gone again . . .

You play a game. You try to feel the wallet pressing against your ass without reaching for it. It feels vacant back there. You really don't want to reach with your hand but you do. And the wallet is *never* there. Then you manage to stand up and then you look through all your pockets: no wallet, ever. I became more and more discouraged with humanity.

Anyhow, then the fight scene was over and Jon Pinchot came over and asked, 'Well?'

'Not quite right.'

'Why?'

'Well, in our fights, the gladiators were more like clowns, they played to the crowd. One guy would land and almost blast the other guy off his feet, then turn to the crowd and say, "Hey, how'd you like that one?"'

'They hammed it up?'

'Yes . . .'

Jon went over to the doubles and spoke to them. They listened. Good old Jon, probably one of the first directors to ever listen directly to the writer. I felt honored. My life had hardly been lucky, now it seemed to be getting so. I could take a little of that.

They shot the fight scene again.

I watched and I have to tell you that I grew weak watching that old dream. I wanted to be one of them, going at it again. Stupid or not, I felt like punching the alley wall. Born to die.

Then it was over. Jon walked over.

'Well?' he asked.

'I liked it . . .'

'Me too,' he said.

Then that was it.

Sarah and I walked back to the booth in the bar.

Illiantovitch was gone. The bar had probably run out of vodka.

Sarah and I ordered and Rick went for another coffee.

'This is one of the best nights I ever had,' said Rick.

'Listen, Rick, you've got to be playing with me. Where have you been spending your nights?'

He just smiled into his coffee cup. He was a wonderful and innocent man.

Then Francine Bowers was back with her notebook.

'How did Jane die?'

'Well, I was with somebody else by that time. We had been split for 2 years and I came by to visit her just before Christmas. She was a maid at this hotel and very popular. Everybody in the hotel had given her a bottle of wine. And there in her room was this little wooden shelf that ran along the wall just below the ceiling and on this shelf there must have been 18 or 19 bottles.

'"If you drink all that liquor, and you will, it will kill you! Don't these people understand that?" I asked her.

'Jane just looked at me.

'"I'm going to take all of these fucking bottles out of here. These people are trying to murder you!'

'Again, she just looked at me. I stayed with her that night and drank 3 of the bottles myself, which brought it down to 15 or 16. In the morning when I left I told her, "Please, don't drink all of them . . ." I came back a week and a half later. Her door was open. There was a large blood stain in the bed. There were no bottles in the room. I located her at the L.A. County Hospital. She was in an alcoholic coma. I sat with her for a long time, just looking at her, wetting her lips with water, brushing the hair out of her eyes. The nurses left us alone. Then, all at once, she opened her eyes and said, "I knew it would be you." Three hours later she was dead.'

'She never had a real chance,' said Francine Bowers.

'She didn't want one. She was the only person I've ever met who had the same contempt for the human race as I did.'

Francine folded up her notebook.

'I'm sure all this is going to help me . . .'

Then she was gone.

And Rick said, 'Pardon me, but I have been studying you all evening and you don't seem to be a vicious man.'

'And neither do you, Rick,' I said.

Chapter Thirty-seven

WE WERE DOWN there a few days later for some daylight shots and it was just after lunch when Jon Pinchot found us. We had not yet entered the bar.

'Wait,' Jon told me, 'the photographer Corbell Veeker will be here any moment. He wants to take some shots of you, Jack and Francine. This guy is known all over the world. He is famous for his shots of women, he really glamorizes them . . .'

So we stood around in the alley behind the bar. There was an admixture of shadow and sunlight there. I expected a long wait but Corbell Veeker arrived within 5 minutes. He was around 55 with a puffy face, pot belly. He wore a scarf and a beret. He had two boys with him, both of them packing equipment. The boys looked frightened and obedient.

There were introductions.

Then Corbell introduced his assistants.

'This is David . . .'

'This is William . . .'

They both gave tiny smiles.

Then Francine arrived. 'Ah, ah, ah!' went Corbell Veeker as he ran up and kissed her.

Then he stepped back.

'Now, now, now . . . Ah! Ah!' he waved his arms. 'This is it! Yes!'

There was an old broken down couch that had been abandoned behind the bar. It caught his eye.

'You,' he looked at me, 'you sit on the couch . . .'

I walked over and sat on the couch. 'Now, Francine, you sit in his lap . . .'

Francine had on a bright red dress with a slitted skirt. She wore red shoes, red stockings and white pearls. She sat on my lap. I looked around and winked at Sarah.

'That's it! Yes!'

'Does my hard ass bother you?' Francine asked me.

'No, it's all right. Don't worry about it.'

'Camera number FOUR!' Corbell Veeker screamed.

David ran up with camera number four and Corbell slung it around his neck, dropped to one knee . . . There was a click and a flash . . .

'FINE! YES! YES!'

Another click, another flash . . .

'YES! YES!'

Click, flash . . .

'FRANCINE, SHOW MORE LEG! THAT'S IT! YES! YES!'

Click and flash, click and flash . . .

He was shooting furiously, with passion . . .

'FILM! FILM!' he screamed.

William ran up with a new load of film, inserted it into the camera, put the exposed film into a special box.

Corbell dropped to both knees, focused, said, 'SHIT, I DON'T WANT THIS CAMERA! CAMERA NUMBER SIX, PLEASE! NOW! NOW!'

David ran up with camera number six, affixed it to Corbell Veeker and took camera number four away.

'MORE LEG, FRANCINE! IT LOOKS GOOD! I LOVE YOU, FRANCINE! YOU ARE THE LAST GREAT STAR IN HOLLYWOOD!'

Click, flash . . . Click, flash . . . again . . . and again . . . and again.

Then Jack Bledsoe arrived.

'JACK, YOU GET ON THE COUCH TOO! ONE ON EACH SIDE! YES! YES!'

Click, flash . . . Click, flash . . .

'FILM! FILM!' Corbell screamed.

The photos were to be for a fancy woman's magazine with a very large circulation.

'ALL RIGHT, YOU GUYS OFF THE COUCH! I WANT FRANCINE ALONE!'

He had her lie lengthwise on the couch, elbow propped on the armrest, one arm thrown over the back, holding a long cigarette. Francine loved it.

Click, click, flash, flash . . .

The last great star in Hollywood.

The boys ran in with new film, new cameras . . . I guess they figured it beat working in a gas station.

Then Corbell noticed the wire fence.

'THE WIRE FENCE!' he screamed.

He had Francine lean provocatively against the wire fence with Jack Bledsoe on one side and me on the other.

'FINE! FINE!'

He loved the wire fence idea and took more and more shots. The wire fence turned him on. Maybe it was the background beyond the wire fence.

Flash, click, flash, click . . .

And then, like that, it was over.

'Thank you very much, everybody . . .'

He kissed Francine again. His boys were busy packing things, gathering things, numbering things. William had a notebook and he wrote everything down in the notebook: shot number, time, subject matter, camera and film used.

Then everybody just walked off and Sarah and I walked into the bar. The regular barflies were there. They were movie stars now and had developed a certain dignity. They had become quieter, as if thinking about great things. I liked them better the old way. The movie was just about finished and I was a little sorry I had missed so many days of shooting but then if you're a horseplayer almost everything else has to go.

Sarah and I were taking it easy. I ordered a beer and she had a red wine.

'You think you'll ever do another screenplay?' she asked.

'I doubt it. You just have to make too many fucking compromises. And you always have to think through the eye of the camera. Will the audience get it? And almost anything upsets or insults a movie audience, while people who read novels and short stories love to be upset and insulted.'

'Well, you're good at that . . .'

Just then Jon Pinchot came into the bar. He took a seat to my left, smiled at us.

'Son of a bitch,' he said.

'What is it?' asked Sarah.

'Has the movie been cancelled again?' I asked.

'No, not that . . . It's something else . . .'

'Like?'

'Jack Bledsoe refused to sign a release for the still photos that were just taken . . .'

'What?'

'Yes, one of Corbell Veeker's boys went over to his trailer with the papers and Jack refused to sign the release for the photos. Then Corbell went over there. Same thing.'

'But why?' I asked. 'Why did he allow himself to be photographed and then refuse to sign the release?'

'I don't know. But we can still go ahead and use the photos of you and Francine. Are you guys going to watch the next shot?'

'Sure . . .'

'I'll come get you . . .'

'Thanks . . .'

Sarah and I sat thinking about it. I suppose that she was thinking about it. I know that I was.

I just decided that actors were different than we were. They had their own reasons for things. You know, when you spend many hours, many years pretending to be a person who you aren't, well, that can do something to you. It's hard enough just trying to be yourself. Think of trying very hard to be somebody that you're not. And then being somebody *else* that you're not. And then somebody else. At first, you know, it could be exciting. But after a while, after being dozens of other people, maybe it would be hard to remember who you were yourself, especially if you had to make up your own lines.

I figured that Jack Bledsoe had gotten lost and decided that they were photographing somebody else and not him so that all that was left for him to do was to refuse to sign the release. It made sense to me. I decided to explain it to Sarah.

I watched her put her wine down and light a cigarette.

Then I thought, well, maybe I'll explain it another time and I took a long good pull at my beer, wondering if they'd use any of those shots of Francine sitting in my lap with her nice hard ass in that fancy woman's magazine . . .

Chapter Thirty-eight

THEN, JUST LIKE that, the 32 days of shooting were over and it was time for the wrap party.

On the first floor was a long bar, some tables and a large dance floor. There was a stairway that led to an upper floor. Essentially it was the film crew and cast, although all of them weren't there and there were other people that I didn't recognize. There was no live band and most of the music coming over the speakers was disco but the drinks at the bar were real. Sarah and I pushed in. There were two lady bartenders. I had a vodka and Sarah had red wine.

One of the lady bartenders recognized me and brought out one of my books. I signed it.

It was crowded and hot in there, a summer night, no air conditioning.

'Let's get another drink and go upstairs,' I suggested to Sarah. 'It's too hot down here.'

'O.K.,' she said.

We made our way up the stairway. It was cooler up there and not so many people. A few people were dancing. As a party it seemed to lack a center but most parties were that way. I started getting depressed. I finished my drink.

'I'm going to get another drink,' I told Sarah, 'You want one?'

'No, you go ahead . . .'

I walked down the stairway but before I could get to the bar a fat round fellow, lots of hair, dark shades, grabbed my hand and started shaking it.

'Chinaski, I've read everything you've ever written, everything!'

'Is that right?' I asked.

He kept shaking my hand.

'I got drunk with you one night at Barney's Beanery! Remember me?'

'No.'

'You mean you don't remember getting drunk with me at Barney's Beanery?'

'No.'

He lifted his shades and perched them on top of his head.

'Now do you remember me?'

'No,' I said, pulled my hand away and walked toward the bar.

'Double vodka,' I told the lady bartender.

She brought it to me. 'I have a girlfriend named Lola,' she said. 'Do you know a Lola?'

'No.'

'She said she was married to you for two years.'

'Not true,' I said.

I moved from the bar, made my way toward the stairway. Here was another heavy fellow, no hair on his head but a big beard.

'Chinaski,' he said.

'Yes?'

'Andre Wells . . . I had a bit part in the movie . . . I'm also a writer . . . I have a novel finished and ready to go. I'd like you to read it. Can I mail you a copy?'

'All right . . .' I gave him my p.o. box number.

'But don't you have a street address?'

'Of course, but mail it to the box number.'

I walked to the stairway. I drank half my drink walking up the stairs. Sarah was talking to a female extra. Then I saw Jon Pinchot. He was standing alone with his drink. I walked over.

'Hank,' he said, 'I'm surprised to see you here . . .'

'And I'm surprised that Firepower put up the money for this . . .'

'They are charging it . . .'

'Oh . . . Well, what's next?'

'We're in the cutting room now, working on it . . . After that, we mix in the music . . . Why don't you come up and see how it's done?'

'When?'

'Anytime. We're working 12 to 14 hours every day.'

'All right . . . Listen, whatever happened to Popppy?'

'Who?'

'The one who put up the ten grand while you were living down at the beach.'

'Oh, she's in Brazil now. We'll take care of her.'

I finished my drink.

'Aren't you going to go down and dance?' I asked Jon.

'Oh no, that's nonsense . . .'

Then somebody called Jon's name.

'Excuse me,' he said, 'and don't forget to come to the cutting room!'

'Sure.'

Then Jon was off across the room.

I walked over to the railing and looked down at the bar. While I had been talking to Jon, Jack Bledsoe and his motorcycle buddies had walked in. His buddies leaned against the bar, backs to the bar, facing the crowd. They each held a beerbottle, except for Jack who had a 7-Up. They were dressed in leather jackets, scarves, leather pants, boots.

I walked over to Sarah. 'I'm going to go down and see Jack Bledsoe and his gang . . . You coming?'

'Sure . . .'

We went on down and Jack introduced us to each of his buddies.

'This is Blackjack Harry . . .'

'Hi, man . . .'

'This is The Scourge . . .'

'Hello there . . .'

'This is The Nightworm . . .'

'Hey, hey!'

'This is Dogcatcher . . .'

'Too much!'

'This is 3-Ball Eddie . . .'

'God damn . . .'

'This is FastFart . . .'

'Pleased to meet ya . . .'

'And Pussykiller . . .'

'Yeah . . .'

That was it. They all seemed to be fine fellows but they looked a little on-stage, leaning back against the bar and holding their beerbottles.

'Jack,' I said, 'you did a great job of acting.'

'And how!' said Sarah.

'Thank you . . .' he flashed his beautiful smile.

'Well,' I said, 'we're going back upstairs, it's too damned hot down here . . . Why don't you come up?'

I motioned to the barmaid for refills.

'You going to write another movie script?' Jack asked.

'I don't think so . . . Too much loss of privacy . . . I just like to sit around and stare at walls . . .'

'If you write one, let me see it.'

'Sure. Listen, why are your boys facing away from the bar like that? They looking for girls?'

'Naw, they've had too many girls. They are just easing up . . .'

'All right, see you, Jack . . .'

'Keep doing your good work,' Sarah said.

We went back upstairs. Soon Jack and his gang were gone.

It wasn't much of a night. I kept going up and down the stairway for drinks. After 3 hours, almost everybody was gone. Sarah and I were leaning over the balcony. Then I saw Jon. I had noticed him dancing earlier. I waved him over.

'Hey, whatever happened to Francine? She didn't make the wrap party.'

'No, there's no media here tonight . . .'

'Got it.'

'I've got to go now,' said Jon. 'Have to get up early and go to the cutting room.'

'All right . . .'

Then Jon was gone.

It was empty downstairs and it was cooler and so we went down to the bar. Sarah and I were the last ones there. Now there was only one lady bartender.

'We'll have one for the road,' I told her.

'I'm supposed to charge you for drinks now,' she said.

'How come?'

'Firepower only rented this place until midnight . . . It's ten after 12 . . . But I'll slip you some drinks anyhow because I like your writing so much, but please don't tell anybody that I did it.'

'My dear, nobody will ever know.'

She poured the drinks. The late disco crowd was beginning to come in. It was time to go. Yes, it was. Our 5 cats were waiting for us. Somehow, I felt sad that the shooting was over. There was something explorative about it. There had been some gamble. We finished our drinks and walked out into the street.

The car was still there. I helped Sarah in and got in on the other side. We belted up. I started the car and soon we were on the Harbor Freeway going south. We were moving back toward everyday normalcy and in a way I liked it and in another way I didn't.

Sarah lit a cigarette. 'We'll feed the cats and then we'll go to sleep.'

'And maybe a drink?' I suggested.

'All right,' said Sarah.

Sarah and I got along all right, sometimes.

Chapter Thirty-nine

A FEW DAYS later we went over to the mixing room. Jon Pinchot and the Film Editor Kay Bronstein were busy at it.

Jon pulled up some chairs for us.

'I'll show it to you uncut. It's still very rough, you know. There's a lot of work still to be done . . .'

'We realize that,' said Sarah.

'We want to do justice to your film,' said Kay. 'I really love it!'

'Thank you,' I said.

'We're mixing in the music now,' said Jon. 'Both Friedman and Fischman are in London working on a new deal. They phone 4 or 5 times a day screaming, "STOP THE MIX! STOP THE MIX!" I pretend not to understand. We've selected some great music but it's going to cost a lot to obtain the rights. Friedman and Fischman want me to use canned music, which won't cost anything but which is *awful*. It would ruin the film! So I am mixing the good music in with the soundtrack so they can't take it out later . . .'

'Have you ever made a movie under these conditions?' I asked.

'No. There is nobody like these two guys. But I love them!'

'You love them?'

'Yes, they are like children. They have heart. Even when they are trying to cut your throat, there is a certain warmth about them. I'd much rather deal with them than with the corporate lawyers who run most of the business in Hollywood.'

Jon cut the lights and we watched. It was being shown on a small screen, like a tv set. The credits rolled. Then there was my name. I was a part of Hollywood, if only for a small moment. I was guilty.

It moved along well. I found nothing wrong with it as it went on.

'I like it, I like it,' I said.

'We've got something here,' Jon said.

Then there was the scene in which Jack and Francine had just met. They are sitting down at the end of the bar. Jack has brought Francine a couple of drinks. Francine has downed them. Jack is sitting with a half bottle of beer. With his right hand he pushes the beer out of sight, says, 'That's it . . .' 'That's what?' Francine asks. Jack goes on to explain that he has no more money, he's broke, can't buy any more drinks . . .

'NO! NO!' I yelled. 'OH, HOLY CHRIST, NO!'

Jon stopped the film.

'What is it?'

'The alcoholics who see this will laugh us right out of town!'

'What's wrong?'

'A drinking man would *never* push a half bottle of beer away and say, "That's it." He'd finish the bottle to the *last* swallow, then say, "That's it . . ."'

'Hank's right,' said Sarah, 'I noticed that also . . .'

'I took 5 shots of that scene and felt that this was the best one . . .'

'Jon, I felt *affronted* when I saw him push that bottle away, it hurt, it was like getting hit in the face!'

'I think I have a shot where there is only a tiny bit left in the beer bottle . . .'

'Even a tiny bit is too much but use that one please, if you have it,' I said.

That's what could happen when you had a director who wasn't an alcoholic and an actor who hated to drink and they were both working in the same film. And an alcoholic writer who preferred to be at the racetrack rather than at the set.

We watched the remainder of the film.

Jon turned on the lights.

'How'd you like it? I mean, this is very rough, you know . . .'

'The music and camera work are great,' said Sarah.

'Baby, how about the writing?' I asked.

'Chinaski is as good as ever,' she said.

'Thank you,' I said.

'The whole cast and crew were always conscious of you,' said Kay, 'even when you weren't there.'

'Ah,' I said.

'But, Hank, what did you think of it?' Jon asked.

'I liked Jack's acting. I felt Francine needed a little more oil in her joints.'

'Francine was very good,' said Jon. 'The film really comes alive when she is on camera.'

'Maybe so. Anyhow, I'm glad to be part of this film and part of her great comeback . . .'

So, to celebrate our good feelings, we locked the cutting room, got into the elevator and got out into the street and into my car and went off to eat. Not Musso's this time but someplace closer, a restaurant about 8 blocks west. It was curious, I thought, the way things got done. It was just one day at a time, day after day and then there it was. In a sense, I felt as if I hadn't yet even written the script. You haven't, some critic might say, as long as you embrace the bad and the obvious in your writing. But what was the difference between a movie critic and the average movie-goer? Answer: the critic didn't have to pay.

'Pull over here,' said Jon, 'this is the place!'

And I did.

Chapter Forty

I WENT BACK to the racetrack. At times I wondered what I was doing out there. And at times I knew. For one, it allowed me to view large numbers of people at their worst, and this kept me in touch with the reality of what humanity consisted of. The greed, the fear, the anger were all there.

There are certain characteristic individuals at every racetrack everywhere, every day. I was probably viewed as one of those characters and I didn't like that. I would have preferred to be invisible. I don't care to hold counsel with the other players. I don't want to discuss horses with them. I don't view the other players with any kind of camaraderie at all. Actually we are playing against each other. The track never has a losing day. The track takes its cut, the state takes its cut, and the cut keeps getting bigger, which means for a player to win consistently he or she must have a decided betting edge, a superior method, a logical insight. The average player plays daily doubles, exactas, triples, pick sixes, or pick nines. They end up with handfuls of useless cardboard. They bet win, they bet place, they bet show. But there is only one bet, and that bet is to *win*. It takes the pressure off. Simplicity is always the secret, to a profound truth, to doing things, to writing, to painting. Life is profound in its simplicity. I think that the racetrack keeps me aware of this.

But, in another sense, the racetrack is a sickness, a fill-in, a cop-out, a substitute for something else that should be faced.

Yet, we all need to escape. The hours are long and must be filled somehow until our death. And there's just not enough glory and excitement to go around. Things quickly get drab and deadly. We awaken in the morning, kick our feet out from under the sheets, place them on the floor and think, ah, shit, what now?

At times, I'd get sick with the need for the racetrack. I'd play the thoroughbreds during the day and then at night I'd find myself playing the quarter horses or the harness races, depending on what was available. And there in the evening I'd see some of the same people that I saw during the day. They were betting at night too. The ultimate sickness.

So I went back to the racetrack and forgot all about the movie and the actors and the crew and the cutting room. The track kept my life simple, although maybe 'stupid' is a better word for it.

At night I usually watched a bit of tv with Sarah, then went upstairs and played with the poem. The poem was what kept the mind from cracking. The poem was what I needed. Really needed.

I was back into this routine for two or three weeks when the good old phone rang. It was Jon Pinchot.

'The film is finished. We are going to have a private screening at Firepower. No press. No critics. I hope you can be there.'

'Sure. Tell me the time and place.'

I wrote it down.

It was a Friday night. I well knew my way to the Firepower building. Sarah was smoking and musing about something. As I drove along I began having some thoughts too. I remember something Jon Pinchot had told me. Long before he found anybody to produce the screenplay, he went all around town each night scouting the bars, looking for just the right bar, for the right barflies. He gave himself a name: 'Bobby'. And he went from bar to bar, night after night. He said he almost became alcoholic. And in all those bars, he said, he never met a woman he'd care to go home with. Sometimes he took a night off and came over to our place with all those photos of the bars he'd visited and put them on the coffee table before me. I'd choose the best ones and he'd say, 'Yes, I will concentrate on these . . .' He always had faith that the screenplay would become a movie.

The screening room was not at Firepower but in a lot behind it.

We drove up. There was a guard there.

'Firepower screening of *The Dance of Jim Beam*,' I told him.

'Go on in . . . take a right . . .' he said.

There. We were bigshots. I drove on in, took a right, parked.

It was a lot full of private studios. I had no idea why Firepower didn't have their own screening room. Their building was huge. But they probably had a damned good reason why they did what they did.

We got out and began looking for the screening room. There were no signs. We seemed to be the only ones about. Yet we were on time. We walked on. Then I saw a couple of slim, movie-studio types leaning against a half-open door. Everybody in the business looked nearly the same — I mean the crews, consultants, so forth, they were all between 26 and 38 years old and were slim and were always talking to each other about something interesting.

'Pardon me,' I asked, 'but is this the screening room for *The Dance of Jim Beam*?'

They both stopped and stared at us as if we had interrupted something important. Then one of them spoke.

'No,' he said.

I don't know what will happen to those fellows after they reach 39. Maybe that's what they were talking about.

We walked on looking for the screening room.

Then standing near an automobile with the motor running was somebody familiar. It was Jon Pinchot standing with the co-producer Lance Edwards.

'Jon, for Christ's sake, where's the screening room?'

'Yeah,' said Sarah, 'where?'

'Oh,' said Jon, 'they moved the location. I tried to phone you but you had already left . . .'

'Well, where is it baby?'

'Yeah, baby,' said Sarah.

'I was looking for you . . . Listen, Lance Edwards is driving over there now. All right if we ride with you, Lance?'

Lance nodded as if he was pissed off. I thought that we were the ones who should have been pissed off. In Hollywood those things sometimes get mixed up.

Jon got in front with Lance and Sarah and I got into the back. They claimed Lance was bashful and that's why he wouldn't talk. I had the feeling that he just didn't give a fuck. One of the tv interviewers, the woman from Italy, had told me, 'I used to work for that son of a bitch! I never met such a cheap bastard! He doesn't pay anything. He doesn't even use his own stationery. He'd use envelopes that people had mailed to him. He'd have me cross out the names and addresses and write new names in and we'd mail the same envelope out again. He'd rip off stamps that weren't cancelled on incoming mail and use them again. One day I was working and I felt his hand on my leg. "Did you lose something?" I asked him. "What do you mean?" he asked. "I mean, did you lose something there on my leg? What are you looking for? If you didn't lose something then take your hand off my fucking leg!" He fired me, without severance pay.'

The car kept driving on. It seemed like a very long drive.

'Hey, Lance,' I said, 'you going to drive us back to our car?'

He nodded as if he were pissed off. Of course he was pissed off: gas expense.

We finally got there, got out and went into the screening room. It was full. Everybody was there. They looked comfortable and at ease. Many of them were holding golden cans of beer.

'Son of a bitch!' I said loudly.

'What is it?' asked Jon.

'All these people have beer! We have NOTHING to drink!'

'Wait! Wait!' said Jon.

He ran off.

Poor Jon.

Sarah and I were being treated like second class citizens. But then, again, what could you expect when the leading man made 750 times as much as the screenplay writer? The public never remembered who wrote the screenplay, just who fucked it up or who made it work, either the director or the actors or whoever. Sarah and I were only slum dwellers.

Jon made it back with two cans of beer for us just as the lights went out and the film came on. *The Dance of Jim Beam*.

I took a gulp of beer in honor of the alcoholics of the world.

And as the film began I flashed back (as they do in the movies) to that morning in the bar when I was young, when I was feeling neither good nor bad, just rather numb, and the bartender said to me:

'You know what, kid?'

'No, what?'

'We're gonna put a gas pipe right through the bar here, right here where you sit all the time and we're going to cap it.'

'A gas pipe?'

'Yeah. And so when you feel like ending it all, you can uncap it and take a few whiffs and go . . .'

'I think that's damned nice of you, Jim,' I said.

Chapter Forty-one

THERE IT WAS. The film was rolling. I was being beaten up in the alley by the bartender. As I've explained before I had small hands which are a terrible disadvantage in a fist fight. This particular bartender had huge hands. To make matters worse, I took a punch very well which allowed me to absorb much more punishment. I had some luck on my side: I didn't have much fear. The fights with the bartender were a way to pass the time. After all, you just couldn't sit on your barstool all day and all night. And there wasn't much pain in the fight. The pain came the next morning and it wasn't so bad if you had made it back to your room.

And by fighting two or three times a week I was getting better at it. Or the bartender was getting worse.

But that had been over four decades before. Now I was sitting in a Hollywood screening room.

No need to recall the film here. Perhaps it's better to tell about a part left out. Later in the film this lady wants to take care of me. She thinks I'm a genius and wants to shield me from the streets. In the film I don't stay in the lady's house but overnight. But in actual life I stayed about 6 weeks.

The lady, Tully, lived in this large house in the Hollywood Hills. She shared it with another lady, Nadine. Both Tully and Nadine were high-powered executives. They were into the entertainment scene: music, publishing, whatever. They seemed to know everybody and there were two or three parties a week, lots of New York types. I didn't like Tully's parties and enter-tained myself by getting totally drunk and insulting as many people as I could.

And living with Nadine was a fellow a bit younger than I. He was a composer or a director or something, temporarily out of work. I didn't like him at first. I kept running into him around the house or out on the patio in the morning when we were both hungover. He always wore this damned scarf.

One morning about 11 a.m. we were both out on the patio sucking on beers, trying to recover from our hangovers. His name was Rich. He looked at me.

'You need another beer?'

'Sure . . . Thank you . . .'

He went into the kitchen, came back out, handed me my beer, then sat down.

Rich took a good swallow. Then he sighed heavily.

'I don't know how much longer I can fool her . . .'

'What?'

'I mean, I don't have any talent of any kind. It's all just bullshit.'

'Beautiful,' I said, 'that's really beautiful. I admire you.'

'Thank you. How about you?' he asked.

'I type. But that's not the problem.'

'What is it?'

'My dick is rubbed raw from fucking. She can't get enough.'

'I have to eat Nadine every night.'

'Jesus . . .'

'Hank, we're just a couple of kept men.'

'Rich, these liberated women have our balls in a sack.'

'I think we should start in on the vodka now,' he said.

'Fine,' I said.

* * *

That evening when our ladies arrived neither of us were able to perform our duties.

Rich lasted another week, then was gone.

After that I often ran into Nadine walking about the house naked, usually when Tully was gone.

'What the hell are you doing?' I finally asked.

'This is my house and if I want to run around with my ass in the wind, that's my business.'

'Come on, Nadine, what is it really? You want some turkey-neck?'

'Not if you were the last man on earth.'

'If I were the last man on earth you'd have to stand in line.'

'You just be glad I don't tell Tully.'

'Well, just stop running around with your pussy dangling.'

'You pig!'

She ran up the stairway, plop, plop, plop. Big ass. A door slammed somewhere. I didn't follow it up. A totally over-rated commodity.

That night when Tully came home she packed me off to Catalina for a week. I think she knew Nadine was in heat.

That wasn't in the film. You can't put everything in a film.

And then back in the screening room, the film was over. There was applause. We all walked around shaking each other's hands, hugging. We were all great, hell yes.

Then Harry Friedman found me. We hugged, then shook hands.

'Harry,' I said, 'you've got a winner.'

'Yes, yes, a great screenplay! Listen, I heard you've done a novel about prostitutes!'

'Yes.'

'I want you to write me a screenplay about that. I want to do it!'

'Sure, Harry, sure . . .'

Then he saw Francine Bowers and rushed toward her. 'Francine, honey doll, you were magnificent!'

Gradually things wound down and the room was almost empty. Sarah and I walked outside.

Lance Edwards and his car were gone. We had the long walk back to our car. It was all right. The night was cool and clear. The movie was finished and would soon be showing. The critics would have their say. I knew that too many movies were made, one after the other after the other. The public saw so many movies that they no longer knew what a movie was and the critics were in the same fix.

Then we were in the car driving back.

'I liked it,' said Sarah, 'only there were parts . . .'

'I know. It's not an immortal movie but it's a good one.'

'Yes, it is . . .'

Then we were on the freeway.

'I'll be glad to see the cats,' said Sarah.

'Me too . . .'

'You going to write another screenplay?'

'I hope not . . .'

'Harry Friedman wants us to come to Cannes, Hank.'

'What? And leave the cats?'

'He said to bring the cats.'

'No way!'

'That's what I told him.'

It had been a good night and there would be others. I cut into the fast lane and went for it.

Chapter Forty-two

CANNES WAS ANOTHER matter. I received a phone call from Pinchot from over there.

'We don't expect to win but we hope we can come close.'

'I think that Jack Bledsoe might get best actor.'

'It is rumored that the French are going to give the Palme d'Or to one of their own.'

Down at Firepower the publicity department kept sending various trade magazines to interview me about the movie. Having broken some cathedral windows in my time, the magazines sensed I was something or somebody they should bait, somebody to get blathering stupid drunk, somebody who could be persuaded to say something stupidly useable. And they got it one stupid night. I said something negative about an actor that I really liked as a person and as an actor. It was a small thing, it described only a small segment of this person. But like his wife told me on the telephone, 'It may have been true but you didn't have to say it.' She was right but in another way she was wrong. We should be free to speak freely especially when we are asked a direct question. But there is the matter of tact. Then there is the matter of too much tact.

Hell, I had been attacked continually over the years but I had somehow found this to be invigorating. I never believed my critics to be anything but assholes. If the world lasts until the next century, I will still be there and the old critics will be dead and forgotten only to be replaced by new critics, new assholes.

So, I was sorry about wounding the actor but maybe actors are just more sensitive than writers. I hope so.

And I stopped giving interviews.

Actually, I would tell anyone who asked that the charge was $1,000 an hour. They would quickly lose interest.

Then Jon Pinchot was on the phone again from Cannes.

'We have problems . . .'

'Like what?'

'Jack Bledsoe won't come out of his hotel room to be inter-viewed . . .'

'I can understand that.'

'No, wait . . . It's because he won't speak to anybody who didn't give his last movie a good review. Problem is, he didn't get many good reviews for that one. The reporters were all waiting in the lobby and Jack said, "No, no interviews, you people don't understand me." A guy held up his hand and said, "Jack, I gave your last movie a good review!" Jack said, "All right, then I'll give *you* an interview." So they set it up. At a certain cafe, at a certain time. Only problem is, Jack doesn't show up.'

'Jon, I guess these actors are more sensitive than writers or directors . . .'

'Sensitive? Well, you can call it that . . .'

'How's Francine doing?'

'Fine. Fine. She talks to everybody. She wears these summery dresses. She speaks well of all of us. She knows that she has made a great comeback. She feels that she is the last of the last of the great ones. She walks about like a goddess. It's a great show.'

'Yeah. How's Friedman?'

'Oh, he's great! He's everywhere, talking and sweating, waving his arms. He's hated by all the powerful people here.

At the same time they fear him because of his tenacity and energy. He disturbs their sleep. They speak of him over their drinks. They want to rip his ass off with their deathrays.'

'No chance. Anything else?'

'Just Jack. If we could only get him out of his hotel room. We did finally get him to agree to appear on one of the most popular tv programs in France. He agreed. Then he didn't arrive.'

'Why did he go to Cannes at all?'

'Damned if I know . . .'

The time went by as time will do. The track was still there. Also, I reread some James Thurber. At his best he was wildly funny. It's just a shame he had such an upper-middle-class viewpoint. He would have made one hell of a bad-assed coal miner.

I also knocked out a handful of poems. The poem has some value, believe me. It keeps you from going totally mad.

Yes.

And then, no. The film didn't win anything at Cannes.

And Sarah began planting new flowers and vegetables in the garden.

And our 5 cats watched us with their ten beautiful eyes.

Chapter Forty-three

AFTER CANNES THERE was still more work in the cutting room to be done. Pinchot was working hard at it.

I had a small part in the movie. I played a barfly in one scene. It was brief but it could have been longer. They cut most of it out. Let me explain. I am sitting there with these other two fellows, we are at the bar, not sitting together but separately. It's the scene where Jack first meets Francine. The three of us, as barflies, are just supposed to sit there like barflies. Once the camera was on us, though, I couldn't help myself. I took a large gulp of beer, rolled it around in my mouth, then shot it back down into the neck of the beerbottle from a good six inches. An excellent trick. Not a drop fell on the bar. I don't know what made me do it. I had never done it before. But that part ended on the cutting room floor.

'Look, Jon,' I said, 'why don't you put that part back in?'

'I can't. Everybody would be asking, "Who the hell is that guy?"'

When you're an extra, you just don't ad-lib.

Anyhow, the time came when there was no more to be done to the film. The date for the release was set.

This particular night about a week before the opening Jon was over at our place and we were sitting around.

'Well, are you going to write us another screenplay? I'm ready when you are.'

'No, Jon, I'm afraid of Hollywood. This is it. Or, I certainly hope that this is it.'

'What are you going to do now?'

'A novel, I guess.'

'About what?'

'You never talk about it first.'

'Why not?'

'It lets the air out of the tires.'

'Hank is always checking his tire pressure,' said Sarah. 'He carries this little gauge around with him. To test his novels.'

'She's right . . . Listen, Jon, is there going to be a premiere for this film?'

'A premiere? Why, no . . .'

'No premiere?' asked Sarah. 'That's ridiculous!'

'Jon,' I said, 'I want a premiere!'

'*You* want a premiere? I can't believe this! Why?'

'Why? For laughs. For bullshit. I want a white stretch limo with a chauffeur, a stock of the best wine, color tv, car phone, cigars . . .'

'Damned right,' said Sarah, 'and Francine will love it!'

'Well,' said Jon, 'I'll see what I can do.'

'Tell Friedman it's for publicity purposes,' said Sarah. 'Tell him it will help the gross.'

'I'll work on it . . .'

'And, Jon,' I reminded him, 'don't forget the white stretch limo.'

Somehow Jon managed it. The night of the premiere came around. Sarah was upstairs getting ready as the white stretch limo came up the drive. The little neighborhood kids had seen it and were already gathering in the yard next door. I went outside and guided the limo up the drive.

'Hank, are you famous?' one of the kids asked.

'Famous? Oh yeah, yeah . . .'

'Hank, can we come along?'

'You wouldn't like it.'

'Yes we would!'

The chauffeur cut the engine and got out.

We shook hands.

'I'm Frank,' he said.

'I'm Hank,' I said.

'You're the writer?'

'Yes. Have you read my stuff?'

'No.'

'Well, I haven't seen you drive either.'

'Oh yes, you have, sir. You just saw me drive up the driveway.'

'That's right, isn't it? Listen, my wife is still getting dressed. It won't be long.'

'What do you write, sir?'

'What do you mean?'

'I mean just that, sir. What do you write?'

The fellow was beginning to piss me off a little. I wasn't used to chauffeurs.

'Well, I write poems, short stories, novels . . .'

'And you wrote a screenplay, sir.'

'Oh. That. Yes.'

'What do you write about, sir?'

'About?'

'Yes, *about* . . .'

'Oh, haha, I write about life, you know. Just life, you know.'

'My mom,' one of the kids said, sticking his head over the fence, 'says he writes *dirty* stuff!'

The chauffeur looked at me. 'Please tell your wife that it's a long drive. We mustn't be late.'

'Says who?'

'Mr Friedman.'

I walked into the house and yelled up the stairway.

'Sarah, the limo is here, hurry . . .'

'He's early . . .'

'I know. But it's Friday night and it's a long trip.'

'I'll be down in a moment. Don't worry. We'll make it.'

I cracked a beer and turned on the tv. There was a fight on ESPN. They were really slugging it out. The fighters were better conditioned now than in my youth. I marveled at the energy they could expend and still keep going and going. The months of roadwork and gymwork that fighters had to endure seemed almost intolerable. And then, those last two or three intense days before a big fight. Condition was the key. Talent and guts were a must but without condition they were negated.

I liked to watch the fights. Somehow it reminded me of writing. You needed the same thing, talent, guts and condition. Only the condition was mental, spiritual. You were never a writer. You had to *become* a writer each time you sat down to the machine. It wasn't that hard once you sat down in front of the machine. What was hard sometimes was finding that chair and sitting in it. Sometimes you couldn't sit in it. Like everybody else in the world, for you, things got in the way: small troubles, big troubles, continuous slammings and bangings. You had to be in condition to endure what was trying to kill you. That's the message I got from watching the fights, or watching the horses run, or the way the jocks kept overcoming bad luck, spills on the track and personal little horrors off the track. I wrote about life, haha. But what really astonished me was the immense courage of some of the people *living* that life. That kept me going.

Sarah came down the stairway. She looked great.

'Let's go!'

I snapped off the tv. Then we were out the door.

I introduced Sarah to the chauffeur.

'Sarah! Sarah! Sarah!' the kids screamed. The kids liked Sarah.

'Can we go with you, Sarah?'

'You'll have to ask your mothers,' she laughed.

Mothers? Didn't anybody ever ask the fathers?

The chauffeur helped us into the back. The limo slowly backed out with the kids following along the fence. Hell, I'd soon be dead and someday about half of them would be sitting down to word processors and writing unimaginably bad shit.

We drove down the steep hill and I got the cork out of the first bottle of wine. I poured two tall glassfulls.

'Here's mud in your eye,' I said to Sarah, clicking our glasses.

'Here's mud in both of our eyes,' she said.

I turned on the tv. It didn't have ESPN. I shut it off.

'Do you know how to get there?' Sarah asked the chauffeur.

'Oh yes . . .'

Sarah looked at me. 'Did you ever think you'd be taking a limo to the premiere of a movie that you had written?'

'Never. I'm just glad I got off of that park bench.'

'I like limos. Don't you like the way they ride?'

'They glide. We're on a glider to hell. Here, let me give you another drink.'

'Great wine . . .'

'Oh yes . . .'

We went up the Harbor freeway north and then we cut onto the San Diego freeway north. I hated the San Diego freeway. It always jammed. Then I noticed a slight rain beginning to fall.

'That's it,' I said, 'it's beginning to rain.' All the cars were going to stop. California drivers didn't know how to drive in the rain. They drove too fast or too slow. Most of them drove too slow.

'We're going to be late,' Sarah said.

'I think so, kid.'

Then it really started to come down. Terror filled the other drivers on the freeway. They peered through their flipping wipers with their tiny soulless eyes. The fuckers should be glad they had wipers. Once I had an old car without them. You want to know about hard driving? Try that. In rainy weather I carried a sliced potato with me. I'd stop the car, clean off the windshield with the potato and drive on. You had to know how to do it: just a very light rub.

But these drivers, now, in their cars, acted as if they were practically on their death beds. You could feel their panic in the downpour of rain. Dumb panic. Useless panic. Wasted panic. You ever want to use your panic, save it for something real.

'Well, baby, we have plenty of wine.'

I poured a bit more.

But I had to allow the chauffeur a bit of credit. He was a pro. He seemed to know which lane would slow down and which would soon move and he slid that limo, that large large limo gently back and forth between lanes, getting all the best of the flow. I almost forgave him for not being one of my readers. I loved professionals who could do what they were supposed to be able to do. They were rare. There were so many inefficient professionals: doctors, lawyers, presidents, plumbers, quarterbacks, dentists, policemen, airline pilots and etc.

'I think we're going to make it,' I told him.

'We might,' he admitted.

'Who's your favorite writer?' I asked.

'Shakespeare.'

'If we make it, I'll forgive you.'

'If we make it, I'll forgive myself.'

I just couldn't engage in conversaton with that mother. He put the stopper to me each time.

Sarah and I just sipped our wine.

And then we were there. The chauffeur pulled up and opened the door. We got out.

It was at the edge of a large shopping mall. The theatre was back in there somewhere.

'Thank you, Frank,' I said.

'You're welcome. I'm going to park now. I'll find you when you come out.'

'How can you find us?'

'I'll find you . . .'

Then he was in the driver's seat and the white stretch limo was gone into traffic. The rain was still falling.

I looked and there were 4 or 5 men with umbrellas waiting for us. It was the open part of the mall and some of the rain drifted in. The men with the umbrellas rushed toward us, looking very very concerned that we might get wet.

I laughed. 'This is ridiculous!'

'I like it!' Sarah laughed.

We all rushed toward each other. Then we moved into the mall. There were cameras flashing. Big time. I had left the park bench behind.

Chapter Forty-four

I SAID TO one of the men as we walked along, 'God damn it, we left our wine bottle in the car! We are going to need a couple of bottles of wine for the movie!'

'I'll get them for you, Mr Chinaski,' the man said. I had no idea who he was. He broke away from the group.

'And don't forget a corkscrew!' I yelled after him.

We moved further into the mall. Far over to our left I could see flashbulbs popping. Then I saw Francine Bowers. She was posing, looking first this way, then that. She was regal. The best of the last.

We followed the men. Then there was a tv camera. More flashbulbs. I recognized the lady as one of the interviewers on an entertainment station.

'Henry Chinaski,' she greeted me.

'How do you do,' I bowed.

Then before she could ask any questions, I said, 'We are worried. We left our wine in the limo. The chauffeur is probably drinking it right now. We need more wine.'

'As the screenwriter, do you like the way the movie turned out?'

'The director handled two difficult actors, the leads, without any problem at all. We used real barflies, none of whom are able to make it out here tonight. The camera work is great and the screenplay is well written.'

'Is this the story of your life?'

'A few days out of a ten year period . . .'

'Thank you, Mr Chinaski, for speaking to us . . .'

'Sure . . .'

Then Jon Pinchot was there. 'Hello, Sarah, hello, Hank . . . Follow me . . .'

There was a small group with cassette recorders. Some flash-bulbs went off. I didn't know who they were. They began asking questions.

'Do you think drinking should be glorified?'

'No more than anything else . . .'

'Isn't drinking a disease?'

'Breathing is a disease.'

'Don't you find drunks obnoxious?'

'Yes, most of them are. So are most teetotalers.'

'But who would be interested in the life of a drunk?'

'Another drunk.'

'Do you consider heavy drinking to be socially acceptable?'

'In Beverly Hills, yes. On skid row, no.'

'Have you "gone Hollywood"?'

'I don't think so.'

'Why did you write this movie?'

'When I write something I never think about why.'

'Who is your favorite male actor?'

'Don't have any.'

'Female.'

'Same answer.'

Jon Pinchot tugged at my sleeve.

'We'd better go. I think the movie is about to begin . . .'

Sarah and I followed him. We were rushed along. Then we were at the theatre. Everybody seemed to be inside.

Then there was the voice behind us: 'WAIT!'

It was the man who had gone for the wine. He had a large paper bag. He ran up and thrust it into my arms.

'You are one of the world's great men!' I told him.

He just turned and ran off.

'Who was that?' I asked Jon. 'Does he work for Firepower?'

'I don't know . . .'

'Come on,' said Sarah, 'we better go in.'

We followed Jon into the lobby. The doors were already closed. Jon pushed them open. It was dark and we followed him down the aisle. The movie had already begun.

'Shit,' I said, 'couldn't they have waited for us? We are the writers!'

'Follow me,' said Jon, 'I saved you two seats.'

We followed him all the way down to the first row, side aisle. There were two seats up against the wall.

'I'll see you later,' said Jon.

There were two girls seated in our same aisle. One of them said to the other, 'I don't know what we are doing here. I really hate Henry Chinaski. He's a disgusting human being!'

I fumbled in the dark for one of the wine bottles and an opener. The screen went from dark to light.

'Henry Chinaski,' the girl went on, 'hates women, he hates children, he's a creepy bitter old fuck, I don't see what people see in him!'

The other girl saw me in the light of the screen and dug her friend in the ribs with her elbow.

'Shhhh . . . I think that's him!'

I opened one bottle for Sarah and one for me. We each lifted them high. Then Sarah said, 'I ought to beat up those cunts!'

'Don't,' I said, 'my enemies are the source of half my income. They hate me so much that it becomes a subliminal love affair.'

We were in a terrible position to view the movie. From where we sat, all the bodies were tall, elongated and thin, and the heads were the worst. Large and misshapen, big foreheads, and yet as big as the foreheads were there seemed to be almost no eyes or mouths or chins to the heads. Also the sound was too loud and badly distorted. The dialog sounded like, 'WHOOO, WOOOO, WULD WAFT TA KRISTOL, YO TO YO . . .'

The premiere of my first and only movie and I couldn't make anything out of it.

I was later to find out that there was another theatre right next door showing our movie at exactly the same time and that it was only half-full.

'Jon didn't plan this very well,' Sarah suggested.

'Well, we'll see it on video cassette some day,' I told her.

'Yeah,' she said.

And we lifted our bottles in unison.

The girls watched us in total fascination and disgust.

The oversized heads with big foreheads kept moving around on the screen.

And the heads spoke loudly to each other.

'FLAM FLAM WOOL WO, TAKA BRAK VO SO . . .'

'YA DOL YA, TEK TA TAM, YA VO DO . . .'

'PREEBERS . . .'

'BRAKA DAM . . .'

'They fucked over my dialogue, Sarah.'

'Uh . . . yeah . . .'

But it was best when the big tall foreheads went for the very tall thin drinks, the drink filled half the screen, and then the drink went somewhere in, under the forehead, and then it was gone, and then there were just undulating empty glasses, changing shape, stretching and contracting, glistening empty glasses from hades. What hangovers those foreheads would have.

Finally, Sarah and I stopped watching the screen and just worked on our wine bottles.

And, with time, the movie ended.

There was some applause and then we waited for the

audience to file out. We waited for a good while. Then we got up and went out.

There were more flashbulbs in the lobby. Handshakes. We ducked that.

We needed the restrooms.

'See you by the potted plant across from the ladies room,' I told Sarah.

I made it to the men's room. In the urinal next to me was a swaying drunk. He looked over.

'Hey, you're Henry Chinaski, aren't ya?'

'No, I'm his brother, Donny.'

The drunk swayed some more, pissing away.

'Chinaski never wrote about no brother.'

'He hates me, that's why.'

'How come?'

'Because I've kicked his ass about 60 or 70 times.'

The drunk didn't know what to think about that. He just kept pissing and swaying. I went over, washed up, got out of there.

I waited by the potted plant. The chauffeur stepped out from behind it.

'I've been instructed to take you to the celebration party.'

'Great," I said, 'as soon as Sarah . . .'

And there was Sarah. 'You know, baby, most chauffeurs wait outside but our man, Frank, he came inside and found us. But he took off his cap so as not to look like a chauffeur.'

'It's been a strange night,' she said.

We followed Frank through the mall. He was about two steps ahead.

'You didn't drink our wine, did you, Frank?'

'No, sir . . .'

'Frank, isn't the first rule for a chauffeur never to leave his limo? Suppose somebody stole the limo, for instance?'

'Sir, nobody would ever steal that piece of crap.'

'You're right.'

As soon as we stepped outside of the mall, Frank put his cap back on. The limo was parked right at the curb.

He helped us into the back seat and we were off.

Chapter Forty-five

THE POST-PREMIERE PARTY was at Copperfield's on La Brea Avenue. Frank pulled up in front, let us out and we moved toward the entrance to more flashbulbs. I got the idea that they didn't know who they were photographing. As long as you got out of a limo you qualified.

We were recognized at the entrance and were let inside to a crowd of people, closely packed in and all holding glasses of red wine in their hands. They stood in groups of 3 or 4 or more, talking or not talking. There was no air conditioning and although it was cool outside, it was hot in there, very hot. There were just too many people sucking in the oxygen.

Sarah and I got our wine and stood there, trying to get it down. The wine was very abrasive. There is nothing worse than cheap red wine unless it's cheap white wine that has been allowed to get warm.

'Who are all these people, Sarah? What do they want here?'

'Some are in the business, some are on the edge of the business and some are just here because they can't think of anyplace else to be.'

'What are they doing?'

'Some are trying to make contacts, others are trying to stay in contact. Some go to every function like this that they are able to. Also there's a smattering of the press.'

The feeling in the air was not good. It was joyless. These

were the survivors, the scramblers, the sharks, the cheapies. The lost souls chatted away and it was hot, hot, hot.

Then a man in an expensive suit came up. 'Aren't you Mr and Mrs Chinaski?'

'Yes,' I said.

'You don't belong down here. You belong upstairs. Follow me.'

We followed him.

We followed him up a stairway and to the second floor. It was not quite as crowded. The man in the expensive suit turned and faced us.

'You mustn't drink the wine they are serving here. I will get you your own bottle.'

'Thanks. Make it two.'

'Of course. I'll be right back . . .'

'Hank, what does all this mean?'

'Accept it. It will never happen again.'

I looked at the crowd. I got the same feeling from them as I got from the crowd downstairs.

'I wonder who that guy is?' I asked.

Then he was back with two bottles of good wine and a corkscrew, plus fresh wine glasses.

'Thank you much,' I said.

'You're welcome,' he said. 'I used to read your column in the *L.A. Free Press*.'

'You don't look that old.'

'I'm not. My dad was a hippie. I read the paper after he was done with it.'

'Can I ask your name?'

'Carl Wilson. I own this place.'

'Oh, I see. Well, thank you again for the good wine.'

'You're welcome. Let me know if you need more.'

'Sure.'

Then he was gone. I opened a bottle and poured two glasses. We gave it a try. Really good wine.

'Now,' I asked Sarah, 'who are these people up here? How are they different than the ones downstairs?'

'They are the same. They just have more pull, better luck. Money, politics, family. Those in the industry bring in their family and friends. Ability and talent are secondary. I know I sound like I'm on a soap-box but that's the way it is.'

'It adds up. Even the so-called best movies seem very bad to me.'

'You'd rather watch a horse race.'

'Of course . . .'

Then Jon Pinchot walked up.

'My god! These people! I feel like I've been covered with shit!' I laughed.

Then Francine Bowers came over. She was elated. She had made her comeback.

'You were good, Francine,' I said.

'Yes,' said Jon.

'You let your hair down,' said Sarah.

'Maybe too much?'

'Not at all,' I said.

'Hey,' said Francine, 'what's that wine you're drinking? It looks like good stuff.'

'Have some,' I tilted the bottle into her glass.

'Me too,' said Jon.

'How come you get his good stuff?' Francine asked.

'The owner's father was a hippie. They both read the *L.A. Free Press*. I used to write a column, "Notes of a Neanderthal Man."'

Then we all stood there not saying anything. There was nothing more to say. The movie was finished.

'Where's Jack Bledsoe?' I asked.

'Oh,' said Jon, 'he doesn't come to these things.'

'Well, I do,' said Francine.

'We do too,' Sarah admitted.

Then there was some beckoning from another group.

'A magazine wants to interview you, Francine. *Movie Mirror*.'

'Of course,' said Francine. 'Forgive me,' she said to us.

'Sure.'

She walked over, stately and proud. I felt good for her. I felt good for anybody who made a comeback after being relegated to the hinterlands.

'You go over there with her, Jon,' said Sarah. 'She'll feel better . . .'

'Should I go too, Sarah?'

'No, Hank, you'll only try to hog the interview. And remember, you charge $1,000 now.'

'That's right . . .'

'All right,' said Jon, 'I'll go over there.'

Then he was gone, over there.

A young man walked up with a tape recorder. 'I'm from the *Herald Examiner*. I do the "Talk and Tell" column. How did you like the way the movie came out?'

'Do you have a thousand dollars?' Sarah asked.

'Sarah, this is just chit-chat, it's all right.'

'Well, how did you like the way the movie turned out?'

'It's a better than average movie. Long after this year's Academy Award movies are forgotten, *The Dance of Jim Beam* will be showing up now and then in the Art houses. And it will pop up on tv from time to time, if the world lasts.'

'You really think so?'

'Yes. And as it's viewed again and again special meanings will be found in the lines and scenes that weren't intended by anyone. Overpraise and underpraise is the norm in our society.'

'Do barflies talk like that?'

'Some of them do until somebody kills them.'

'You seem to rate this movie pretty high.'

'It's not that good. It's only that the others are so bad.'

'What do you consider to be the greatest movie that you have ever seen?'

'*Eraserhead*.'

'*Eraserhead*?'

'Yes.'

'And what's next on your list?'

'*Who's Afraid of Virginia Woolf?*'

Then Carl Wilson was back. 'Chinaski, there's a guy downstairs who claims he knows you. He wants to come up. One John Galt.'

'Let him up here, please.'

'Well, thank you, Chinaski,' said the *Herald-Examiner* man.

'You're welcome.'

I uncorked the second bottle and poured us a couple more. Sarah held her booze remarkably well. She only became talkative when we were alone together. And then she talked good sense, mostly.

Then, there he was John Galt. Big John Galt. He walked up.

'Hank and I never shake hands,' he smiled. 'Hello, Sarah,' he said, 'got this guy under control?'

'Yes, John.'

Damn, I thought, I know so many guys named John.

The biblical names hung on. John, Mark, Peter, Paul.

Big John Galt looked good. His eyes had gotten kinder. Kindness came finally to the better ones. There was less self-interest. Less fear. Less competitive gamesmanship.

'You're looking good, baby,' I told him.

'You look better now than you did 25 years ago,' he said.

'Better booze, John.'

'It's the vitamins and health foods,' said Sarah. 'No red meat, no salt, no sugar.'

'If this ever gets out my book sales are going to plummet, John.'

'Your stuff will always sell, Hank. A child can read it.'

Big John Galt. God damn, what a life-saver he had been. Working for the post office, I had gone over to his place instead of eating or sleeping or doing all the other things. Big John was always there. A lady supported him. The ladies always supported Big John. 'Hank, when I work, I'm not happy. I want to be happy,' he would say.

There was always this big bowl of speed sitting on the coffee table between us. It was usually filled to the brim with pills and capsules. 'Have some.'

I would dip in and eat them like candy. 'John, this shit is going to destroy your brain.' 'Each man is different, Hank, what destroys one doesn't affect another.'

Marvelous nights of bullshit. I brought my own beer and popped the pills. John was the best-read man I had ever met, but not pedantic. But he was odd. Maybe it was the speed.

Sometimes at 3 or 4 a.m. he'd get the urge to raid garbage cans and backyards. I'd go with him. 'I want *this*.' 'Shit, John, it's just an old left boot somebody threw away.' 'I want it.'

His whole house was filled with trash. Piles of it everywhere. When you wanted to sit on the couch you'd have to push a mound of trash to one side. And his walls were pasted over with mottos and odd newspaper headlines. All the stuff was way off key. Like the last words of the earth's last maniac. In the cellar of his house were thousands of books stacked up and they were swollen and wet and rotted with the damp. He had read them all and come away quite well. All he needed to survive was a shoestring and you'd better not get in a chess game with him, or a struggle to the death. He was a marvel. I do suppose in those days I had a fair amount of self-pity and he made me aware of that. Mainly, those times and those hours were *entertaining*. I fed off of Big John Galt when there was nothing else around. He was a writer too. And later I got lucky with the word and he didn't. He could write a very powerful poem but in between times there were spaces where he just seemed vacant. He explained it to me, 'I don't want to be famous, I just want to feel good.' He was one of the best readers of poetry, his or anybody else's, that I had ever heard. He was a beautiful man. And later, after my luck, when I'd mention Big John Galt here and there, I'd get the same feedback, 'I don't see what Chinaski sees in that old blow-hard.' Those who had accepted me and my work wouldn't accept him and his work and I wondered if maybe my writing was made for fools? Which I couldn't help. A bird flies, a snake crawls, I change typewriter ribbons.

Anyhow, it felt good seeing John Galt once again. He had a new lady with him.

'This is Lisa,' he said. 'She writes poetry too.'

Lisa jumped right in and began talking. She talked up a storm and John just stood there. Maybe it was an off night for her but she sounded like an old time Female Libber. Which is all right, for them, except they tend to eat up the oxygen and it was already too hot in there for lack of fresh air. She went on and on, telling us everything. John and she often read together. Did I ever hear of Babs Danish? 'No,' I told her. Well, Babs Danish was *black* and she was *female* and when she read she wore big earrings and she was very passionate and the earrings jumped up and down and her brother Tip provided a musical backdrop for her readings. I should hear her.

'Hank doesn't go to poetry readings,' Sarah said, 'but I've heard Babs Danish and I like her very much.'

'John and I and Babs are reading at Beyond Baroque next Wednesday night, will you come?'

'I probably will,' said Sarah. And she probably would.

I took a long look at John Galt then. He looked gentle and good but I saw a deep pain in his eyes that I had never seen before. For a man who had wanted to be happy he looked like a man who had lost two pawns in the early rounds of a chess match without gaining an advantage.

Then the *Herald Examiner* man was back.

'Mr Chinaski,' he said, 'I wanted to ask you another question.'

I introduced him to John Galt and Lisa.

'John Galt,' I said, 'is the great undiscovered poet in America. This man helped me to go on when all else said stop. I want you to interview John Galt.'

'Well, Mr Galt?'

'Hank and I knew each other maybe 20 years ago . . .'

Sarah and I drifted off.

'Looks like with Lisa John's got a full nine innings on his hands,' I said.

'Maybe it's good for him.'

'Maybe.'

More people had come upstairs. It seemed that nobody had left. What was there? Contacts? Opportunities? Was it worth it? Wasn't it better not to be in show business? No, no. Who wants to be a gardener or a taxi driver? Who wants to be a tax accountant? Weren't we all artists? Weren't our minds better than that? Better to suffer this way rather than the other. At least it looks better.

Our second bottle was almost empty.

Then Jon Pinchot returned.

'Jack Bledsoe is here. He wants to see you.'

'Where is he?'

'He's over there, by the doorway.'

And sure enough, there was Jack Bledsoe, just leaning in the doorway with his famous and sensitive smile.

Sarah and I walked over. I reached out and Jack and I shook hands.

I thought of John Galt's saying, 'Hank and I never shake hands.'

'Good show, Jack, great acting. I'm really glad you were aboard.'

'Did I put it over?'

'I think you did.'

'I didn't want to get too much of your voice in there or too much of your slouch . . .'

'You didn't.'

'I just wanted to come by to say hello to you.'

That one struck me. I didn't know how to react.

'Well, hell, baby, we can get drunk together anytime.'

'I don't drink.'

'Oh, yeah . . . Well, thank you, Jack, glad you came by. How about one for the road anyhow?'

'No, I'm going . . .'

Then he turned and walked down the stairway.

He was alone. No bodyguards, no bikers. Nice kid, nice smile.

Goodbye, Jack Bledsoe.

I wormed another bottle out of Carl Wilson and Sarah and I stood around with the other people but actually nothing was occurring. Just people standing around. Maybe they were waiting for me to get drunk and insane and abusive like I sometimes did at parties. But I doubted that. They were just dull inside. There was nothing for them to do but stay within the self that was not quite there. That wasn't too painful. It was a soft place to be.

With me, my main vision for life was to avoid as many people as possible. The less people I saw the better I felt. I met one other man, once, who shared my philosophy, Sam the Whorehouse Man. He lived in the court behind mine in East Hollywood. He was on ATD.

'Hank,' he told me, 'when I was doing time, I was always in trouble. The warden kept throwing me in the hole. But I *liked* the hole. The warden would come around and lift the lid and look in, and he asked me one time, "HAVE YOU HAD ENOUGH? ARE YOU READY TO COME OUT OF THERE?" I took a piece of my shit and threw it up and hit him in the face. He closed the lid and left me down there. I just stayed in there. When the warden came back he didn't lift the lid all the way. "WELL, HAVE YOU HAD ENOUGH YET?" "NOT AT ALL," I yelled back. Finally the warden had me pulled out of there. "HE ENJOYS IT TOO MUCH," he told the guards. "GET HIS ASS OUT OF THERE!"'

Sam was a great guy, then he got to gambling. He couldn't pay his rent, he was always in Gardena, he slept in the crappers there and began gambling again as soon as he woke up. Finally Sam got tossed out of his apartment. I traced him to a tiny room down in the Korean district. He was sitting in a corner.

'Hank, all I can do is drink milk but it comes right up. But the doctors say there is nothing wrong with me.'

Two weeks later he was dead. This man who shared my philosophy about people.

'Listen,' I said to Sarah, 'there's nothing happening here. This is death. Let's leave.'

'We have all the free drinks we want . . .'

'It's not worth it.'

'But the night is young, maybe something will happen.'

'Not unless I make it happen and I'm not in the mood.'

'Let's wait just a little while . . .'

I knew what she meant. For us it was the end of Hollywood. All in all, she cared more for that world than I did. Not much, but some. She had begun studying to be an actor.

Still it was just people standing, that's all. The women weren't beautiful and the men weren't interesting. It was duller than dull. The dullness actually hurt.

'I'm going to crack unless we get out of here,' I told Sarah.

'All right,' she said, 'let's leave.'

Good old Frank was downstairs with the limo.

'You're leaving early,' he said.

'Uh huh,' I said.

Frank placed us in the back and we found a new bottle of wine in the limo. We uncorked it as our trusty man found the Harbor Freeway south.

'Hey, Frank, want a drink?'

'Sure as shit, man!'

He hit a button and the little glass partition dropped. I slipped the bottle through.

As Frank drove the limo along he took a hit from the wine bottle. I don't know but somehow it all looked very strange and funny and Sarah and I started laughing.

At last, the night was alive.

Chapter Forty-six

AFTER THAT, NOT much. The movie opened in 3 or 4 theatres in town. People began bothering me at the racetrack.

'Did you write that movie?'

'Yes.'

'I thought you were a horseplayer.'

'I am. Now, if you will excuse me . . .'

Some people had a nice way of approaching. Others were terrors. They saw you and their eyes widened and then came the rush toward you. I learned to recognize that look and when I saw it I would duck down some side aisle, make a quick turn. I'm sure that I ran away from a lot of people who had no intention of bothering me. I knew in time that things would get back to normal and that once again I'd just be another old guy at the track like all the other old guys.

The reviews of *The Dance of Jim Beam* were both good and bad. *The New York Times* gave it a wondrous review but *Jim Beam* upset the lady at *The New Yorker*. Rick Talbot said it was one of the ten best movies of the year.

Then there were odd moments. One night I was upstairs and Sarah hollered up, 'They are reviewing *The Dance of Jim Beam*!'

It was Wexler and Selby on a cable station. When I arrived they were showing the shot where Jack Bledsoe is throwing Francine Bowers's clothing out of their 6th floor window. Then the shot ended.

Selby shook his head and limp-wristed the movie away:

'AWFUL! TERRIBLE! This has to be the *worst* movie of the year! Here we have this . . . *bum* . . . with his pants down around his ankles! He's filthy, uncaring . . . obnoxious! All he wants to do is beat up the bartender! From time to time he writes poems on torn pieces of paper! But mostly we see this scum-bag . . . sucking on bottles of wine or begging for drinks at the bar! In one bar scene we see two ladies fighting to their very *death* over him. Impossible! NOBODY, NOBODY would ever care for this man! Who could care for him? We rate movies from one to ten here. Is there any way I can give this a minus one?'

Sure enough, up on the screen appeared a minus one.

Then Wexler started. 'I agree with your view but I give it a two. I think there was one funny scene, where he takes a bath in the tub with the dog.'

'Oh no,' said Selby, 'that was stupid . . .'

After a month the movie was still playing at 3 or 4 theatres. Then it opened in a theatre near San Pedro and we decided to go see it. After all, we had never seen it on a large screen except the time of the premiere and the huge elongated heads.

We drove to a small mall and parked where we could see the theatre. And on the marquee were the words, *The Dance of Jim Beam*. That was a thrill, seeing that.

I had seen most of my movies as a kid, all very horrible movies. Fred Astaire and Ginger Rogers. Jeanette McDonald and Nelson Eddy. Bob Hope. Tyrone Power. The Three Stooges. Cary Grant. Those movies shook and rattled your brains, left you without hope or energy. I sat in those movie houses, sickened in the gut and soul.

We sat in the parking lot and waited for the end of the afternoon showing.

'Maybe nobody is in there,' I said. 'Maybe nobody will come out.'

'They're in there, Hank . . .'

We waited. Then the movie was over and they started coming out.

'There's 3,' said Sarah.

'5,' I said.

'7.'

'8.'

'Eleven . . .'

I felt better. They kept coming. I gave up counting.

Then they were all out of there. It would soon be time for the early evening show.

'Do you think anybody else does this, Sarah?'

'What?'

'This sitting and watching to see how many people are going in and out of your movie?'

'I'm sure we're not the first.'

More time went by.

'Where are the people?' I asked. 'Maybe nobody's coming!'

'They'll be here.'

Just then, sure enough, old model cars began pulling in, circling, looking for places to park. One guy got out with a wine bottle in a paper sack.

'The drunks are coming to check for accuracy,' I laughed.

'They'll find it,' said my dear wife.

'As a historian of drink I don't have a peer.'

'That's because none of them have lived as long as you. What's your secret?'

'Never get out of bed before noon.'

It looked like a fair crowd going in. We walked on over to the theatre. I stood at the ticket booth. 'Two,' I told the girl, 'one senior.'

Then the fellow took our tickets, ripped them and we walked in. Coming attractions were playing full volume. We got two seats to the side but far back, and waited. There seemed to be at least 100 people in there.

Then, at the last moment, two young people, male and female, mid-twenties, tall and slender, took the seats in front of us.

The coming attractions were over and then there was *The Dance of Jim Beam*. The credits appeared. And the movie began. I had seen it on video 3 or 4 times and had it fairly well memorized. Ah, it was the story of my life. Who else could jam it down their throats like that? But actually, it wasn't meant to be that self-concerned. I only wanted to show what strange and desperate lives some drunks live and I was the one drunk I knew best.

I had been preceded by some good drinkers. Eugene O'Neill, Faulkner, Hemingway, Jack London. The booze loosened those typewriter keys, gave them some spark and gamble.

The movie ran on.

'Do you think anybody knows that you're here?' Sarah asked.

'No, I look pretty much like anybody else.'

'Does that bother you?'

'Yes, I don't like to look like anybody else.'

The tall slender male in front of us turned and said, 'Please, I'd like to watch the movie.'

'I'm sorry,' I said.

The movie continued. Then there was a sudden indecency and the girl in front of us winced and said, 'Oh no.'

'It's all right, Darlene,' said her tall companion.

Darlene got over that and then there was a simple scene where a lady in the bar is bragging about how she gives the best head in town. The lady says, 'Nobody in this town can swallow paste like I can!'

Darlene covered her face and said, 'I can't believe it . . .'

'It's all right, honey,' said her male cohort.

Darlene continued her face-covering act throughout the movie but neither Darlene or her boyfriend left.

Then the movie was over and the people slowly left their seats. We waited. Well, I had seen a lot worse movies, especially in the thirties.

Sarah and I got up and moved up the aisle toward the exit. We walked to the car, sat there watching them pull out. I rolled down the windows and we had a smoke.

Then an old car drove slowly past in front of us. In it was a single man. He saw us and began waving. He had a crazy smile upon his face. I waved back, then he was gone.

'He spotted you,' said Sarah.

'Yes, that was funny.'

'Yeah.'

We drove back home just like from any other movie.

We got back to the place and I opened a bottle of good red wine. The blood of the gods.

The news was on tv. The news was bad.

We sat and drank and watched tv until Johnny Carson came on. There he was, perfectly clothed. His hand kept darting to the knot of his necktie, he was subconsciously worried about his appearance. Johnny went into his monologue and E d's booming false laughter could be heard from the sidelines. It paid well.

'What are you going to do now?' Sarah asked.

'About what?'

'I mean, the movie is really over.'

'Oh, yes.'

'What will you do?'

'There are the horses.'

'Besides the horses.'

'Oh, hell, I'll write a novel about writing the screenplay and making the movie.'

'Sure, I guess you can do that.'
'I can, I think.'
'What are you going to call it?'
'*Hollywood*.'
'*Hollywood*?'
'Yes . . .'
And this is it.

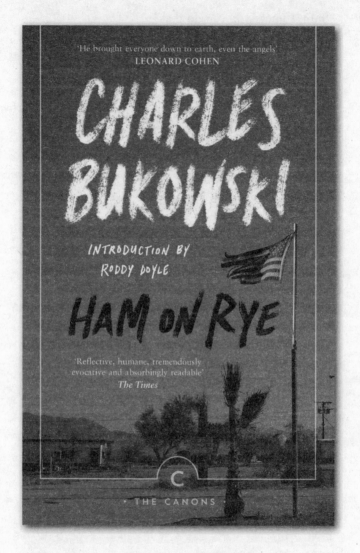

'He brought everyone down to earth, even the angels'
LEONARD COHEN

CHARLES BUKOWSKI

INTRODUCTION BY
RODDY DOYLE

HAM ON RYE

'Reflective, humane, tremendously
evocative and absorbingly readable'
The Times

· THE CANONS ·

'Both powerful [and] extremely funny'
Sunday Telegraph

CANON GATE

'Strikingly original'
Guardian

CANON▌▌GATE

'Pure pleasure - a perpetual-motion machine of
no-stakes elation and champagne fizz' *New Yorker*

SEX & RAGE

ADVICE TO YOUNG LADIES
EAGER FOR A GOOD TIME

EVE BABITZ

C

· THE CANONS ·

'Cool, sharp and delicious'
Elizabeth Day

CANON❚❚GATE